THE BROKEN COVENANT
A CRIME THRILLER

WHEN HONOR DIES
BOOK 3

ROBERT VAUGHAN

ROUGH
EDGES
PRESS

The Broken Covenant
Paperback Edition
Copyright © 2024 (As Revised) Robert Vaughan

Rough Edges Press
An Imprint of Wolfpack Publishing
1707 E. Diana Street
Tampa, FL 33610

roughedgespress.com

Paperback ISBN 978-1-68549-373-8
eBook ISBN 978-1-68549-372-1

THE BROKEN COVENANT

CHAPTER 1

BEVERLY HILLS, CALIFORNIA SEPTEMBER 1929

The underwater lights caused the swimming pool to give off a shimmering, turquoise glow. The perfume of a dozen blooming flowers scented the air as nocturnal creatures raised their throat pouches or agitated their back legs in melodious song. Overhead, the cold vault of darkness was ablaze with heavenly bodies, from the iridescent moon, to the bright star of Venus, down to a barely discernible light blue dusting of distant stars.

Deke Clark, considered by many to be one of the most talented movie directors in Hollywood, was standing at the open door of the bedroom, looking out. The backyard was surrounded by a high brick wall and landscaped with mature shrubbery and hedgerows to provide maximum privacy.

"Deke?" a woman's voice called from the shadows of the bedroom.

Deke turned toward her, saw that she was naked, then

sighed in appreciation. Katie Starr never ceased to amaze him, for upon first glance, she was sedate, almost mousy looking. She could, however, project a sexuality that was as powerful as any aphrodisiac. And because Katie Starr could project that same smoldering sexuality in the flickering light and shadow of celluloid, she had become one of the most popular film stars in Hollywood.

"Hello there," Deke said.

"Do you like?" Katie asked. She teased him by putting one leg in front of the other, then turning her body in profile and raising one arm to affect a statuesque pose.

"Oh yes," Deke replied, nodding his head. "I like. I like very much."

"If you like very much, why are you leaving?"

"It's after midnight."

"So what happens after midnight? Does your Duesenberg turn into a pumpkin?" Katie asked.

Deke chuckled. "No," he answered. "But Tamara does turn into a witch."

"I thought you said your wife doesn't care what you do outside the marriage."

"She doesn't."

"Then why don't you stay the night?"

"She doesn't care what I do," Deke explained. "But she does care how it looks. We must maintain the facade of a happy marriage."

"I see," Katie said in a tone of voice that indicated, clearly, that she did not see.

"I don't think you do see, Katie. Not really." He sighed. "I'm not at all sure that I do. But I do hope you understand that I truly love you. I am bound by certain constraints to behave in a particular way...to follow specific rules. But beyond those constraints and rules there is room in my life only for you. You do believe me, don't you? Please tell me that you believe me."

"Yes," Katie said. "I believe you."

"Good." Deke said. "It is very important to me that you understand, not only what I am going through, but also how much I truly love you."

"And I love you," Katie replied.

"We have that," Deke said. "No one can take that from us."

"Deke?"

"Yes?"

"Why didn't you tell me that you got the job of directing *Aerodrome*?"

Deke paused for just a moment, then he turned back toward her. "How did you find out?"

"I have eyes and ears in Sid Friedman's office. Is it true? Are you going to direct the film?"

"Yes," Deke said.

"Why, Deke, I think that is truly wonderful!" Katie gushed. "But why didn't you tell me? You know how important that film is to me. It will be the first time we have ever worked together."

"I, uh, was asked to keep it secret," Deke said.

"Secret?"

"Yes. You know, until Sid makes a public announcement."

"Well, darling, why keep it secret from me? Were you afraid I might call the newspapers and tell them?" Katie ground out the cigarette. "I am so excited for you...for us! I can't believe you didn't tell me."

"Well, I... just thought it best not to, that's all."

Katie looked at him in surprise for a moment, then she smiled. "Oh, I understand," she said. "Why you sweet, wonderful, foolish man. You are afraid of what it might do to our relationship if we made a movie together, aren't you?"

"It has happened in the past," Deke said. 'Two people

can be very much in love but the strain and pressure of working on the same movie can tear them apart."

Katie put her arms around his neck and leaned into him, then kissed him on the lips. When she pulled her face away to look into his eyes, she formed an arch so that her nude body was pressed against him.

"Darling, don't you know that could never happen to us?" she asked. "You are the director; I am the actress. I know how to follow orders. And I'm no prima donna. You can ask any director who has ever worked with me."

Gently, but firmly, Deke extracted himself from her embrace. "Listen," he said. "I really do have to go. The last thing we want is for Tamara to tighten the noose on me."

"All right," Katie said. She made a sweeping move with her arm. "Run home to your mama, little boy." Though there was a biting edge to her words, she eased the impact of them with a smile. "I'll be waiting here when she lets you out to play again."

Deke smiled. "Good," he said. "Because when I start looking for a playmate, you are the one I am going to come looking for."

"And it is good news about you being selected to be the director for *Aerodrome*. Regardless of what you think, I think it will be wonderful for us to have the chance to work together."

Deke reached for his hat. "I'll see you tomorrow night at the Maxie Award banquet," he said.

"The Maxie Award," Katie said. She groaned. "Oh, why did you even have to remind me? I could have forgotten all about it and been just as happy."

"Why would you want to do that?" Deke asked in surprise.

"Because I'm one of the nominees, remember?" Katie replied.

"I know you are. And I should think that would be all the more reason why you would want to go."

"Huh-uh," Katie said. "You forget, Mr. Clark, that I have been nominated twice for the Oscar. Last year I had to sit there and smile and pretend I was very happy for Janet Gaynor. This year, I flashed the ivories at Mary Pickford. I thought it was over with for the year, but no, I get nominated for the Maxie and I have to go through that ordeal all over again."

"Well, you know what they say. The third time is the charm," Deke said. "Who knows? Maybe you'll win. You will be there, won't you?"

"Well, of course I'll be there," Katie answered. "I mean you can't really afford to stay away from something like this. But I have to tell you, I'm not going to get my hopes up this time."

"Then I'll get my hopes up for you." Deke stopped just before he left and blew her a kiss. "I'll lock the door on the way out," he said. "You don't even have to leave the bedroom."

"Neither do you," Katie said wistfully.

Powerful searchlight beams swept the night sky while harried policeman blew whistles and waved their arms frantically to keep the traffic moving in front of the Top Hat Restaurant. Red velvet ropes passed through polished-brass poles to hold back the movie fans who had crowded the sidewalk outside the restaurant, straining to get a look at what was going on inside.

This was one of the most important events of the year and for over an hour limousines had glided up to the red-carpeted curb in well-bred silence to deposit the wealthiest and most successful icons of Hollywood. When the last guest arrived, the doors of the restaurant were closed, sealing out the curious public. Only the most elite were granted entry into the hallowed banquet room. There, all eyes and ears were focused on the president of the Motion Picture Guild, who was, at that moment, standing behind the speaker's podium, addressing his distinguished audience.

The Motion Picture Guild was one of the most influential organizations in the industry, though its chief competitor, the Motion Picture Academy of Arts and Sciences, had, with the advent of the Academy Award, or "Oscar," presentations, become better known to the outside world.

The Motion Picture Guild was making an attempt to counter the hoopla of the Oscars with its own award. This was the first year of the "Motion Picture Award for Excellence," or, as the Motion Picture Guild wanted it to be known, the "Maxie."

"The Maxie will be the single most prestigious award in the motion-picture industry," the Motion Picture Guild publicity mills gushed, "for it is only one award, given to only one person per year." This was, of course, a snide reference to the fact that the "Oscars" were given away in so many categories that it was hard to remember the winners without a program.

A few minutes earlier the president of the Guild had been introduced to announce this year's winner of the Maxie and to make the presentation. He was doing that now.

"The person we are honoring tonight is the true story of the American dream," he said. "Picture, if you will, someone raised far away from the glamour and glitter of Hollywood. This person has a burning ambition to be a motion-picture star. Now imagine that person getting on a train and coming all the way across this wide and great country of ours, little knowing what lay ahead, and, once here, being subjected to the ordeal of a screen test." Here the speaker paused and looked out over his audience of distinguished motion-picture personalities. "I imagine a few of you know what that is like," he said, eliciting the laugh he was looking for. "And then something magic happened," he continued. "A bit of starlight here, some pixie dust there, and a brush from an angel's wing managed to turn this young, shy, hopeful girl into one of Hollywood's most glamorous and best-loved stars. Ladies and gentlemen, it is with great pride that I, as president of the Motion Picture Guild, declare that this year's winner of the Maxie is none other than... Miss Katie Starr!"

The room erupted into loud and enthusiastic applause. At the Galaxy Pictures table where Katie was sitting with her studio-provided escort, Deke Clark stood, then another person stood, and another still, until soon not only the Galaxy table but the entire room was giving her a standing ovation.

"Katie, my dear, we are all so proud of you," Tamara Welles said. In addition to being Deke's wife, Tamara was an established star in her own right. It had been some time since she had made a film but she was still a person of tremendous influence, though that was now due as much to her wise investments as to her popularity with the moviegoing public. It was rumored that she owned the biggest block of shares of Galaxy Pictures and Katie had reason to believe that the rumor was true.

Katie Starr walked up to the podium and acknowledged the cheers with eyes that were glistening with tears. She waited until the applause stopped and the audience retook their seats. "I cannot tell you what a thrill this is," she said into the microphone. "I am extremely pleased that you found my past work worthy. I hope my future work justifies your confidence. Thank you, ladies and gentlemen. Thank you from the bottom of my heart."

There was more applause and more cheers as Katie took her seat again. The program was then turned over to the orchestra leader who dedicated the first number "Beautiful Katie" to the guest of honor for the evening.

Sitting at the table with Katie were several other Galaxy Pictures stars and officials. The head of the studio was Sid Friedman and he applauded loudest and longest as Katie returned to the table with her Maxie.

"Well, Katie," he said as he held Katie's chair for her. "I know this is a personal victory for you tonight but I hope you won't be too selfish to let me share some of the pride with you. After all, you are Galaxy's brightest star."

"Thank you," Katie said. She gave the trophy, a crystal obelisk surmounted by a golden movie camera, to Larry Cohen, who looked at it appreciatively and then passed it on to Benny Gold. Larry Cohen and Benny Gold were members of the board of directors of Galaxy Pictures. After admiring it for a moment, they passed the Maxie around for the others to see.

"I'll let all of you take a look at it...as long as you remember who it belongs to," Katie said

"Ha! Not much problem there," Sid replied. "How proud you must feel."

"I do feel proud," Katie said. "Though I must confess that I'm not sure why I was selected. There are so many other actors and actresses whose contributions to the industry have been much greater than mine."

"Well, that's the beauty of it, don't you see?" Sid said, laughing. "Our business is nothing if it is not capricious. How else can one explain stardom?"

"How do you explain stardom? Well, you heard our president, didn't you?" Larry said. "Starlight, pixie dust, and angels' wings."

"Here, here," the president agreed, coming to the

table at that particular moment. "May I join this table of honor?"

"Of course." Sid snapped his fingers and pointed to one of the lesser luminaries at the table. "George, get our president a chair."

"Right away, Mr. Friedman," the young man responded.

"I must admit that winning the Maxie is quite an honor," Katie admitted. "But I'm not quite ready to lean back and rest on my laurels. I hope to make many more contributions."

"I should certainly hope so," the Guild president said. "Your fans will absolutely demand it."

"Oh, and she will make many more contributions," Sid extolled. "In fact, I have two or three hot properties that I'm looking at right now, that I think would be just right for her."

"Well, keep looking at properties if you want to. But I have to tell you that I can't think about anything else now except *Aerodrome*," Katie said. "There is no doubt in my mind that the role of Molly Tremaine was created just for me. And now that I know who is directing it, I am even more excited about working on the picture." She looked pointedly at Deke Clark, who suddenly found something very interesting to stare at on his plate. Tamara, on the other hand, stared across the table at Katie with an unbroken gaze and a smile that Katie could only describe as smug.

"Sid, what is it?" Katie asked, suddenly feeling a sense of foreboding. "What's going on here?"

Sid cleared his throat, then picked up a glass of water and took a sip. "Actually, Katie, I wanted to talk to you about that tomorrow," he said.

"Tomorrow? What's the matter with tonight?" Katie asked. "I mean if you want to make the best deal with me, I assure you, you aren't going to catch me in any more receptive mood than I am right now. After all, this is my night, isn't it?"

"Yes, it is," Sid said. "And it is well deserved, not only for the work you have done in the past, but also for the many wonderful things you are going to do in the future." He paused for a long moment. "But *Aerodrome* isn't one of them. Katie, I don't feel that part is for you."

"What?" Katie asked. "Sid, what are you talking about? I'm the one who brought the book to you in the first place, remember? I'm the one who convinced you to do the film. You didn't even want to do it." She looked across the table at Deke again. "You knew this, didn't you?" she asked. "You knew this, that's why you didn't tell me you were directing. Well, I have news for you, mister. If you think—"

"Katie, it wasn't my doing," Deke said interrupted her before she could get into the details of their conversation from the night before. "I wanted you in that role. I asked for you."

Katie looked at Sid. "Is that true?" she asked.

"Yes."

"Then I don't understand. Deke is the director, isn't he? Are you saying he has no say in his own movie?"

"The terms of our agreement give me the final word on casting," Sid said. "And I just don't see you in that role."

"Any particular reason why?"

"Katie, the nurse in the story, Molly Tremaine, is supposed to be a well-bred, cultured member of the upper class."

"So, what are you saying, Sid? That I'm low-class?" Katie snapped.

"Oh no, darling, nothing like that," Sid replied quickly. "Nothing like that at all. But your voice does have a certain...shall we say...ethnic quality to it that I feel would not be good for this particular role."

"I want this role, Sid," Katie said. "I want this role more than I have ever wanted any role in my life. You know that my brother was an aviator during the war. Because of that this role is very meaningful to me."

"I'm sorry, but my mind is made up," Sid said. He waved his hand toward the crowded room. "When I arranged this award tonight, I thought it would—" he started to say, then paused. "I mean—"

"Wait a minute, hold on, here," Katie interrupted. "What are you saying, Sid? Are you telling me that you arranged for me to win the Maxie? Is this so-called honor I received tonight supposed to compensate me for losing the role in *Aerodrome*?"

"Katie, you didn't lose the role," Sid said. "You have to have something before you can lose it and you never had the role, not from the very beginning. I have another person in mind for that part, and have had from day one."

Though no one else at the table was taking part in the conversation, they were following it very closely, the better to relate what they saw and heard to those gossip columnists who would pay handsomely for such information. With this latest revelation, however, the president of the Motion Picture Guild could no longer remain quiet.

"Who do you have in mind, Sid?" he asked. "Are you willing to share that?"

"No, not yet," Sid replied. "You know how these things are. They play better if they are released in their own sweet time. I really didn't intend to let it be known yet that Deke was directing the film. But the cat is out of the bag and there is nothing I can do about that. However, I don't intend to cheat the young lady I have chosen out of the spotlight that is rightly hers by announcing it prematurely. No, sir, you'll get no announcement from me tonight. But I promise, I will make my choice known soon."

"Are you behind this, Tamara?" Katie asked.

"Really, dear, aren't you getting unduly upset over one little role?" Tamara said. "There is such a thing as professionalism, you know. Show a little respect for your position. After all, you are the winner of the Maxie Award. That's a great honor and it entails a certain degree of responsibility. I don't mind telling you, the way you are acting, I'm beginning to wish anyone but you had won. In fact, I'm beginning to wish I had done a movie this year so I would have been eligible."

Katie flashed a smile at Tamara, but there was little warmth in it. Pointedly she began running her hand up and down the crystal obelisk, stroking it suggestively. "Why, whatever would you do with something like this, Tamara?" she asked. "From what I hear, you can't handle anything that is long and hard."

"Katie!" Sid gasped. "You have said enough! The decision has been made. It's over now."

"No," Katie said, standing abruptly. "It's just beginning."

ONE WEEK LATER

Katie Starr stood at the front window watching her chauffeur polish the Packard beneath the portico lights. The car didn't need it; it was already shining so much that a million starbursts glistened from deep inside the midnight blue. The chauffeur was just killing time while waiting and Katie had kept him waiting for well over an hour.

Behind Katie. the phone rang and when she heard her

maid Alma walking toward it, she called out to her. "Let it ring, Alma."

"But Miss Starr, it could be important," Alma said.

"I said, let it ring."

"Yes, ma'am."

Katie looked over at the clock that was sitting on the marble mantel. It was ten minutes after nine. The party had started at eight. Now, she decided. Now it was time to go.

CHAPTER 2

Hal McPherson hung up the phone and looked over at Sid Friedman. "No answer?" he said.

"What do you mean, no answer? Goddamnit, somebody has to be there. The butler, the maid, somebody."

"Maybe so, but nobody answered."

"What the hell kind of game is that bitch playing?" Sid asked. "Surely she isn't planning to come tonight. She wouldn't be that gauche, would she?"

"I wouldn't think so, Sid," Hal assured him.

"Don't be so sure," Lee Williams cautioned, crossing his arms then laying a long, slender, perfectly manicured finger on his cheek. "Katie Starr has more balls than most men I know."

"And you should know," Hal said. "You've certainly felt enough of them."

"What's the matter, sweetie, jealous that you aren't getting your share?" Lee replied.

"Knock it off, you two. You're like a couple of frustrated old maids," Sid said. He ran his hand through his hair in frustration. "I've got to get back to the party. Hal, you watch one entrance, Lee, you watch the other."

"What do we do if we see her?" Lee asked.

"Shit, I don't know," Sid admitted. "We couldn't turn her away...not without making a scene. But at least you can come give me warning."

"I think you are worrying about nothing," Hal said. "She won't be here, you can mark my words on that."

"Oh yes, she will," Lee minced in a singsong voice. "She'll be here with bells on."

Sid watched his two so-called assistants leave, then he returned to the main part of the house to mingle with his guests. This party was important to him and he had no intention of letting it be spoiled just because Miss Katie Starr hadn't gotten her way.

This party was to celebrate the completion and imminent release of Sid's and Galaxy Pictures', latest film, *Arabian Pleasures*. Before he started production on it, Sid had convinced the board of directors at Galaxy to issue him carte blanche. As a result, *Arabian Pleasures* was the most expensive picture the studio had ever made and was, in fact, the third most expensive picture in the history of the business. Although *Arabian Pleasures* hadn't even been released, Sid had already gone to the board to submit the budget for his next picture, *Aerodrome*. Amazingly, *Aerodrome* was to have an even higher budget.

"But I give you my personal guarantee that you won't regret it," Sid promised the board. "With the new sound technology and special effects, we'll make enough money from *Arabian Pleasures* to pay for both films. That means that everything we make from *Aerodrome* will be pure profit."

Already the studio publicity mills were filling the newspapers, fan magazines, and trade publications with stories about *Aerodrome*. In addition, it looked as if the first half of the gamble was about to pay off, because the reviewers who had been granted a special viewing of *Arabian Pleasures* raved about it.

"*Arabian Pleasures* is dazzling, delightful, delicious," one reviewer said.

"Outstrips its name, for surely no pleasure in all of Arabia can equal the pleasure of watching this picture," another suggested.

"A surefire Oscar winner," a third predicted.

"Will be the standard by which all future pictures are measured," Variety insisted.

Tonight, Sid's Beverly Hills estate, Dreamcastle, was the place to be. Every other would-be host in Hollywood knew this as well, because at least a dozen other events had been cancelled in order not to compete with the doings at Dreamcastle.

Even though the party had been going on for an hour, guests were still arriving. Out front, white-sidewalled tires crunched on the crushed marble gravel of the curved driveway as chauffeur-driven Cadillacs, Lincolns, Packards, and Duesenbergs deposited their passengers. Obsequious servants held open doors and helped the luminaries exit the cars while others stood by, ready to provide valet parking for the guests who had driven themselves.

Once inside, the guests were entertained by music, not from the ordinary party band of five or six pieces, but by an entire orchestra, full of woodwinds and brasses and strings and a whole range of percussion instruments. It was pointed out to everyone that this was the same orchestra that had played the score for the picture they were all celebrating. Despite the size of the band, however, the music was nearly drowned out by the chatter and the laughter and the clink of glasses as the partygoers drank in happy abandon, totally oblivious of the act that had made Prohibition the law of the land.

There were several bars working openly, despite the fact that among the guests were the mayor, a couple of judges, the police commissioner, and half a dozen city council members. For those who didn't care to go to a bar, waiters glided from room to room, carrying silver trays laden with various types of mixed drinks as well as the ubiquitous champagne.

In addition to the many established stars in attendance, there were also scores of beautiful young women trying to become stars, hoping to be noticed by someone who could give them their big break. Whenever they encountered such a person, they wasted no time in finding the opportunity to show a long, white flash of inner thigh, or the creamy globes of young, firm breasts.

There were an equal number of handsome young men, elegantly dressed in tuxedos and black ties, and while the young women were flirting with the older men, the handsome young men attempted to gain some advantage by arousing the sexual fantasies of the neglected, middle-aged wives of the more influential producers and directors. Later, these same young men and young women would get together in the corners of the garden, where they would grope each other as they laughed over their escapades.

Though no photographers or newspaper reporters were actually allowed into the party (these functions were taken care of by studio publicity), there were many representatives of the press waiting just outside Dreamcastle, taking pictures of the arriving limousines and hurrying over to get a few words from whoever the celebrity was that the limousine deposited.

"Hey! Hey, there's this year's Maxie winner! That's Katie Starr!" one of the reporters suddenly shouted and flashbulbs began going off as Katie stepped out of her car.

"Oh shit," Hal said, realizing now that not only had he been wrong but he would also have to listen to Lee saying, "I told you so." Hal took a deep breath then hurried back inside to tell Sid the bad news.

Katie Starr's dark, almond-shaped eyes flashed in the ambient light as she looked around at the impromptu welcoming committee. Her dark hair was cut short, like a living "cloche hat," and was accented by a diamond-encrusted tiara. Her white-sequined dress was off the shoulders and ended, fashionably, just above the knees. She was lithe, fluid, and extremely sexy, the very qualities that had made her one of Hollywood's most glamorous stars.

"Hey, Katie, where's your Maxie? Didn't you bring it with you?"

"I was going to wear it as an earring," Katie teased. "But I thought I had better wait until I win another so I can have a matched set."

The reporters laughed appreciatively. "No kidding, Katie, what are you doing here?" one of them asked.

"That should be obvious, shouldn't it?" Katie answered, flashing a wide, and practiced smile. "I've come to help my dear friend Sid celebrate the finish of *Arabian Pleasures*. I saw some of the rushes and I can assure you it is a wonderful picture."

"But don't you feel that your being here is a little awkward?"

"Awkward? No, I don't think so. Why should it be awkward? What an unusual question for you to ask."

"Well, because everyone knows you wanted the female lead in *Aerodrome* but you got turned down," the reporter said.

Katie smiled again. "I'm afraid your information is

wrong," she said. "The decision as to who will play that part hasn't been made."

"What are you talking about, Katie? Of course it has been made. It has been rumored ever since Maxie night. It was made official three days ago. My goodness, you have to know about it by now. They've been running it in papers all over the country."

"Sure, everybody knows that, Katie," another reporter put in. "Joan Leland has been cast as Molly Tremaine."

"That's true, Katie. As a matter of fact, she's here tonight," the first reporter explained. "The way we get it, this is not only a party to celebrate the release of *Arabian Pleasures*, it is also to introduce Joan Leland as Molly Tremaine."

"Yes, yes," Katie said. "Miss Leland is a very sweet girl and I know they have been considering her for the part."

The reporters and photographers looked at each other with obvious surprise. One of them shook his head, then made a circling motion with his finger, as if to say that Katie had lost her mind.

Katie saw the motion and laughed easily, confidently. "Trust me, boys," she, said. "I know what I'm talking about. Now, if you will excuse me, I really must get inside to the party."

"What the hell is going on here?" one of the reporters asked as Katie left them to go on inside Dreamcastle.

"Beats me," another replied. "But I'll tell you the truth. If Katie Starr says the part hasn't been cast yet, I'm going to at least listen to her. She packs a lot of weight around here."

"She does, I'll admit," the first reporter replied. "But not as much as Sid Friedman and if he says the picture is cast, then the picture is cast."

"I'll reserve judgment on that," the doubter said.

Once inside the door, Katie reached out to grab a champagne cocktail from the tray of one of the circulating waiters, then she sipped it as she wandered around the room. She saw Sid, surrounded by several of his guests. She also saw Joan Leland standing by his side. Though the buxom blonde needed no introduction, Sid was, very pointedly, introducing her to everyone who came by.

Joan Leland had cultivated the art of looking directly into the eyes of whoever was speaking to her as if, for that particular moment at least, her interlocutor was the most important person in the world. Her light blue eyes flashed on command and she had a beautiful smile. She also wore her blond hair long, thereby defying the prevailing trend, and she had a little habit of brushing a wayward lock of it back from her face, a suggestion of intimacy that men reacted to.

Nodding and answering greetings from several well-wishers, Katie worked her way through the large crowd until she could approach Sid. When she walked up to Sid and Joan, she saw an instant's hesitation in the producer's eyes, as if he wasn't sure just what she had in mind. She saw during that instant that he was actually afraid of her and as soon as she realized that, she knew also that she actually relished that feeling.

"Katie, darling, so good of you to come to the party," Sid said nervously, extending his left hand to her, palm down. "I must tell you that there were quite a few who swore that you wouldn't dare show your face here. But I said no, Katie is a trouper, a real pro. She'll be here, congratulating Joan, laughing and having as good a time as anyone else, and basking in her own glory of having won the Maxie. You mark my words, I said, Katie is that kind of person. Now, didn't I say that, fellas?" he appealed to Hal and Lee. "Didn't I tell you she would be here?"

"That's what you said, Sid. You surely did," Lee agreed.

"There's no doubt about it, Miss Starr, Sid is your greatest admirer," Hal added.

"I'm sure the lady knows that," Sid said. "Oh, you've met Joan Leland, haven't you?"

Katie smiled sweetly at Joan. "Yes, of course I have. How lovely you look tonight, Joan."

"Thank you. Listen, Miss Starr, I hope you don't have any hard feelings over the fact that I got the part you wanted," Joan said.

"Oh, no hard feelings at all," Katie said. "But"—she held her finger up as if cautioning Joan—"I wouldn't start studying the lines just yet, if I were you."

"What…what do you mean? Mr. Friedman, what does she mean?"

"Nothing," Sid said. He forced a laugh. "She's joking with you, that's all. You should know what a kidder she is. She's always kidding about something. But listen, Katie, everyone doesn't know you like I do. You ought not to tease like that. People might get the wrong idea."

"Oh well, we wouldn't want people getting the wrong idea, would we?" Katie replied. "By the way, I hope you don't mind, but I've taken the liberty of asking my brother to join us here at the party tonight."

"Your brother? I thought…I thought he was in New York."

"He was. But after the little conversation you and I had the other day, I decided to call him. He has always taken an interest in my career, you know, even way back when I was still under exclusive contract to Sammy Solinger. You do remember Sammy Solinger, don't you? Anyway, after I told him that you were having a difficult time making up your mind, he decided to come out here to see if he could make you listen to reason."

The smile left Sid's lips and his face began to turn red. His eyes bulged with fear and beads of perspiration broke out on his upper lip.

"Oh, I see some people I simply must say hello to," Katie said. "Would you excuse me, Sid? And Joan, you are such a talent. I do hope you find a part, real soon."

Sid, Hal, and Lee watched in shocked silence as Katie walked away.

"The nerve of that woman," Joan finally said. "Telling me she hopes I find a part real soon. And what does she mean, Mr. Friedman, when she says her brother is coming out here to make you listen to reason?"

"Shut up," Sid said brusquely.

"Mr. Friedman! You can't talk to me that way! I'll see my agent, he'll—"

"I said, shut the hell up," Sid growled. He turned to one of his two toadies. "Hal, find Larry Cohen and Bernie Gold," he said. "Ask them to...no, by God, tell them, to meet me in my study."

"Right away, Sid."

"And you, Lee. Round up a couple of security guards. Make sure they are armed."

"Did you say make certain they are armed?"

"With guns," Sid said. "Big guns. The bigger the better."

"What do you want me to do with them once I have them?" Lee asked.

"Tell them not to let me out of their sight. No, don't do that. Tell them—tell them to just stand by for further instructions."

"Okay, Sid, if you're sure that's what you want," Lee said, hurrying off to accomplish his errand.

When Larry Cohen and Bernie Gold came into Sid's study a few minutes later they found him pouring himself a good, stiff drink from a cut-glass decanter. He filled the glass almost to the top then raised it to his lips, his hand, shaking visibly.

"Sid, Sid, what is it? What's going on?" Larry asked.

"It's Katie Starr."

"She's raising hell because you cast Joan Leland?" Larry asked. "Well, let her. If she makes too much noise about it, the publicity will kill her, it won't kill us."

"Funny you should use that word," Sid said, tossing his drink down as if it were water.

"What word?"

"Kill."

"It's a figure of speech. I don't mean it literally."

"I do," Sid said. He poured himself another glass of whiskey. "Or, more importantly, Katie's brother does. She's called him to come out here. To make me 'listen to reason,'" he added.

"So what? Who is her brother supposed to be? Some tough guy, or something?" Larry asked.

"You remember Sammy Solinger, don't you?"

"Sammy Solinger? No, I don't think so."

"He was a little before your time, Larry," Bernie interjected. "But I remember him." He looked at Sid. "He was the first person out here to have Katie under contract, wasn't he?"

"Yes."

"What does he have to do with anything?"

"Katie's brother came out to talk to Sammy to make him listen to reason. Only Solinger didn't listen to reason. Do you remember what happened to him?"

"I know he turned up dead. But he was a small-time schmuck and he was always screwing people. He just screwed the wrong person one time too often, that's all."

"He didn't just turn up dead, if you recall," Sid said. "His head was served up for lunch, nestled in a bed of lettuce on a tray of deli meats and cheeses. And the wrong person he screwed was Katie Starr, or, more specifically, her brother."

"My God! Really?" Larry gasped.

"Yeah, now that you mention it, I do remember how they found him," Bernie said. "As I recall, his valet was setting the table for lunch and when he took the cover off the serving dish, there was Sammy's head." Despite the gruesomeness of the statement, Bernie chuckled. "The truth is, ol' Sammy got a lot more notice after he was dead than he ever did while he was alive."

"Maybe you also remember that Katie Starr had been trying to get out of an exclusive contract with him at the time."

"Yeah, now that I think about it, I believe I do remember that."

"The way the story goes, Katie's brother came to negotiate for her, but Solinger refused to release her from the contract. Shortly afterward..." Sid made a sound with his mouth then drew his hand across his neck in a cutting motion.

"Nobody was ever charged with that," Bernie reminded him.

"Of course not. When you're in that business you are smart enough to cover your tracks."

"What business? Say, who the hell is Katie's brother, anyway?" Larry asked.

"His name is Sangremano," Sid said. "Johnny Sangremano."

Bernie went white. "Johnny Sangremano?" he said in a small voice. "Wait a minute. You mean the mobster? My God, are you telling me that Johnny Sangremano is Katie Starr's brother?"

"That's right."

"Jesus, he's big time, isn't he? I mean, he's like Al Capone."

"Who are you kidding, he's like Al Capone? Al Capone won't dare mess with him."

"And he's coming here?"

"Yes. Tonight."

"What are you going to do?" Bernie asked fearfully.

Sid put his empty glass down and wiped his mouth with the back of his hand. "I'm not sure," he finally said. He took a deep breath. "But I don't think he could really get away with something like the Solinger business again. And certainly not in a place as public as this. What's more, I think he knows it. Something tells me he is coming here to run a big bluff."

"So what, exactly, do you have in mind?" Larry asked.

"I don't know, but I just feel that if we keep our wits and our courage, we can stand up to him," Sid said.

"You mean you think we should call his bluff?" Larry asked.

"Like Solinger did?" Bernie added, pointedly.

"Solinger was small potatoes, you said so yourself," Sid replied. "He didn't have any friends when he was alive and he had fewer after he was dead. But we're not like that. We are highly visible people in a very visible industry."

"I don't know," Bernie hedged. "These big-time mobsters don't play by the same set of rules as the rest of the world. If this guy wanted to kill us, he could do it."

"Yeah, but that's just it," Sid said. "I don't think he wants to kill us...he wants something from us. He wants me to cast his sister in the role of Molly Tremaine. And I sure as hell can't do that if I'm dead, now, can I?"

"No," Bernie agreed. "No, I guess not."

"Then all we have to do is agree to stick together."

"Listen, Tamara Welles is out there. Maybe we should get her in here," Bernie said.

"Why do we want her in here?"

"Because she is the biggest individual stockholder of Galaxy Pictures, that's why. And she is the one who insisted that you not cast Katie in the picture."

"She just suggested, she didn't insist," Sid said.

"Yes, but her suggestion is backed with an awful lot of stock and an even larger number of proxies," Larry reminded him.

"It might be good to have her in here," Bernie said again.

"No," Sid replied. "Anyway, what is she going to do, hold up her proxies for the man? No, thank you. The day I have to hide behind a woman's skirts, or proxies, is the day I quit this business. Let's just leave Tamara out of it."

"Okay, if you say so," Bernie said.

"Sid, are you sure you know what you're doing?" Larry asked.

"Listen, just trust me," Sid said. "He's not going to try anything here at the party. And after he leaves, we'll raise so much stink he won't dare try anything at all."

There was a quiet knock on the door of the library and Sid looked at the others for a moment, then he went to the door. Lee was standing on the other side, and behind him was a tall, dark, impeccably dressed, very handsome man.

"Mr. Sangremano?" Sid asked over Lee's shoulder.

The visitor smiled easily, then moved past Lee and stuck out his hand. "Johnny Sangremano," he said. "Mr. Friedman, it's very nice of you to take the time to speak with me."

Sid was a little taken aback...he hadn't actually indicated to Sangremano that he would speak with him. But of course, there was no way he wasn't going to and Sangremano knew that. "Yes, well, do come in, won't you, Mr. Sangremano? I'd like you to meet my associates, Mr. Gold and Mr. Cohen." As Johnny shook hands with each of Sid's associates, Sid spoke quietly to Lee. "Did Hal contact those...people...like I asked him to?"

"They're right out here, Sid," Lee replied.

"Good, good. Uh, tell them not to wander too far off."

"You want me to come in or wait out here?" Lee asked.

"Wait outside," Sid replied. When he turned around he saw that Johnny, without asking, had poured himself a drink. Also, without being asked, he had sat down.

"Please, gentlemen, have a seat," Johnny invited, as if this meeting were taking place in his home instead of Dreamcastle.

"Thank you," Sid said dryly, though he believed his sarcasm was lost.

"By the way, I watched *Arabian Pleasures* this afternoon," Johnny said. "I want to congratulate you gentlemen, especially you, Mr. Friedman. I thought it was a very good picture. I especially liked the battle scenes between the nomads and the French Foreign Legion."

"You watched it when?" Larry asked.

"This afternoon," Johnny replied easily. "Well, more like this evening, actually. I just finished seeing it. That's why I was a little late in coming to your party. I know my tardiness was rude and I do hope you will forgive me."

"Wait a minute," Sid said. "It is impossible for you to have just watched *Arabian Pleasures*. We haven't made any duplicates yet, there is only the master copy and it's locked up in a vault."

"Yes, I know," Johnny replied.

Sid laughed. "So why are you telling us you saw the picture?"

"Because I did see it," Johnny said in the same easily tone. He took a piece of paper out of his pocket and handed it to Sid. "Perhaps you'll recognize this."

"What's that?" Larry asked.

Sid looked at the paper, then he looked up at Johnny, his face reflecting confusion and anger.

"This is my certification that the film is a master copy," he said. "How did you get hold of this? It is supposed to be in the can with the film."

"It was," Johnny said. "But I thought I might need it to prove to you that I actually saw the picture. And I now see that I wasn't mistaken."

"All right," Sid said. "All right, so you got to someone in the film vault and he let you screen the picture. The question is, why? And what does that have to do with your sister playing Molly Tremaine?"

"Oh," Johnny said. "Well, actually, I don't believe I have suggested that my sister play Molly Tremaine. Why do you ask? Are you considering her for the part?"

"No, goddamnit, I am not considering her for the part," Sid replied. "That role is already filled. Joan Leland is going to be my Molly Tremaine."

"Well, then I wish Miss Leland all the luck," Johnny said. "I've never seen her in anything, but if you think she is better than Katherine, then she must be very good indeed. And, of course, you are the one who is best qualified to make those decisions. I certainly would never want to make them for you."

Sid got a very confused expression on his face and when he looked at his two associates, he saw that they were just as confused as he was.

"I don't understand," Bernie said. "You aren't here to try and talk Sid into casting your sister?"

"Oh no," Johnny replied. "Nothing like that. As I said, that is Mr. Friedman's decision to make. Actually, I'm here to talk about *Arabian Pleasures*."

"*Arabian Pleasures*? What do you have to do with *Arabian Pleasures*?" Sid asked, even more confused now than he had been.

"As I said, it is a very good movie. It's a shame no one will be able to see it."

"No one will be able to see it? What are you talking about?" Larry asked.

"Look here, you guinea bastard!" Sid exploded. "Did you do something to the master copy? Because if you did, that's grand larceny and I'll have your ass put under the goddamned jail!"

"Relax, relax," Johnny said easily. "I didn't do anything to your master copy. It's still in the vault where you left it, and how you left it."

"Then...what are you talking about...nobody will be able to see it? Why the hell not?"

"Perhaps you have forgotten, Mr. Friedman," Johnny said, as if explaining something to a child, "that there is more to the motion-picture industry than just making films. If the theaters don't show the film, the picture can't make any money. And the theaters, Mr. Friedman, are not going to show *Arabian Pleasures*."

"Would you mind telling me just why the hell they won't?"

"It's a simple matter of distribution," Johnny explained. "You see, before the theaters can show the films, they must get them from a distributor. It may interest you to know that through direct ownership and, uh, let us say, certain ironclad alliances, I control the distribution for over fifteen hundred theaters across the country. This includes, by the way, at least eighty percent or more of all the theaters in New York, Chicago, Boston, Detroit, Philadelphia, Atlanta, Louisville, Cleveland, St. Louis, Kansas City, New Orleans, Denver, and San Francisco."

"You control them?" Sid asked in a weak voice.

"Well, either I or my business associates control them," Johnny replied. "And I can tell you now, Mr.

Friedman, that we have no intention of distributing
Arabian Pleasures

"What?" Sid exploded. "Why the hell not?"

"Let's just say that I am not too happy with the
casting in that picture," Johnny replied. "The man who
played Jacques Gameau, for example. What was his
name?"

"John Delaney," Sid said. "What do you have against
him? He is a marvelous actor."

"Really? I thought he was rather weak. And if that is
an example of the kind of miscasting we are going to get
from Galaxy Pictures, then perhaps I should avoid
Galaxy Pictures altogether. Unless, of course, I see some
indication that in the future you will be more selective in
your casting."

"Such as Katie Starr instead of Joan Leland?" Sid said.

Johnny smiled. "That would be a start," he said.

"Well, you can just shove that notion right up your
ass," Sid snorted. "Because it's not going to happen."

"I see." The easy smile had still not left Johnny's face.
"Gentlemen, I once heard that you should never attempt
to teach a pig to sing. It will only waste your time and
annoy the pig. I am evidently wasting my time here." He
got up to leave.

"No! No, wait," Bernie called out. "Sid, for God's
sake, don't you realize what is happening here? He has
us by the goddamned balls! If our picture is kept out of
fifteen hundred theaters, there is no way in hell it will
ever pay out. We'll go belly up."

"He's bluffing," Sid said. "I'll go to the theater owners
personally. If we have to, by god, we'll bypass the
distributors."

The telephone rang.

"Oh, perhaps you had better answer that, Mr. Friedman," Johnny suggested. "I took the liberty of putting

through a long-distance telephone call to Max Austin in New York. As you know, he owns three hundred and twenty theaters. I thought you might want to talk to him."

"What do you mean you put through a long-distance call?" Friedman asked. He pointed to the phone. "There's no way you could've done that. This is my private line here. There aren't more than seven or eight people who know this number."

"Why don't you answer the phone?" Johnny suggested again.

"All right, wise guy, I will. Hello," Friedman said, picking up the phone. "What? My long-distance call to New York. Uh, yeah, operator, go ahead, put him on." He covered the mouthpiece of the phone and looked up at Johnny. "Okay, so you found out my private number. Big deal. We'll see who Max listens to. I've got a few favors of my own I can call in. I guarantee you, Mr. Big-time Mobster, we'll show in every theater in the country, and we'll fill all the seats. Yes, Max!" he said when someone answered from the other end. "Max, this is Sid Friedman! Yes, that Sid Friedman," he added, laughing. "Well, I'm honored that you are honored. Listen, Max, I'm sure you've heard that we're about to release *Arabian Pleasures*. Yes, yes, everything you've heard about it is true. It is a wonderful picture and it's going to make a lot of money for everyone, especially for the theater owners," he added, laughing. "So, Max, I was thinking, as a publicity gimmick, and also to help you out, I might send the two stars of the picture to New York for a series of personal appearances. They'll be completely at your disposal, Max. Hell, they'll even stand in the lobby and greet the customers if you want them to. Now, what do you think about that, Mr. Max Austin? Does Sid Friedman know how to treat his theater owners, or what?"

Max said something on the other end of the phone, and though the others in the room could hear his voice, they couldn't understand exactly what he was saying. They got a pretty good idea of what it might be, however, by the expression on Sid's face. It went from a broad, confident smile, to shock, then anger.

"What do you mean you won't be showing this film?" Sid shouted into the phone. "My God, man, don't you know this may be the biggest money-making film ever?"

Another unintelligible reply.

"You owe me, Max! Goddamnit, you owe me, you sonofabitch!" Sid slammed the phone down, then looked at Johnny.

"Go ahead," Johnny invited. "Call in all your favors. You might manage to get a showing in Boise."

Sid pinched the bridge of his nose. Finally, he sighed. "It is too late to make any changes in the casting of *Arabian Pleasures*," he said.

"Yes, that is unfortunate, but I understand."

"Suppose...suppose I made a few changes in the tentative casting of *Aerodrome*, to show you that I am sensitive to the problem? Do you think you might reconsider your objections to *Arabian Pleasures*?"

"I think we might be able to work something out," Johnny replied.

"I'll have to reevaluate the entire cast, you understand," Sid said. "And that might take several days. But suppose, in the meantime, I made just one significant change, sort of as a 'good faith' gesture? Would that ensure the distribution of *Arabian Pleasures*?"

"I'm sure it would," Johnny said. "If the change is one that I agree with."

Sid pinched the bridge of his nose for a long, long time before he spoke again. "I was thinking of something along the lines of replacing Joan Leland with Katie Starr," he finally said.

Johnny finished the rest of his drink and stood up then, smiling broadly. "I think that would be an excellent move," he said. "And I'm so glad the idea was yours. Gentlemen, I will be glad to personally see to it that *Arabian Pleasures* is distributed. I think it will be a mutually profitable exercise. But now, if you will excuse my leaving early, I really must get back to the airport. I'm flying back to New York. I have to return to the city as quickly as I possibly can in order to make certain that all my distributors get the good word."

Johnny left the library without being shown the way out. Bernie Gold, Larry Cohen, and Sid Friedman remained behind. Sid was still sitting in his chair, still pinching the bridge of his nose. When Gold and Cohen saw that tears were running down his face, they looked away in embarrassed silence.

"That sonofabitch," Sid said, his shoulders shaking as he sobbed. 'That miserable, low-life sonofabitch."

CHAPTER 3

UPSTATE NEW YORK

Mike Kelly slapped at a mosquito on his forehead and when he pulled his hand down, it was covered with blood. Whether the blood was his or the blood of one of the mosquito's previous victims, Mike didn't know. He did know that the mosquitoes were driving him nuts and he wished he had put on a little more of the foul-smelling repellent.

"They're not bothering you?" he asked his partner, Jason Vandervort.

"My blood is blue, remember?" Jason replied. "Mosquitoes don't like blue blood."

"It figures," Mike replied. He checked the magazine in his submachine gun, though he had checked it numerous times already, then he pulled a tree branch aside to look toward the house.

It was a sprawling two-story farmhouse. The fact that there was a barn with no livestock and a machine shed with no machinery gave further testimony, if such testimony were needed, that this was no ordinary farmhouse. This was a meeting place, a "safe house" for gangsters and right now it was the hideout for a gang of outlaws who, three days earlier, had robbed a bank in New Jersey, killing a teller and a bank guard in the process.

"There's Bill's signal," Jason hissed. "He and Joe are in position."

Bill Carmack and Joe Provenzano were the other two members of the team of FBI men. They had come to make an early-morning arrest of the six bank robbers. They had tracked the outlaws here through a combination of luck, an eyewitness report, and some good police work. Now they were waiting for dawn to make the arrest, to eliminate the possibility of anyone getting away in the darkness.

"I think they must be getting ready to leave," Mike said. "I've been seeing movement through the windows for the last few minutes."

"Yeah, me too. And it's been quite a while since I smelled the bacon cooking. They've obviously had their breakfast by now. Too bad I can't say the same about us."

"Get ready," Mike said. "Someone's coming out the back door."

The man who came out the back door walked over to one of the two cars that were parked under the tree.

"What do we do now?" Jason hissed. "We can't just let him leave, can we?"

"He's not going anywhere," Mike insisted. "All the money is inside, remember?"

"Yeah, I guess you're right."

The outlaw slipped into the gray Dodge, stepped on the starter, shifted the gear, then backed it up to the back door. He left it sitting there with the doors open and the engine running while he went over to the blue Ford and moved it back in line with the Dodge.

"They're getting ready to leave," Mike said. "Can you still see Bill or Joe?"

"Yeah."

"Give them a signal to get ready."

Jason caught Bill's attention, then he pointed to the two cars the robber had moved into position. Bill nodded back.

"They're ready," Jason said.

"Here they come," Mike hissed.

The back door opened again and this time six men came out. One of them was carrying a couple of bank sacks. Mike stood up.

"Freeze!" he shouted. "You're surrounded by federal agents!"

"Cops!" one of the outlaws shouted, and he pulled a gun and fired toward Mike.

"Return fire!" Mike shouted, ducking back down quickly while at the same time squeezing off a burst from his Thompson submachine gun.

Three of the gangsters turned around and ran back into the house. The other three got into the lead car and tried to drive away, firing through the windows at Mike and Jason as they did so.

Mike squeezed off another burst of fire, this time aiming for the car's engine. He punctured the radiator and was rewarded with a gush of steam. Other bullets knocked out the windshield and the front tire. The car turned over and slid on its side for several feet, then was perfectly still. Crouching low, Mike ran to the car, then looked down inside. One of the occupants appeared to be dead, but the other two were moving, though groggily.

"Out of the car," Mike ordered, opening the door so they could climb out. As each of the robbers exited, Mike cuffed them, then he brought them back over to the trees where he and Jason had been waiting.

Just as he reached the trees a bullet popped by his ear, so close that he could feel the concussion.

"Damn!" Mike said, dropping to his knees and looking back toward the house.

"They're on the second floor," Jason said. "And they have rifles."

"Yeah, well, I guess no one said this was going to be easy," Mike replied.

Jason put down his submachine gun and pulled his pistol.

"What are you doing?" Mike asked.

"I'm going after them."

"One pistol against three rifles? That's not the best of odds, is it?"

Jason smiled. "Well, I'm not exactly going to put it between my teeth and charge," he replied. Bending over low enough to be shielded by a long row of honeysuckle vines, Jason ran to the far corner of the house. Mike watched him dart from there to a tall elm tree. Once there, Jason climbed the tree, then worked his way out onto a limb that protruded over the roof of the house. A moment later, Jason was on the roof, gun in hand, waving back at Mike.

Mike sprayed a long burst of fire toward the house, shooting low enough to make certain there was no possibility of hitting Jason with a stray bullet while, at the same time, keeping the robbers' attention away from the roof of the house. The robbers fired back and Mike could hear the bullets cutting through the leaves, just overhead.

Suddenly Mike heard shots from the other side of the house, then, a moment later, Bill shouted at him.

"One was trying to come out the back way, Mike! We got him!"

"That means there are only two of you left!" Mike shouted to the house. "Why don't you give up?"

"Why don't you come in here and get us, lawman?" one of the robbers replied.

Just as the robbers were issuing their challenge, Jason was reaching out to grab a tree limb. He used it to launch himself, feet first, through one of the windows. There was a tremendous crashing noise as he burst through the glass, and that, plus the surprise of his entry, left the robbers too startled to respond. Jason was on his feet with his gun in his hand before they could even turn around.

"What the hell?" one of them shouted.

Jason chuckled. "Excuse my dropping in like this. But you did say come in, didn't you?"

GREEN MOUNTAINS, VERMONT, ONE WEEK LATER

The leader of the group was Mike Kelly. Mike was an Irishman whose father and both grandfathers had been New York City policemen. Mike might have joined the city police force as well had he not found so many police officers corrupted by the mob. When he learned of the existence of a Federal Bureau of Investigation, answerable not to a corrupt city hall but to the federal government, he joined.

The next person after Mike to join the Bureau was Mike's cousin, Bill Carmack. Like Mike, Bill was a third-generation police officer and had actually been a member of the New York Police Department when Mike recruited him. Bill was now second-in-command.

The third man to come into the organization was Joe Provenzano. Joe had also been a policeman when he joined. Unlike Mike and Bill, however, Joe had no family history of police work. By becoming a law-enforcement officer, Joe was actually following a profession that was anathema to his family and peers. Joe was a first-generation Italian-American, and many of Joe's family and friends were "connected," involved in one way or another with the Mafia. Al Provenzano, Joe's uncle, was, in fact, the consigliere or chief counselor to Johnny Sangremano, godfather of the Sangremano Family.

With his Italian background, and of course his knowledge of the language, Joe was an invaluable resource in the fight against the Mafia.

Mike had actually learned of the Mafia many years earlier, not from Joe Provenzano but from Johnny Sangremano, a man who had been Mike's best friend. At the time Mike and Johnny were barnstorming their way across the United States in a war-surplus airplane. Being a police officer was the most distant thing from Mike's mind, just as Johnny Sangremano had no intention of entering his family's "business." Despite their best intentions, however, an unexpected tide of events swept away those early resolutions. Today, Agent Mike Kelly was head of the "Blood Oath Society," a small but elite force within the Bureau of Investigation, which was sworn to do battle against the Mafia. And Johnny Sangremano, who had survived the death of his father and the gangland murders of his two brothers, was now one of the top Mafia leaders in New York. Once the closest of friends, the two men were now the bitterest of enemies.

The last man to join the Bureau and the Blood Oath Society was Jason Vandervort. Mike's allusion to Jason's blue blood referred to the fact that Jason's father was one of the wealthiest men in America. Many years earlier, Jason Vandervort's father and no more than a dozen of his peers, had met with J. P. Morgan in his private library, where they pledged their personal fortunes to stop the collapse of the nation's banking system. Their efforts, largely unknown and unappreciated by the American public, had prevented a catastrophic depression from ruining the country.

The Vandervort fortune had actually increased over the last twenty years, but the younger Jason Vandervort was neither interested nor involved in the family investment business. He had turned his back on all that in order to become a member of the Federal Bureau of Investigation. Jason's dedication to his career was so complete that if someone told him he would have to give up his share of the family wealth in order to continue to serve in the Bureau, he would have done so without hesitation.

Fortunately, no one had made such an offer; thus Jason Vandervort was able to have his cake and eat it too. And because Jason was a generous young man, his good fortune was also the good fortune of the other three men with whom he was closest. It was in that spirit of sharing that all four were now enjoying a much-needed vacation at Jason's father's mountain cabin in Vermont.

The cabin had once belonged to Ethan Allen and had been used by him to foray the Green Mountain Boys to fight in the Revolutionary War. The Blood Oath Society, whereby Mike, Bill, Joe, and Jason took the blood oath of allegiance to each other, and enmity to the Mafia, was also started here.

The four had arrived at the cabin earlier in the day, and now Jason was reading, Mike was repairing a kerosene lamp, and Joe and Bill were out on the banks of the river, trying to catch enough fish for their supper.

"Do you think they'll actually catch anything?" Jason asked.

Mike looked up from the lantern. "Could be. But remember, you're talking about a couple of guys who grew up in the heart of the city and who never saw a fish that wasn't laid out on a bed of ice."

"They are resourceful, though."

"Oh yes," Mike said. "There is that to say for them. They are resourceful."

Mike and Jason heard a pistol shot, then another, then another. Curious, Jason walked over to the door and looked out.

"Do you see anything?" Mike asked.

They heard another pistol shot then, the unmistakable sound of laughter.

"No," Jason said. "But whatever it is, they seem to be having a good time with it."

"Probably practicing," Mike suggested.

"Why do they need to practice? They are the two best shots in the Bureau now."

Mike smiled. "How do you think they got that way?"

"Touché," Jason replied.

"Hello, the cabin!" someone shouted a little bit later.

"It's them," Jason said, putting his book down and walking over to the door.

"Get the skillet ready! We've got fish!" Joe called.

"I'll be damned," Jason said. He turned toward Mike. "Did you hear that? They say they've got fish."

"I heard it," Mike said, putting the pieces of the lantern aside. "But I don't believe it."

Half a minute later Bill and Joe came into the cabin and opened the little wicker basket to show off half a dozen good-sized fish.

"What do you think of these babies?" Joe asked.

"They're beautiful," Mike said, genuinely impressed. "I didn't think you could do it."

"What, you mean ye were of little faith?" Bill asked.

"That he was," Jason said, laughing with them. "And

I have to confess that I, too, had my doubts. What kind of bait did you use?"

"Thirty-eight Special," Joe said.

"What? What are you talking about?"

Joe chuckled. "Well, we couldn't get the damn things to take anything from the hook," he said. "So we just tossed some breadcrumbs out on the water and when the fish came up to nibble, we shot them."

"You mean that's what all the shooting was about, a while ago?"

"Yeah," Bill said. "It works real well. You should try it sometime."

"Here, give them to me," Jason offered. "However you got them, they have to be cooked. And if you are as innovative about cooking them as you were with catching them... I think I had better do it."

Later, after a supper of fish and fried potatoes, Mike related a telephone conversation he had had with J. Edgar Hoover just before he left the office in New York. "He sent his congratulations on a job well done," Mike said. "He was particularly pleased with how quickly we cleared up that bank robbery."

"I should think so," Jason said. "Is that all he wanted?"

"Well, no," Mike admitted. "Not exactly."

"What does that mean? Not exactly?" Bill asked suspiciously.

"He wants us to form a special task force," Mike said. He moved his index finger in a circle, taking in the four of them. "Us," he said, more specifically.

"You mean the Blood Oath Society?"

Mike nodded. "Yes," he said.

Outside of these four men, only one other person in the Bureau was even aware of the existence of the Blood

Oath Society. That man was J. Edgar Hoover. Hoover was, in fact, a member of the Blood Oath Society.

"Mike, you don't mean he has finally agreed to let us work openly against the Mafia?" Bill asked.

Mike shook his head. "I'm afraid not," he replied. "You know how he feels about that. According to him, there is no such thing as organized crime, let alone the Mafia."

"Then I don't get it. What does he want the task force to look for?" Joe asked.

"Communists," Mike replied.

"Communists?" Bill sputtered. "Are you serious? He wants us to waste our time looking for Communists?"

"Well, you know how he feels about them," Mike said. "He is convinced that communism is the biggest threat this country faces."

"Where are these Communists supposed to be?" Jason asked. He chuckled. "I don't know that I've ever even seen one. Certainly not around the Long Island Country Club."

"It's up to us to find them," Mike said.

"What did you tell him?" Bill wanted to know.

"I told him we would form the special task force and we would look for Communists."

"You're not serious."

"Don't dismiss it out of hand. It's not all bad," Mike said. "In order to find these Communists, we have been given the most sweeping mandate ever given to a special task force of the Bureau. Under the guise of Communist hunting, we can go anywhere we need to go and investigate anything we think needs investigating. We don't have to be asked by the local authorities."

"You mean we could investigate the Mafia?" Jason asked, suddenly getting the picture.

Mike smiled. "Especially the Mafia. It's just a personal theory, you understand, but what better way would the Communists have of undermining our country than by organizing the various criminal mobs across the country?"

Bill laughed. "You sly sonofabitch," he said. "We've been trying to get a mandate like that ever since we started."

"I know," Mike replied. "But until now we just never realized which button had to be pushed. Now we know."

LONG ISLAND, NEW YORK

Don Luca Vaglichio, the head of the Vaglichio Family, sat in his big leather chair and puffed contentedly on a Havana cigar as he listened to his brother Mario. Luca was in his middle fifties, about five feet seven, with a broad face, heavy brows, and high cheekbones. He tended to squint whenever he was discussing anything intently, which, because of the cheekbones and brows, turned his eyes into narrow slits. Mario was Luca's younger brother. Except for the dark hair and eyes, the two looked nothing alike. Mario had, in fact, been quite a handsome man in his youth. Mario's interests were a bit more diversified than Luca's, and he was a bit more cultured, but no one ever made the mistake of thinking he was less dangerous. Like his brother Luca, Mario could be a very brutal man.

The Vaglichios controlled all of Long Island and the Bronx. The lines of control were strictly drawn, having been established by years of brutal gangland war. During those long years of war, the bitterest rivals had been the Vaglichios and the Sangremanos. It had been a particularly bloody war for both families, and when Johnny Sangremano's oldest brother was killed by the Vaglichios, he retaliated by killing Luca and Mario's father, dropping a bomb from an airplane on the Vaglichio's fortress stronghold.

The war was over now and an uneasy peace existed between the two families, though there was still a great deal of bad blood between them. This meeting was, in fact, to discuss the latest bone of contention.

"It's the same way it was when we first started moving whiskey," Mario was saying. "You remember how Tony Sangremano didn't want to have anything to do with it? He wouldn't sell booze in his territory and he wouldn't let nobody else do it either."

"What are you asking me if I remember?" Luca replied. "Of course I remember. Pop got killed in the war that started."

"I'm afraid we've got the same thing going again, only this time it's dope. Johnny doesn't want anything to do with the dope, so he doesn't sell any, and he won't let any of our people in there either."

"Maybe he's holdin' it off for himself, same as they did with the whiskey," Luca suggested. "I mean, you see how quick they jumped in once Vinnie was in charge. And after Vinnie was killed, Johnny kept the business goin'."

Ben Costaconti spoke then. Ben was the consigliere to the Vaglichio Family and had been since it was headed by the old man. "I don't think it's the same thing, Don Luca," he said. "With the whiskey we all knew that Vinnie was in favor of it, so we figured that the Sangremanos would eventually get around to it. But Johnny is the only one left now and he hates the dope. No, I don't think the Sangremanos are ever going to come around on this."

"What are you tellin' me?" Luca asked. "Are you tellin' me that the blacks aren't dealin' in Sangremano's territory? Black dope pushers, they'll go anywhere, those guys. They're crazy, and just because Johnny says he don't want them in there, that ain't goin' to stop them."

"There's a little dealing going on," Ben admitted. "But only nickel and dime stuff. The truth is, we aren't going to make any progress in the dope department, without starting an all-out war and I think we all agree that that is something we do not want."

"No," Luca agreed. "We don't want another war. Not that I don't think we could take Sangremano, you understand," he added quickly, using his cigar as a pointer. "And I tell you the truth, I still wouldn't mind seein' that sonofabitch dead after what he did to Pop."

"We can't do that," Ben said. "Maybe we're stronger than the Sangremano Family, but we couldn't take on all the other Families as well, and the terms of our peace say that whoever breaks the peace will be the enemy of all."

"Yeah, yeah, I know, I know," Luca said, waving the explanation off.

"Luca," Mario suggested. "There is a place where Sangremano is vulnerable."

"Yeah? Where's that?"

"The movies."

"The movies? What do you mean, the movies?"

"Tell him, Ben," Mario said.

"The Sangremano Family controls the distribution of every film that plays in the city...not just in their territory, but the entire city. I can't imagine that the other Families are too happy about that."

"Yeah, well, he's had that for a long time," Luca said. "That's penny-ante stuff. Nobody cares."

"Luca, do you have any idea how much money that damned movie, Arabian Pleasures has made for the Sangremano Family since it was released?" Mario asked.

"No," Luca answered. "You're the movie fan. I don't

pay much attention to that sort of thing. I never go to the movies."

"Believe me, it isn't penny-ante," Mario said. "Movies are not only good entertainment, they are good business. And Johnny Sangremano gets a cut off every ticket sold in the city. Every ticket."

"Last week Sangremano's cut from the theaters in our territory alone was more than we got from prostitution, numbers, bookies, and policy combined."

"What?" Luca gasped.

"His total income from all the theaters all over the city was more than we made from everything, booze and dope included. And he still has all his other businesses going for him," Ben said.

"I had no idea the sonofabitch was making so much money out of that," Luca said.

"Johnny Sangremano is cleaning up," Mario said bitterly. "Cleaning up, mind you, from our people in our theaters, in our territory. And it's not right, damn it. He has no right coming into our territory like that."

Luca took his cigar from his mouth and stared at the end for a moment before he looked up at his consigliere. "Ben, what about that? Can't we go to council and get this resolved? I mean you're right about the other Families. Surely they can't be any happier with this situation than we are."

"I have discussed it with the other consigliereis, Don Luca," Ben replied. "And there is really nothing we can go to the council with. I mean, as far as the theaters themselves are concerned, all the Families already control the ones within their own territory. On Long Island and in the Bronx, for example, we control all the concessions, we say who gets hired and who gets fired. Strictly speaking, the Sangremano Family has not crossed territorial lines."

"Ben is right, Luca," Mario explained. "He has not

crossed territorial lines, but there's not a theater on Long Island or the Bronx that can show a damn thing without Johnny Sangremano's approval. And everything we do show, he gets a piece of. That means that without crossing territorial lines, Sangremano controls the entire city."

"How can he do that?" Luca asked.

"It all has to do with distribution," Ben answered. "It just so happens that all the distributors are physically located in Sangremano territory."

"And we can't get pictures for our theaters unless we go through them," Mario added.

"Can't we get them from somewhere else?" Luca asked. "Another distributor in another town?"

"No," Mario said.

"Why the hell not? Seems like a simple thing."

"If we try to get the pictures from somewhere else, we're going to run into roadblocks all over the place. First of all, the distributors themselves have contracts with all the production companies, guaranteeing territorial integrity."

"What's that mean?" Luca asked.

"It means that when a distributor in Boston or Philadelphia gets a picture, they sign a contract stating they will not attempt to distribute it outside a specific territory," Mario said.

"So they break the contract," Luca suggested. "What the hell, are you tellin' me we can't get a contract broken?"

"It's not as simple as that," Ben interjected. "That could also bring up a question of copyright infringement. And that's a federal violation."

Luca laughed. "Yeah, and so is sellin' dope and whiskey, but we're doin' pretty well by it."

"I was just telling you the legal ramifications," Ben

said. 'The real restriction would be in violating iron-clad agreements Sangremano has worked out with other Families in other cities. You see, once everyone realized what a sweet deal the Sangremanos had going for them in the movie distribution business in New York, they began organizing the distributors in their own territories. After that, they made agreements with each other. If we try and violate any of those agreements, we're going to pick up a lot of enemies."

"Then what you are saying is, there's nothing we can do about it," Luca said.

Ben Costaconti took out a gold cigarette case and extracted a cigarette. He tapped it down, then lit it before he replied. "No," he said. "I'm not saying there is nothing we can do about it. As a matter of fact, your brother has come up with an idea I think you should listen to."

"What's your idea?"

"Luca, have you heard anything about Johnny's sister, Katie Starr, and the new picture she is going to be in?" Mario asked.

"No," Luca said with a wave of his hand. "I mean, I know Katherine does something in the movies, but like I say, I don't keep up with all of it."

"Well, just to bring you up-to-date," Mario said, "Galaxy Pictures is about to begin production on a new film called *Aerodrome*. Have you heard anything about it?"

"No, I can't say as I have," Luca admitted.

"It's a picture about the airplanes and the war. It's a little like Wings, only with sound."

"Okay, what about it?" Luca asked.

"Well, an interesting development has occurred," Mario explained. "At least, I think it is interesting. It seems that when the picture was first announced, an actress named Joan Leland was supposed to star in it.

Then, quite unexpectedly, the studio announced a change. Show him the story, Ben."

Ben unfolded the newspaper he had been carrying and pointed to a story. "Katie Starr is to star in *Aerodrome*," the story says.

"So," Luca replied. "They changed their minds. People do that. What does that have to do with us?"

Mario chuckled. "If you weren't such an old stick-in-the-mud about the movies, you would see just how unusual something like this is. You see, when they first said Joan Leland was going to star in the movie, there was all sorts of hoopla surrounding the announcement. America's newest and brightest star, they called her. Then, without the slightest explanation as to why, they released the information that not Joan Leland but Katie Starr had the role. So I got curious and I decided to see if I could find out why."

"And did you find out?"

"Yes," Mario answered. "It seems that our friend Johnny Sangremano made a special trip out to Hollywood to get the producer to 'listen to reason.' "

"Listen to reason?" Luca nodded his head. He knew that "listen to reason" was a euphemism the Sangremanos used when they wanted to force someone to do something. They would hold it out like a feather but the feather would be concealing a stiletto. "What you are saying is, Sangremano forced the producer to change his mind?"

"Exactly."

"I'll be damned. You know, I always wondered how his sister got to be in the movies. All this time it was because of Johnny."

"Oh, don't underestimate Katherine's acting ability," Mario said quickly. "She really is a star in her own right, with or without her brother's help. But the point is, for whatever reason, they didn't want her to be in this movie, and now she is."

"Okay," Luca said. "So how do we figure in this? I mean, what's in it for us, our knowing this information?"

"If what I heard is true, and I've no reason to doubt it, then you have to believe that the producer of the movie considers Johnny Sangremano his enemy. And you know what they say... "The enemy of our enemy is our friend.' If we can make one producer our friend, we can make many producers our friends," Mario said.

"Sonofabitch!" Luca said. "I see what you're gettin' at now! Let Johnny Sangremano control all the distributors he wants. If we can control the production companies who make the films, we will be in the driver's seat, not Johnny Sangremano."

"Now you've got the picture," Mario agreed, nodding, and smiling broadly. "What do you think?"

"Brother, I think you and I are going to take us a trip out to California," Luca said.

CHAPTER 4

Johnny Sangremano's home, which was also on Long Island, was large by any standard. He had built it to resemble a villa that once caught his fancy when he was in France during the war. Like that villa, Johnny's house had nineteen rooms, turrets, dormer windows, and a red tile roof. The twenty-five well-tended acres on which it sat ran from the portico in front, across the clipped grass lawn, around handful marble statues, through a formal garden, across flagstone walks, by a large swimming pool, and finally ended at a boat house and dock down at the shore.

There were only two ways to reach the house. One was by private road, the other was from the bay. The private road was guarded twenty-four hours a day, every day, and there were enough underground impediments in the bay to force any approaching boat to use a specific channel. Johnny Sangremano did not like "drop-in" visitors and the precautions he took with the private road and water access were to ensure that no one would be able to pay him an unexpected visit. Despite all of Johnny's precautions, however, he had not been able to protect his wife. She, like his brothers and so many of his soldiers, had fallen, a victim in the wars. That had been two years ago, but the memory was as green and as painful as if it had happened yesterday.

Johnny had been hot and sticky from his trip into the city, so the moment he returned home, he decided to take a swim. He put on his swimsuit then went downstairs and outside. The surface of the bright, blue pool flashed with sunbursts. The gently undulating water was so inviting that he ran through the grass, dashed across the tile coping, and dived right in.

Johnny plummeted down through the water, then opened his eyes as he flattened out his dive to glide just above the blue tiles, far beneath the surface. That was when he passed over the cold, unblinking stare of his wife, Clara, lying nude at the bottom of the pool. Tiny bubbles of blood were still rising from the slit in her throat.

To the rest of the world, Clara's murder was just another Mafia killing. But to Johnny, her death was like losing a piece of himself, a part of his own soul. It was, he decided, a terrible payment for being a member of the Mafia.

The word "Mafia" was never used by its actual members or by those who were subject to its power. The members called it the Arm, the Clique, the Outfit, the Tradition, the Office, the Honored Society, the Combination, La Cosa Nostra, and the Family, with a capital "F," but never Mafia.

The Mafia had been founded for noble purposes in the 1600s as an underground army to fight against the oppressive rule of the Bourbons. When it began, the Mafia's aims were honorable and it thrived on strong kinship bonds and on a code of ethics and masculine honor.

Any noble purpose the Mafia may have once served, however, had long since been overshadowed by the greed of those people who, getting a taste of power, were unwilling to relinquish it. As a result, the Mafia moved into all aspects of criminal activity, from something as simple as a ten-cent bet wagered on punch cards, to something as complex and brutal as enforcing their rule by murder.

Johnny had never planned to occupy the position of godfather of his own Mafia Family. When Johnny's father, Giuseppe, died, the position went, as it should have, to the oldest son, Tony. But first, Tony, and then the second son, Vinnie, were killed in a gang war, and that left no way out for Johnny. He had no choice but to assume the mantle of responsibility, worn for so long by his father. Thus it was that Johnny Sangremano, Giuseppe's youngest son, was now "Don" Sangremano.

Don Sangremano, who was in his office at the back of the ground floor of his house, popped another lemon drop into his mouth then leaned back in his chair. On the other side of his desk, one of his lieutenants was giving a report.

"The blacks are our biggest problem, Godfather," Frankie Sarducci, the man giving the report, said.

"What is it, heroin?" Johnny asked.

"No, not heroin. Oh, there's a little horse being dealt here and there, but not enough to worry about. We're keepin' it out pretty good. But that ain't what I'm talkin' about. It's whores, is what I'm talkin' about."

"Whores?"

"The blacks are moving their whores right down into our territory. I mean, they got no respect at all for territory lines."

"Black whores or white whores?"

"They're black," Frankie said. "There's a couple that are really beautiful girls."

Johnny chuckled. "You sound interested."

"What, me? No way, godfather, not me," Frankie insisted. "I'm a married man. Besides which, every time I want a little something strange, I don't go no further than the whores that work for us. After all, I got loyalty, you know."

"I was just teasing," Johnny said.

"Yeah, oh well, yeah." Frankie said laughed, though it was obvious he hadn't really seen the humor. "Anyway, like I was sayin', there's two or three you can't really tell whether they're white or colored. And it don't look good, those girls workin' our neighborhood. It'll maybe give some others the idea they can come in too."

"Who's the head man?" Johnny asked.

"The head man?"

"Who's in charge of the hookers?"

"Oh well, that's just it," Frankie replied. "It don't seem like there really is any one person in charge. It's like a goddamn Chinese fire drill or somethin'. I mean, sure, the girls have their pimps and all. But I don't think there's any one colored man that we could go to to get things all straightened out. It ain't like dealin' with another Family. I mean, if we want to do somethin', we're goin' to have to do it to all of 'em, one at a time."

"What exactly did you have in mind?" Johnny asked.

"I was thinkin' maybe we could make things sort of uncomfortable for them. You know what I mean?" Frankie said. "Maybe rough 'em up a little."

Johnny wagged his head no. "I don't go for rough stuff with women," he said.

"Well, we got to do somethin'," Frankie insisted. "We can't just let them get away with it."

Johnny stroked his chin for a moment before he spoke again. "All right," he said. "This is what we'll do. Get some of the boys together and round up the girls. Don't hurt them. I'm going to be hard on anyone who hurts any of them. Round them up and take them somewhere, way the hell on the other side of the city or something, and dump them off."

"What about their pimps?"

"If their pimps give you any trouble, you can break a few heads," Johnny said.

Frankie smiled broadly. "Yeah, I'm goin' to like that. Okay, boss, I got you," he said.

"Oh, and Frankie?" Johnny called out, reaching for another lemon drop as Frankie started out the door.

"Yeah, boss?"

"Maybe you had better take personal charge of them."

"Don't worry none about them. I'll look after them, personal," Frankie promised.

Al Provenzano was sitting in a chair on the side of the room and he chuckled as Frankie left. "That's a little like setting a cat to watch a bowl of cream, isn't it?" he asked.

"It may be," Johnny agreed. "But at least if the cream gets licked up, we'll know who did it. Now, is there anything else we need to take care of today?"

"No," Al replied. "Oh," he added, holding up a finger. "The clipping service sent us over another batch of articles dealing with Katherine."

"What are they saying?" Johnny asked.

Al smiled. "They're all good. Most of them are saying they don't understand why Katherine wasn't cast in that role in the first place."

"We owe anything for any of those?"

"We've got a couple of stringers out working for us, yes," Al said. "But quite a few are straight articles."

"Reward the guys we got working for us," Johnny said.

"Yes, Godfather."

Johnny looked at Al. "Al, how many times have I told you, you don't have to call me that. I remember when you took me to my first Communion, for crying out loud."

"I don't call you that because I have to, Johnny," Al said. "I call you that because I want to. It's not good for the others to hear me call you Johnny."

Johnny smiled and shook his head. "Okay, Al, whatever you say. You're the consigliere. Listen, if there's nothing else, I'm going to be gone for a while."

"You're going flying?"

"Yeah," Johnny said. "Would you like to come along?"

"No, thank you," Al replied with a chuckle. "You seem to do most of your flying upside-down or at some other odd angle. I'll take my flying in an airliner, straight and level. But you go ahead and have a good time. I'll take care of anything that comes up."

"Thanks," Johnny said. He opened the top drawer of his desk and took out his old leather flying helmet. He had worn this same helmet not only during the war but also during his barnstorming days with Mike Kelly. "Be seeing you, Al." Johnny stuck the cap down in his pocket, then went out through the back door.

One of the advantages of living on such a large estate was that there was enough room for Johnny to have his own private airstrip. Behind the automobile garage, there was an aircraft hangar and in the hangar a midnight-blue-and-orange Curtis-Robbin biplane. The fabric of the plane had been doped, painted, and hand-rubbed so many times that it glistened like a mirror. Only the silver propeller spinner was shining more brightly than the fabric itself.

Johnny pushed the airplane out of the hangar, then climbed into the rear seat, the mechanic put his hand on the prop and when Johnny gave him a nod, jerked it around. The engine caught on the first try and Johnny started out to the airstrip. A few minutes later the airplane was off the ground and clawing for altitude.

Johnny headed out over the truck farms of the island. Just ahead of him was a big billowing pile of whipped cream...actually a cumulus cloud. Johnny knew better than to try to fly right through it, of course, for often the big soft cushiony-looking clouds hid hurricane-force wind that could toss an airplane around like a cork at sea or, worse, rip the wings off. It was sometimes nice to skirt around the edges of the cloud, though, catching long streamers of mist on the wing tips. Also, by flying just alongside, one had the illusion of tremendous speed.

Johnny loved flying, not only the physical sensation of it but also because being up in the cool, clean air got him away from everything. Up here he wasn't a Mafia don with the fate of hundreds of people in his hands. Up here he was an aviator, as free as a bird, and the only person's fate he controlled was his own.

There had been times when Johnny considered pointing the nose of the airplane to the west and flying away. He could go somewhere else, change his name, and get a job flying. Why not? Clara was gone and they had had no children. Who would miss him? He could get Mike and they could both go.

But even as he was thinking about it he knew that Mike wouldn't go with him. Mike was caught up now in his work as an agent for the Bureau of Investigation. And if Mike wouldn't go with him, Johnny didn't want to go either.

There had been a time, though. There had been a time when he and Mike had nearly left everything behind to take a job flying the airmail. Johnny squinted his eyes and stared through the spinning prop of his shiny new airplane. In this way, he could almost picture the old DH-4 he and Mike had flown into St. Louis in order to interview for jobs as airmail pilots.

After crossing the Mississippi River just north of the Eads Bridge, the DH-4 had begun descending. It circled once around the city, then landed at Lambert Field. They had taxied to a stop in a spot pointed out to them by a line boy, then, after they killed the engine, climbed down from their airplane.

"Do you want fuel?" the line boy had asked.

"No" Johnny answered. "Just leave it there."

"Leave it? Don't worry about that, mister. There's no way I'm going to try to move this thing. It looks like it's about to fall apart," the line boy said derisively.

The airplane was definitely beginning to show signs of fatigue and wear. It had already accumulated many hours of flying time with no maintenance except what Mike and Johnny were able to provide themselves. With no money for actual replacement parts, the two men managed to keep their airplane flying by using pieces of baling wire for control cable, garden hose for fuel and oil lines, and ash, pine, or elm instead of the hard-to-get spruce to replace or repair damaged spars and ribs. Wherever a cornstalk or a stick had poked a hole in the fabric, they patched it with pieces of cloth cut from flour and feed sacks. The rocker-arm oil leak that had never been adequately repaired continued to pump away and by now had smeared a large brown stain from the nose halfway back to the empennage. The DH-4 was no more than a vagabond collection of stained, bent, and patched bits and pieces of wood, cloth, and wire that somehow held together. It was a refugee from the junkyard and as they walked away from it Mike looked back to see it sitting right in the middle of a long line of shiny new Curtis-Robbins. The contrast between the new airplanes and the one they had been flying was so vivid that Mike groaned.

"What is it?" Johnny asked.

"Look," Mike said, pointing back toward the airplane. "The boy is right. That's not an airplane, that's a collection of junk parts, moving through the air in the same direction at the same time."

"Yeah, I guess it is kind of ugly, isn't it?"

"Ugly? It would have to improve a lot to be ugly," Mike suggested.

"Never mind. If Robertson Aviation will take us on as airmail pilots, we can afford to get our plane fixed up real nice."

"Fixed up? The only thing we could do to fix up that thing is take the old airplane off the propeller and put a new one on."

"And then replace the propeller," Johnny added, laughing.

Now, though the money he was making in the Mafia allowed him to own an airplane that was as nice as anything in the skies, Johnny had a strange longing for that old DH-4. Why did things happen as they did? Why couldn't he and Mike have taken that job and left all this behind? Why was it that two men who were meant to be friends for life were now bitter enemies?

Johnny felt a stinging in his eyes and a lump in his throat and with a frustrated shout into the wind, he flipped the airplane over onto its back, then pulled the nose down into a power dive. As the propeller wound up tighter and tighter and the wind howled through the struts and braces, he had a momentary desire to fly the airplane straight down into the ground, and as he thought about it he wasn't sure that he wouldn't do it.

Johnny's dive was lined up on a barn and he watched as the barn got bigger, and bigger still, until it filled the entire windscreen. He saw a couple of people run out of the house next to the barn. At first, they looked up at him with no more than idle curiosity; then, as the airplane continued to scream down in its dive, the two people on the ground panicked and began running. It wasn't until Johnny saw them start to run that he pulled himself out of his self-induced trance. He hauled back on the stick and the nose came up. The sudden pull-up at the bottom of the dive caused all the blood to run out of his head and he blacked out for a moment, not regaining consciousness until he was at the top end of the swoop, nearing a stall. He moved the stick forward just before the stall developed and he found himself flying straight and level at about five thousand feet. When he looked back down at the barn and the house, the small Long Island farm was nearly a mile below and two miles behind him. He hauled the airplane around in a hundred-and-eighty degree turn and started for home.

"Exit Johnny Sangremano, aviator and free spirit," he said. "Enter Don Sangremano, godfather and capo di capi."

HOLLYWOOD

Sid Friedman was leaning against the front of an army truck, looking out over the line of World War I biplanes. They were French Nieuports and German Fokkers and they were painted in the colors of the American 94th, "Hat-in-Ring" squadron, and the "Flying Circus," squadron of the great German ace Baron von Richthofen.

Though he was actually at a small, rural airport a few miles outside Los Angeles, it looked as if he were somewhere in France. The little airport had been converted by the magic of Hollywood into an exact duplicate ... or at least the set designer's idea of a duplicate of a World War aerodrome.

In addition to the line of French Nieuports and German Fokkers, there were also hangars, barracks, flagpoles flying the French tricolor, as well as several trucks, cars, and motorcycles, all painted in military camouflages. Scores of uniformed men scurried about the field, some working on airplanes, others marching. Sid looked on with appreciation for the magic he had wrought. If Eddie Rickenbacker were to suddenly appear here, he would surely believe himself back in France.

Deke Clark's Duesenberg drove up, its bright yellow color standing out amid the row of olive-drab trucks and cars. Deke got out and started toward Sid. He was carrying a riding quirt, an affectation started by Erich von Stroheim.

Right now Deke Clark was considered one of Hollywood's best directors and Sid had considered himself very lucky to get him to direct *Aerodrome*. There had been some difficulty in the beginning because Deke had wanted Katie in the role of Molly Tremaine, whereas Sid wanted Joan Leland. The irony was that Deke's wife, Tamara, backed Sid in his choice.

Now, due to circumstances beyond their control, Katie was back on the picture. But that hadn't made things go any easier between Sid and Deke. As the director, Deke thought he should have the final word on everything— how the sets were to look, what actors to use, and how to shoot. But Sid knew a little about picture making also and he had too much riding on *Aerodrome* to surrender complete control.

"I'd like a word with you, Sid," Deke began and the tone of his voice told Sid this was about to be another confrontation.

"You don't mean a word, do you, Deke? What you really mean is, you would like several words with me."

"Yes," Deke said. He pointed toward the line of airplanes. "What do you see out there?"

"What do you mean, what do I see out there? I see airplanes, men, trucks, buildings," Sid replied. "What is it specifically you want me to see."

"What I want you to see, Sid, you cannot see," Deke replied. "You can't see it, I can't see it, the audience won't be able to see it, because it isn't there."

"Deke, would you mind telling me just what the hell you are babbling about?" Sid asked in exasperation.

"Dust."

"Dust?"

"There is no dust," Deke said. "When the airplane motors are running, there should be dust. When you look out across here, you should be able to see a cloud of dust, covering everything in an ethereal haze. But there is no dust, Sid. Do you know why there is no dust?"

"You're goddamn right I know why there is no dust," Sid replied. "I had the runways, roads, and grounds oiled to keep the dust down."

"I need my ethereal haze, Sid," Deke said pointedly.

"For God's sake, Deke, we can't have a cloud of dust covering everything out here," Sid insisted. "For one thing it gets into the lenses and the camera mechanisms. For another the mechanics tell me it could get into the airplane engines and screw things up. Hell, it could even cause an accident."

"We have technicians to take care of the cameras, and stuntmen to fly the airplanes. They are paid to take risks, just like I am paid to produce the best picture possible. Now, do I get my dust or not?"

"Not," Sid said.

Deke spun on his heel, then started for his car. Just

before he got in, he turned to look back at Sid, pointing his riding quirt at him. "I want this well documented, Sid. If I submit my resignation to the board, I want them to know it is because I got no support from you."

"Is the thought of your resigning supposed to frighten me, Deke? What are you going to do, go crying home to your wife?"

"I don't need to go to my wife," Deke said. "I know and you know that the board would never have gone along with such a large budget for *Aerodrome* if you hadn't convinced them that I would direct the picture."

"Then direct the picture for chrissake, and leave the producing to me."

"If you don't quit bungling everything, there won't be a picture to produce," Deke growled. He got back into his car, slammed the door, then drove away with his tires spinning. If he had wanted to throw up a lot of dust, though, he was disappointed. Sid had already seen to that.

"Sid?" Lee called to him.

Sid looked around and saw Lee standing on the other side of the truck. "What is it, Lee? You look white as a sheet."

"He's here, Sid. Why is he here? We're doing everything he told us to do."

"Who is here?" Sid asked.

"The Italian."

"Sangremano?"

"No, not him," Lee said. "But it has to be someone Sangremano sent. He's certainly Italian looking, stout, dark, actually, rather handsome in a frightening way." Lee shivered. "He is wearing very expensive shoes and a suit unlike anything I've ever seen."

"Who is he?"

"I don't know," Lee said. "He gave me his name, but

it's one of those names that ends in a vowel. Who the hell can remember such names?"

Sid ran his hand through his hair nervously. "Where is he now?"

"He's out at the gate. The security guards wouldn't let him through."

"Tell him I'm not here," Sid said. "Send him away."

"All right," Lee agreed. "If you really think that's wise. I mean, someone like that, he'll just come back. Or worse, wait. And if he waits and sees you come out later, well, who knows what he'll do?" Lee shrugged.

"Shit," Sid said. "I don't need all this. I've got a prima donna actress, an egomaniacal director, and more airplanes to look after than the entire U.S. Flying Service. And now I have to deal with some strong-armed goon Katie's brother sent out here to check up on me." He sighed. "All right, tell the sonofabitch he can come in. Then notify security."

"What do you want me to tell security?"

"Nothing in particular, I guess," Sid said. "Just have them stand by."

"All right. Oh, and Sid, don't do anything to make him mad, okay? I mean, if he does something awful to you, I'm going to be very, very sick."

"That's comforting, Lee. That's very comforting," Sid said.

Lee disappeared, then returned a second later with the man he had described. The suit was a dark, double-breasted pinstripe. Perhaps Lee had never seen one like that, but Sid had seen many such suits in the old days, on Hester Street, back in New York. For just a moment he could almost smell the street and hear the sounds of his youth. And as such men frightened him when he was a child, that sense of fright returned. His fear wasn't allevi-ated by the man's broad smile and extended hand.

"Mr. Friedman," the man said. "My name is Mario Vaglichio. It is so good of you to see me."

"Before we go any further, Mr. Vaglichio," Sid said. "Were you sent by Johnny Sangremano?"

The smile on Mario's face changed. The change was subtle and though Sid wouldn't have thought it possible, it made his visitor even more frightening.

"No, Mr. Friedman," Mario said. "I wasn't sent by Johnny Sangremano. Johnny Sangremano doesn't even know I am here and I think it would be best for you and me both if he didn't find out."

Now Sid's fear began to change to curiosity, but it was to be a while before he could have that curiosity satisfied because an airplane was taking off at that moment. Its engine roared loudly as it rushed down the runway, then lifted into the air.

"Are you shooting pictures now, Mr. Friedman?" Mario asked, pointing to the airplane that was taking off.

"No, these are just the pilots and mechanics, getting the airplanes ready," he said. "We've had to gather these old crates from all over. We found them in empty fields, airports, and barns. Most of them hadn't been flown in years and we have to get them in shape."

"I see. I must confess to you, Mr. Friedman, that I have always been fascinated by the motion-picture industry," Mario said. "My brother is less infatuated than I am, but I could spend a whole day out here watching all this."

"Yes, but you didn't come out here to look at airplanes, did you, Mr. Vaglichio?"

"Oh, uh, no. No, I didn't," Mario said, turning away from the activity out on the field and back to Sid. "Well, first, let me tell you that Johnny Sangremano is no friend of mine. We're in the same business, but we have two different ways of doing things. I have a sense of honor and respect for my fellowman. Sangremano has no concern for who gets in his way when he wants something. Are you following me on all this, Mr. Freidman?"

Sid shook his head. "No, I can't say that I am."

"Then suppose I give you a for instance. For instance, it was in all the papers that Joan Leland was going to play the lead role in *Aerodrome*. Then all the newspapers said it was going to be Katherine Sangremano."

"You mean Katie Starr."

"Yes, Katie Starr, if you wish," Mario said. "So tell me, Mr. Friedman, was the change really your idea? Did you really want Katherine in your movie?"

"Katie Starr is an immensely popular actress," Sid hedged. "She would be an asset to anyone's picture."

"Mr. Friedman, I'm afraid you're not being on the level with me," Mario said. "If we're going to do some business together, we have to be honest with each other. Now, do you still wish to tell me how you really wanted Katherine in the first place, or do you want to do some serious talking?"

Lee came wandering around the front of the truck then and called out, "Sid, is everything all right?"

"Get out of here." Sid dismissed his assistant with an irritated wave of his hand.

"If you say so, Sid," Lee replied contritely, withdrawing quickly to the other side of the truck.

"See if this isn't what happened, Sid. I can call you Sid, can't I?"

Sid nodded but did not speak.

"Okay, good. Now, the way I figure it is Johnny come here to talk to you, didn't he? To see if he could make you listen to reason."

Sid's eyes grew wide and a sudden line of perspiration burst out on his upper lip. Mario saw his reaction and chuckled.

"Yes, I thought so. Well, don't you worry about it. You and I are going to do some business here that will take care of all that."

"What...what kind of business?" Sid asked nervously.

"Friendly business." Mario chuckled. "You see, Mr. Friedman, if you aren't Johnny Sangremano's friend, that means you are his enemy. And as the saying goes, the enemy of my enemy is my friend. You and I are going to be friends. You do want us to be friends, don't you, Mr. Friedman?"

"Yes, I guess so."

"You guess so?"

"Look, Mr. Vaglichio, right now I've got a star I don't want and a director I can't get along with. The last thing I need is any more trouble from anyone. So if you want to be my friend, the answer is yes. I'll be your friend. I'll be anyone's friend. Whatever it takes to get this picture finished, I will do."

"I understand," Mario said with a benevolent smile.

CHAPTER 5

Deke was sitting beside his swimming pool, nursing a martini when his wife and Alex Jensen came home. Alex was a beautiful young actress whose credits were thus far quite limited. With her dark eyes and hair and smooth olive complexion, she had been used as a stand-in for Katie Starr, though on a few occasions she had managed to get a walk-on part on her own. She had aspirations to greater things, however, and knew that a friendship with Tamara Welles could work in her favor. And because Alex was a bright young girl, she perceived quickly just what was expected of her in maintaining a "friendship" with Tamara Welles.

"Hello, Deke, I didn't think you would be home," Tamara said as she set the package she was carrying down on a table by the edge of the pool. "My, my, Alex and I did have a day of it, didn't we, Alex, dear?"

"Oh yes," Alex replied enthusiastically. "We must have shopped in every store in town. And thanks to Tamara I have so many lovely things now that I hardly know what to do with them."

"I'm sure you will figure something out," Deke replied dryly.

"Well, of course she will," Tamara replied with a scolding glance toward her husband. "If one is going to get ahead in this business, one must look as if one is already there." Tamara smiled possessively at the young actress. "After all, she can't be a stand-in for Katie Starr all her career."

"Tamara, do you mind if I try some of them on now?" Alex asked.

"Of course not, dear. I would love to have you model for me."

"Okay. I'll give you a show," Alex promised.

She took an armful of packages with her and walked around to the other side of the pool.

Tamara watched Alex walk away then turned to Deke. "So tell me, Deke, how was your day?"

"I had another run-in with Sid Friedman," Deke answered. "That man is utterly impossible. Why everyone insists on calling him a genius is beyond me."

"Perhaps it has something to do with the amount of profit his movies show," Tamara suggested.

"Profit? Is that all there is to this business?"

"Isn't that enough?"

"No," Deke insisted. "There are also such things as artistic integrity. And that is a commodity of which Sid Friedman is in short supply. I wish you would speak to him, Tamara. I wish you would tell him that on any question dealing with the artistic integrity of this film, I am to have the last word."

Tamara chuckled. "Deke, Deke, Deke. My dear, sensitive Deke. Do try and work with him, will you? After all, you do have your girlfriend on the picture with you now. I would think that would be enough for you. There is a tremendous amount of money tied up in this production and it wouldn't look good for the producer and the director to be at each other's throat all the time."

"Is that it?" Deke replied. "Is that all the support I get from you? Try and work with him? One would think, Tamara, that seeing as how you are my wife, you would be just a little more on my side."

"Oh, come, come, Deke," Tamara chided. "We both know why I am your wife." She was watching Alex change clothes on the other side of the pool. Alex was in her panties and bra now as she reached for one of the new dresses. Tamara continued to watch appreciatively until the young girl was partially covered, then she turned back to her husband. "Being married helps me maintain the illusion of normalcy whatever that means. And it allows your career to be associated with my name. So far the arrangement has worked out quite nicely, don't you agree? I don't interfere in your love life and you don't interfere in mine. I haven't been touched with the brush of scandal and your career has skyrocketed. Now, let's not change the rules of our relationship at this late date. You don't ask me to coerce Sid Friedman into changing what is already a proven success for making movies, and I won't ask you to procure young girls for my sexual pleasure." Tamara smiled pointedly at Deke, then looked back at Alex, who was now turning and preening as she modeled her dress. "Oh yes, Alex, dear. That is lovely," she called across the pool to her. "Perfectly lovely."

Deke stood and picked up his book. "Well," he said, "I'll leave you two ladies to your own pursuits. I have other things to do."

"You are sure you don't want to stay around?"

"That might be a little awkward for Alex, don't you think?"

"On the contrary. I think Alex might find it quite exciting. She is such an exhibitionist, you know. That's one of the things I love about her."

"Well, thank you for the invitation, but no thanks." Deke started to leave.

"Oh, Deke," Tamara called. Deke stopped and turned toward her. "You'll be going to see Katie, I presume?"

"I thought I might," Deke admitted. "I want to talk over a few scenes with her."

Tamara smiled. "Yes, I'm sure you do want to talk over a few scenes," she said sarcastically. "Although one has to wonder what there is to talk about? As brazen as she was about forcing herself into the picture, I'm sure she considers her own judgment about how a scene is to be played infallible."

"She's not like that," Deke insisted. "Actually, she's a very nice person."

"Of course she is. And her brother is a very nice person too. The mere fact that a few hundred people have wound up dead because they disagreed with him means nothing."

"I'm sure it's not anywhere near that many," Deke said.

"Well then, that makes it all right, doesn't it?" Tamara replied. "By the way, Deke, dear, you don't have that woman thinking you are about to divorce me so you can marry her, do you?"

"No, not really," Deke said.

"Because if you do," Tamara went on, "I think you should disabuse her of the idea. Dally with her all you want, and you'll have no trouble with me. But I will be greatly upset if you attempt to divorce me."

"Why, Tamara," Deke said. "Whatever would make you think I want to divorce you? As you said, our marriage is perfectly symbiotic."

Later, before Deke left the house to keep his dinner

appointment with Katie, he glanced through the bedroom window toward the pool. His wife and Alex were naked. Deke sat in the shadows of the bedroom, smoking a cigarette while he watched.

Deke's voyeurism didn't bother Tamara. Indeed, her earlier suggestion that he stay for a while, was a sincere invitation to indulge it. She had made many such offers to let him watch her with another woman, but he had spurned them all with a great show of indignation. The indignation was to hide the disgust he felt with himself for actually wanting to do it.

As it happened, he knew that Tamara was aware that he occasionally watched, but so far she had not made an issue of it. Deke decided that it was because Tamara derived more enjoyment from her exhibitionism than any satisfaction she would get from exposing his own hypocrisy. It worked out well for both of them.

————

The fronds of the palm tree shimmered in the glow from the underwater lights of the sparkling swimming pool, making a subdued clacking sound as they waved back and forth in the soft night breeze. Katie Starr was aware of these things as she sat on the diving board, but she didn't know why she was there. Her mind was muddled and confused.

Katie was nude and she could feel the rough textured surface of the board pressing against her naked thighs. One long, shapely leg hung down toward the pool, her toes just touching the water. Her other leg was drawn up onto the board and she leaned into it with her chin on her knee and her breasts pressed flat. Her hair was dry and soft since she hadn't been in the pool...so what was she doing out here?

Suddenly she remembered the horror she had just seen...or had she really seen it?

She turned her head and looked over toward the pool house. Please, God, she thought, don't let him be there. Please don't let him be there. This is a dream, a hallucination.

But he was there. He, like she, was totally naked. He was also dead. Deke Clark was lying naked, on his back, on a lounge chair, alongside Katie Starr's swimming pool. A bullet hole was in his forehead, small, ugly, and more black than red.

When did this happen? Why couldn't she remember and why wasn't she screaming from the horror of it? It was all achingly real to her, and yet there was still a strange, dreamlike quality to things. Time wasn't whizzing away, it was creeping by in agonizingly slow seconds.

Katie wondered how long she had been cognizant. Was it seconds, minutes, hours? Had she been sitting in this same position all night, staring at this dead man without really seeing him?

Katie tried hard, but she couldn't remember beyond the dinner. The dinner, yes. She hadn't actually recalled it until this very moment. They had eaten on the glass table by the pool. Alma had made a quiche and left detailed instructions on how it was to be reheated.

Where was Alma? Surely Alma would know what had happened. No, wait, she had given her maid the day off. There had been no one in the house tonight except Deke and her. That was because Deke said he wanted to talk to her, alone.

"There is something you are going to have to understand," Deke had told her. "I am not going to divorce my wife."

"You mean she won't give you one?" Katie had asked.

"No. I mean I'm not going to ask her," Deke had replied.

"I see," Katie said.

"No, I'm not sure you do see. I've told you, but I don't think you understand."

"All right, you told me. So what do we do now?"

"There is no need for us to do anything. When you think about it, nothing has to change," Deke said. "We can go on just as we have been."

"In other words you want to continue to be married to your wife, but you want the key to my bedroom. Is that it?"

"Yes, basically. Katie, please try to understand. It's a matter of business. My wife is a very powerful person in this industry. A messy divorce could not only ruin me, it could hurt many other innocent people. Even you wouldn't escape unscathed. And it's you, above all others, that I want to protect. I love you, don't you see?"

"You love me?"

"Yes. Katie, please say that you understand."

"More quiche?" Katie had asked.

Now Katie looked over toward the lounge chair and saw her clothes. She had the vaguest recollection of having had sex, though she wasn't sure if she had. Why couldn't she remember?

Six blocks away from Katie and the house and the swimming pool and the dead body, Officer Arnie Stone hung up the receiver at the telephone call box and walked back over to the police car. His partner, Jerry Farrell, was just finishing a doughnut, and he licked the sugar off the tips of his fingers.

"The station have anything for us?" Jerry asked.

"Yeah," Arnie replied. "There's a report of a domestic disturbance about six blocks from here."

"Shit, it's nearly midnight. Couldn't they have waited

a few more minutes to call it in? The next relief could've handled it."

"It's probably nothin' more than some wife throwin' a skillet at her ol' man," Arnie said.

"Ain't that somethin'? You'd think anyone rich enough to live out here would know how to behave themselves."

Arnie chuckled as he slipped in behind the wheel. "Jerry, I been on the force out here since long before any of these fancy houses were built, and I've answered hundreds of domestic disturbances. Let me tell you something. You take the richest person you can find, take off his clothes, and dunk him once in the sewer, and you got a person no different from the turds the wagons bring in every night. A human being is a human being. Some of 'em have more money than others, that's all."

"Ha," Jerry said. "Listen to the department philosopher."

It took less than five minutes. Jerry counted down the numbers until they found the house they were looking for. "There it is," he said.

Arnie pulled into a long curving brick driveway.

Lined on each side by a perfectly trimmed hedge, it led to a large stucco, two-story, Spanish-style house with a red tile roof. Both officers got out of the car and Jerry walked up to ring the doorbell. They could hear the chimes echoing from inside.

"Can't be much of a disturbance," Arnie said. "I don't hear anything."

"Me neither," Jerry replied. He rang the doorbell a second time.

"Come on," Arnie suggested. "Let's have a look around back."

"You want to go around back? What for?"

"Haven't you always wanted to see what the back of

one of these fancy places looked like?" Arnie asked. "Well, now is your chance. Besides, I've got an itch in my nose."

"Hey, good police work," Jerry replied sarcastically. "Tell me, Officer, how did you happen onto the scene of the crime? Well, Mr. Prosecutor, my partner had an itch in his nose."

"Come on," Arnie said, ignoring Jerry's sarcasm.

The house was in the middle of two acres of ground, and as they went around back, they walked through a formal garden, across a tennis court, and finally to a high white fence. They pushed on the gate and it swung open. Beyond the gate was a large flagstone terrace, and beyond the terrace, a bright blue swimming pool. On the other side of the pool stood a beautiful young woman, completely nude. She was holding a pistol in her hand, looking down on the body of a nude man.

"Holy shit!" Arnie said. He and Jerry both pulled their guns.

"Drop your gun, miss!" Arnie called to her.

The woman looked over at the two police officers. It was obvious she hadn't been aware of their presence until this very moment, but she seemed neither shocked nor frightened. She held the gun down by her side, making no effort to drop it.

"I said drop your gun!" Arnie shouted again.

The woman looked down at her hand, then opened it and let the gun drop. She watched, almost disinterestedly, as the two police officers approached her, walking around the pool.

"Would you step back, please, miss?" Arnie asked.

The woman stepped back while Arnie dropped to one knee beside the man. He put his hand to the man's neck to check for a pulse, but he already knew that he was dead. He had seen enough of them to know. He looked at the bullet hole in the man's forehead and saw the marks of powder burns.

"Is he dead?" Jerry asked.

"Yeah." Arnie sighed and stood up. "She must've put the gun barrel right to his forehead when she pulled the trigger."

"Arnie," Jerry said, pointing to the woman. "Arnie, do you know who this is?"

"No," Arnie answered. "Do you?"

"Hell yes, of course I do. Don't you ever go to the movies? This here is Katie Starr."

"Katie Starr?" It was obvious the name didn't mean anything to him.

"Katie Starr. Goddamn, don't tell me you've never heard of Katie Starr? She's one of the most famous actresses there is."

"Yeah, I think I've heard of her," Arnie said. He looked at the naked young woman. "Is that true, miss?" Arnie asked. "Are you Katie Starr?"

"Yes," the woman answered. She was standing about ten feet away, looking on impassively. She seemed totally unconcerned that there was a dead man by her pool and equally unconcerned that she was naked.

"Jesus, what a cool bitch she is," Arnie said.

"Who is this man, Miss Starr?" Jerry asked.

"Deke."

"Deke?"

"Deke Clark."

"Holy shit," Jerry said.

"What is it? Do you mean you have heard of him too?" Arnie asked.

"Yes, of course I have. He's a director. One of the best."

"You mean he was a director," Arnie replied. "He's dead meat now." He looked over at the still-impassive young woman. "Miss Starr, would you get dressed, now, please?"

"What?"

"Would you get dressed, please?"

"Okay."

Katie walked over to the lounge chair and started putting on her clothes. She stepped into her panties with as little embarrassment as if she were dressing in her own bathroom. Then she pulled on the red-sequined dress, which she wore without a bra.

"Jerry, go into the house and find a phone, would you? Call dispatch and tell them what we have here."

"Okay," Jerry replied.

"Miss Starr, did you kill this man?" Arnie asked.

"No," Katie answered calmly. She paused for a moment. "At least I don't think I did."

"You don't think you did?"

"I can't remember."

"You can't remember whether or not you committed murder?" Arnie asked.

"No. May I sit down?"

"Yeah, sure, go ahead," Arnie replied.

Arnie walked over to the lounge chair where the man's body lay and looked closely at the cushion. He smiled. Those were pecker tracks if ever he had seen pecker tracks. Of course, it would take a lab report to validate the presence of semen, but he didn't need a lab report to convince him. He looked up at the top of the cushion just under the corpse's head. There was very little blood, but Arnie knew that a bullet in the brain, with no exit wound, actually bled very little.

Katie got up and started moving. Arnie looked toward her.

"Where are you going?"

"To the bathroom," Katie replied pointing to the pool house. "I'm going to be sick."

"Just a minute." Arnie looked into the bathroom and, convinced that there was neither a way for her to escape nor to do harm to herself, nodded his assent.

Katie went inside and closed the door. Arnie could hear her retching while he continued to look around. The gun was a small .25-caliber automatic. That meant that the empty brass cartridge would have been ejected. If he could find it, it might give him a clue as to where the gun was fired. Arnie held his hand down over the deceased's head, looking right into his flat, dead eyes. He made an imaginary gun with his hand, then pulled the trigger. He looked around the lounge about the distance the casing would be ejected and he saw it. It was lying under a small table. He smiled in triumph.

At about that time several officers came through the fence. There were two plainclothes detectives with the uniforms, so Arnie knew that his own investigation was over. For him, it would be back to a police car. From now on it would be up to the glamour boys from homicide.

"I'm Detective Largent, this is Detective Murphy. Where's the woman?" one of the detectives asked.

"She's in the bathroom," Arnie replied.

"The bathroom? Damn!" Detective Largent nodded toward Detective Murphy, and Murphy jerked open the door. Katie was standing at the sink washing her hands. Murphy pulled her away quickly.

"What...what are you doing?" Katie shouted in alarm.

Detective Largent sighed. "If she had any powder stains on her hand, they're gone now," he said.

"I'm sorry, I didn't think."

"That's all right," the detective said. "You aren't paid to think. I am." He looked around. "I wonder where the empty shell casing is."

"I have no idea," Arnie replied.

When Tamara Welles answered the doorbell, she saw Alex Jensen standing there, smiling at her. Alex was wearing the black silk lounging pajamas Tamara had bought for her during their afternoon shopping spree. From the way the pajamas were clinging to her body, she was wearing nothing beneath them.

"Why, Alex," Tamara said, inhaling sharply. "How lovely you look!"

"Do you really think so?" Alex turned slowly to show the garment off. "I hope you don't mind that I came back."

"Mind? No, I don't mind at all," Tamara said. "You will remember when you left, I told you you were welcome to stay."

"I felt uncomfortable with Deke around," Alex said.

"Oh, don't bother about Deke," Tamara said, dismissing him with a wave of her hand. "He lives his life and I live mine. Anyway, he isn't back yet. I imagine he is still with his little Italian whore. What are you doing still standing there? Don't you want to come in?"

Alex smiled, then stepped inside and put her arms around Tamara's neck. She leaned into the older woman, pressing her body to Tamara's, mashing her small, hard breasts against Tamara's larger, softer ones.

"Ooooh," Tamara said, shivering with ecstasy. "You wicked, wicked, little girl."

———

Tamara lay in bed, looking at the shadows on her bedroom wall, cast there by the high, silver moon. Beside her Alex was asleep. In the moonlight, her nude body was a beautiful piece of sculpture done in silver and black. Tamara let her hand drift to the young girl's thigh, right at the pelvic bone. The sensations of smooth flesh, sharp bone, and soft hair were delightful to the touch, a subtle pleasure Tamara could enjoy almost as much as she had enjoyed the actual sex.

Alex was a delightful creature, perhaps more sensuous than anyone Tamara had ever been with before. It was quickly obvious to her that Alex wasn't in the relationship just for the benefit it would do to her own career. She actually enjoyed it. In fact, Tamara was beginning to get concerned that Alex might be enjoying it a little too much.

Much of Tamara's delight with living this kind of a life was in the variety one could experience. She would have to explain that to Alex. Thus far, Alex had no idea of the pleasures of promiscuity. She was still too enamored with the forbidden delights of lesbian love. Tamara wasn't really worried, though. Alex was too much the sensualist to limit herself to one partner. She would learn, then she would thank Tamara for opening the new doors for her.

The phone rang then, and its sudden intrusion into the dark caused Tamara to jump. She reached over to pick it up and brought it into bed with her.

"Hello?"

"Mrs. Clark?" a man's voice asked.

Tamara, who wasn't used to be referred to as Mrs. Clark, had to think a moment before she could answer.

"Yes, this is Mrs. Clark."

"Mrs. Clark, this is the Beverly Hills Police Department. Would you allow one of our officers to pay you a visit tonight?"

"Tonight? Why?"

"I'd rather not tell you over the phone, Mrs. Clark. It's rather bad news, I'm afraid."

"About my husband?"

"Yes."

"You can tell me."

The police officer on the phone hesitated for a moment.

"For heaven's sake, what is it?" Tamara asked. "I'm not some weak sister about to pass out."

"I'm afraid your husband is dead."

Tamara was silent for a long moment, then she said, "Don't bother to send anyone out here tonight. If he's already dead, it'll keep until morning."

"Very well, Mrs. Clark, whatever you say," the police officer replied dryly.

"What is it?" Alex asked as Tamara hung up the phone.

"Nothing," Tamara said. "Go back to sleep."

Katie was standing in a little green room at police headquarters. Last night, when they offered her one phone call, she tried to call New York and was prevented from doing so. This morning, when they received her assurance that she would pay for the long-distance call, they let her put it through.

Katie was frightened now. She had never been more frightened in her life. She had been brought in here in handcuffs, fingerprinted, then put in a jail cell. She, Katie Starr, had actually been put in a jail cell along with two dozen other women, most of whom were prostitutes. For a while, she had been cushioned against her surroundings by some strange lethargy that was working on her. But that lethargy was gone now, and the steel bars looked hard, the bright lights harsh, and the guards frightening.

There were two police officers and a matron in the room with Katie, keeping a close eye on her as she gave the long-distance operator the number she wanted to call in Long Island, New York.

"Godfather, it is the long-distance operator," Frankie said, sticking his head into the room where Johnny and Al were talking.

"Long distance? Where is it from?"

"California," Frankie said.

Johnny smiled. "I'll take it," he said. "It's probably my sister." He picked up the telephone on his desk.

"Hello?"

"Mr. Sangremano? Mr. John Sangremano?" an operator's voice asked.

"Yes, speaking."

"Hold the line, please, long distance calling from Los Angeles, California. Go ahead, miss, your party is on the line."

"Johnny?"

"Katherine, is that you?" Johnny asked. "Gee, it's really good to hear from you, kid. How are you doing?"

"I'm in jail, Johnny. Deke is dead, and the police think I did it."

CHAPTER 6

The rising sun slipped in through the slit in the window curtain, falling on Johnny's face and causing him to wake up. He sat there in his seat for a moment, his head leaning against the window, listening to the steady, reassuring throb of the Tri-motor Ford's engines, then he pulled the curtain aside so he could look out. The bottom of the high wing and the suspended engine nacelle glowed pink from the sun, which was a bright red orb behind them, now just a disk width above the lip of the horizon. Far below, he could see the wooded hills and cultivated farmland of Middle America, though he wasn't sure exactly where they were. The stewardess, seeing that he was awake, came back to his seat.

"Would you care for some coffee and a sweet roll?" she asked.

"Yes, thank you," Johnny replied. He looked at his watch. "Will we be landing anywhere, soon?"

"We'll be in Springfield, Missouri, in about an hour," the stewardess answered pleasantly.

"Will I have time to make a long-distance telephone call to California?"

"Yes, sir, I think so," the stewardess replied. "The airplane will have to be serviced and refueled. You realize, of course, that in California right now, it is just past three in the morning."

"That's all right," Johnny said. "I'm paying the person I'm calling enough to wake him up. Oh, and bring coffee and a sweet roll for my friend back there, too, would you, please?" he asked.

The stewardess looked at the seat behind Johnny. "Your friend is still asleep," she said.

"He won't be," Johnny promised.

"As long as he is mad at you, and not me."

Johnny smiled. "Honey, people don't get mad at me," he said.

The stewardess returned Johnny's smile. "You know, for some reason I believe you."

When the stewardess left to get the coffee and rolls, Johnny turned around to the seat behind him. As the stewardess had indicated, Al Provenzano was asleep.

"Al," Johnny said. "Al, wake up."

Al grunted once, then opened his eyes. "Good morning," he mumbled.

"We need to talk," Johnny invited.

"Okay," Al answered.

"We'll be making a landing in a little while," Johnny said. "I want you to call and make sure things went all right. I wouldn't want to think that Katherine is still sitting there in jail."

"I secured the services of one of the most prestigious law firms in the city," Al said. "And I transferred a hundred thousand dollars to the bank there, to secure the bail. I'm sure she is out by now."

"Yeah, well, I just want to double-check on it, that's all."

"Sure, I don't blame you," Al said. "It pains me to think of sweet little Katherine spending even so much as one hour in jail, let alone an entire night."

"The first thing we do when we get there," Johnny said, "is go see her and make sure she's okay. The next thing is to find out what happened, and then to put things right."

The stewardess returned then with the coffee and sweet rolls. She served them both, then withdrew.

"Well, it is obviously a mistake of some kind," Al said after the stewardess left. He was talking loudly enough to be heard above the roaring engines, though not loudly enough to be heard by anyone else. "Katherine didn't kill that man."

Johnny took a sip of his coffee, then stared out the window for a long moment before he answered. "Yeah, well, I wish I could be as certain of that as you are."

"What are you saying? Johnny, you don't think there is any way she could have really done it, do you?"

"Katherine has changed a lot since she went to California," Johnny said. "In a lot of ways she's more Katie Starr than she is Katherine Sangremano. You take this guy who was killed. She was seeing him, you know. There's no doubt in my mind about that. She was seeing him and he was a married man."

"Well, of course she was seeing him," Al defended. "He was going to direct *Aerodrome* and Katherine was going to star in it. It's only natural that they would have to see each other from time to time to work out details of how the part was to be played and so forth."

Johnny chuckled softly, then reached back across the seat to put his hand on Al's shoulder. "Al, my friend," he said. "I am touched by your loyalty to my sister and to my family. But not even you can find a reason for why my sister and the director of this movie had to conduct their meetings naked."

"Springfield," the stewardess said, moving quickly through the aisle to gather up cups and saucers. "We're landing in Springfield."

Johnny sat with his hands folded in his lap as he looked through the window while the plane started its approach into the Springfield airport. He thought of what must be going on in the flight deck right now as the pilot and copilot were busy with power settings, flap adjustments, and approach angles. It wasn't just fanciful musing; Johnny was an excellent pilot and, had circumstances been different, might himself be flying this, or a similar plane.

The Springfield runway was marked with bright yellow straw baskets and Johnny watched them come closer and closer until he felt the wheels touch down and the plane begin to roll across the well-kept sod. A few minutes later they were onto the hard-surface area, taxiing up to the terminal. The pilot wheeled the plane around into position, then killed all three engines, flooding the interior with an avalanche of silence.

"Folks, we'll be here for exactly forty minutes," the stewardess said. "Those passengers who are going on through, be sure to take your tickets with you so that you can be preboarded before the new passengers."

Next to the Ford Tri-motor was a Fokker. Behind them, the engine of a Stinson Reliant mail plane roared loudly, its tail already lifted as the pilot raced down the runway on his takeoff run. Johnny and Al stepped out of the plane then walked by an arriving fuel truck on their way to the terminal building.

While Al made a series of telephone calls Johnny

bought and read the paper he found at the airport terminal newsstand.

ACTRESS HELD ON SUSPICION OF MURDER OF DIRECTOR

Motion-picture fans around the country were shocked yesterday when they woke up to find that Katie Starr, one of America's best-loved actresses, was being held for murder.

Not since the famous murder trial of Fatty Arbuckle has there been a scandal to compare with this in the Hollywood community.

Sources say that Katie Starr was discovered unclothed, the murder weapon in her hand, standing over the naked body of Deke Clark, a well-known motion-picture director. According to some insiders, Katie Starr and Deke Clark were carrying on a torrid romance, that despite the fact that Deke Clark was already married to Tamara Welles, another well-known movie star.

Sid Friedman, head of Galaxy Pictures, expressed his sympathy to the widow and declared a one-day cessation of all activity in memory of the man he calls "the greatest director in our industry." When asked about Katie Starr, Mr. Friedman declined to comment, stating he would prefer to wait until she has had her day in court. Mr. Friedman was unsure about the future of <u>Aerodrome</u>, the new picture Galaxy was about to begin shooting. <u>Aerodrome</u> was to have been directed by Deke Clark and feature Katie Starr.

"At this point, it is much too early to be discussing what is going to become of Aerodrome. Mr. Friedman said.

"She's okay," Al said, coming over to sit down beside Johnny. "Bail was made and she's home, resting."

"Good," Johnny said, folding the paper and putting it aside.

"Oh, and I found out another bit of interesting news. Do you know who is out there?"

"Who?"

"The Vaglichio brothers."

NEW YORK, LOWER EAST SIDE

The smell of spaghetti sauce and sausage permeated the house. The rose-colored speaker horn on the Victrola in the parlor filled the room with the tenor strains of an Enrico Caruso. Children chased each other, from room to room, laughing and hiding behind furniture and the adults. Every woman in the house was at work preparing the big family dinner that was being held to celebrate the upcoming wedding of Joe Provenzano's cousin, Sophia. The men sat in the parlor, smoking, drinking homemade wine, and talking.

In the front closet, along with the hats and umbrellas, were stored several guns, for guns weren't welcome at such an affair. The fact that Joe's gun was the legal firearm of a law enforcement officer, whereas the other weapons were the illegal firearms of "connected" people, was understood, though not mentioned.

There were very few people in Joe's family who approved of his chosen profession, but by unspoken agreement, they never talked about it. It was understood that Joe parked his badge with his gun when he came into the house. Joe never pumped any of his relatives for information, and given the normal taciturn behavior of the men, plus the Mafia code of silence—the omerta—there would have been little point in trying. In any case, a truce was generally in effect between Joe, the federal law-enforcement officer, and his uncles and cousins, who either belonged to, or worked for, the Mafia.

Much of the talk today was about the murder of the Hollywood director and the fact that Katherine Sangremano was being charged with the crime.

"I've known Katherine since she was a little girl," one of the men said. "I don't think she could do such a thing."

"Listen, don't fool yourself. She is a Sangremano, isn't she?" another replied. "The Sangremanos are tough people. They've always been tough."

"But we're not talking about Giuseppe, nor even Johnny. We're talking about Katherine."

"Nevertheless, she is a Sangremano."

"Not anymore she isn't. Now she calls herself Katie Starr."

"She could call herself the Madonna as far as I'm concerned. She is still a Sangremano."

"Don't be foolish. Who would be so blasphemous as to call themselves Madonna?" another asked.

Sophia came into the room to announce that dinner was about ready.

"Ah, Sophia, such a pretty girl," one of the men said. "Your man is crazy to let you out of his sight for one moment."

"Not crazy," another said. "He trusts her."

"The trust must go both ways," Sophia replied. "I am here alone, yes. But he is in Hollywood, California, where he is surrounded by beautiful girls."

Joe said nothing, but he saw a flicker of alarm in the eyes of several of his relatives, and he realized that Sophia had just divulged some information that was classified. Quickly one of the other men changed the subject.

"So dinner is ready, you say? Well, let's go, then. The smells of cooking have been driving me crazy all day. I could eat a horse."

"Could you really, Papa?" a small boy asked, intrigued by the announcement. "Could you really eat a horse?"

The others laughed and Sophia's slip was put aside. Moments later it was forgotten by all but Joe. According to the rules of the game, Joe never pumped anyone for information, but if any happened to come his way, it was fair game.

"This is why I find it so interesting," Joe explained to Mike the next day. "Sophia's fiancé is a soldier for the Vaglichio Family. And he's not even a very high-ranking soldier, so if he is out there, the Vaglichios must be out there in some strength."

"Johnny Sangremano is out there, too, don't forget," Bill pointed out.

"Yes," Mike answered, stroking his chin. "Well, we know why Sangremano is out there. He is trying to help his sister. The question is, why are the Vaglichios there?"

"Do you have any ideas, Joe?" Jason asked.

"Not a one," Joe admitted. "In fact, until that chance remark by Sophia yesterday, I didn't even know about it."

"Well, if Johnny Sangremano and the Vaglichios are out there, that should certainly be good news for the New York police," Bill said.

"But not so good for the Los Angeles police," Jason put in quickly.

"I'll bet I know why they are out there," Mike said.

"Why?"

Mike smiled broadly. "Well, it's obvious, isn't it? It's all a Communist plot to infiltrate the studios."

"The Communists?" Jason said. "Mike, are you out of your mind?"

Bill laughed. "No," he said. "I don't think so. I don't think so at all."

"Yeah," Joe added, also laughing. "I think our boss has a point there. There might very well be Communists behind this."

"And we'll never know until we go out there and conduct a thorough investigation," Mike concluded.

By now Jason realized that Mike was planning to use the premise of Communist infiltration as an excuse to go to California.

"How soon do we leave?" he asked, showing that he, too, understood.

"As soon as we can pack and get train tickets," Mike replied.

Johnny Sangremano was standing alongside his sister's swimming pool, looking down at the chaise lounge where Deke Clark's body was found. He heard the French doors to the back of the house open and close, then the light footsteps of someone walking across the patio toward him.

"Were you screwing him?" Johnny asked without turning around.

Katie gasped. "Johnny!"

Johnny turned toward her and saw that she was wearing a short, sleeveless sundress. She was also wearing a pair of dark sunglasses.

"I asked if you were screwing him," he said again. He reached up and took off her sunglasses. "And I want to look into your eyes while you answer me."

"We...we were in love," Katie said.

"Yeah, I can see how much you were in love. You were so in love that you killed him."

"I didn't do it," Katie said quickly. "Yes, we were having sex, but I didn't kill him."

"You were having sex? You were having sex with a married man?" Johnny shouted angrily. "That's what I hear from my own sister? Is that what being a movie star has done for you?"

"If I can't be honest with you, Johnny, who can I be honest with?" Katie replied.

"But you didn't kill him?"

"No."

"You told the police you didn't know whether you did or not," Johnny challenged.

"I don't care what I told the police, I didn't do it."

"If you didn't do it, who did?"

"I don't know," Katie said.

"Goddamnit, you were here," Johnny said. "I'm not the police, Katherine. I'm your brother. I'm trying to help you. Now, you must have seen, or heard, something."

"I don't remember anything about that night," Katie insisted. "I remember having dinner, but then I must've blacked out, because the next thing I knew I was sitting on the end of the diving board and Deke was lying over here, dead. I don't know who did do it, but I know I didn't."

"How do you know?"

"I just know, that's all. Johnny, I loved him."

"But he wasn't going to divorce his wife and marry you, was he?"

"No."

"There are some who would say that is motive enough."

"Do you say that?" Katie asked.

Johnny stroked his chin for a moment. "No," he said. "If you tell me you didn't kill him, that's good enough for me."

Tears sprang to Katie's eyes. "Oh, thank God," she said. She put her arms around Johnny's neck and he embraced her, letting her cry on his shoulder. "It's awful enough," she said between sobs, "losing someone you love. But on top of that, to be accused of his murder, is almost unbearable. And if you believed that I did it, too, I don't know if I could take that."

"There, there," Johnny said, patting his sister on the back. "It'll be all right. Don't cry now. Don't worry. It'll be all right." He took a handkerchief from his pocket and gave it to her. "Here, wipe your eyes and blow your nose."

"Thanks," Katie said, making use of the handkerchief.

"Katie, do you have any idea what the Vaglichios are doing out here?"

"The Vaglichios? I don't know. I didn't know they were here."

"They're here, all right."

"Well, if they are, I haven't seen any of them. And anyway, even if they are here, it has nothing to do with me. I'm not a part of your business."

Johnny laughed, though it was a mirthless laugh. "Except when it is convenient for you," he said.

"You mean because I called you to talk to Sid Friedman about the movie?" Katie replied.

"You didn't call anyone else, did you?"

"Yes, but that has nothing to do with your business. I called you because you were my brother."

"Come on, Katie, if I worked on the docks, would you have called me to talk to Friedman for you?"

"Sure I would have," Katie said. Then she laughed. "It just wouldn't have been as effective, that's all. Johnny, you aren't upset with me for calling you, are you?"

"No, of course not," Johnny replied. "I'm glad you called. I mean, if I can't help my own family, then what good is everything I've done?"

"Yes," Katie replied. "Well, I appreciate all you have done for me, I really do. But I'm afraid I've really done it this time. There is no way you are going to be able to help me get out of this mess. You might believe I'm innocent but the police think I killed Deke and there's no way I can prove that I didn't."

Johnny smiled. "Katie, you don't understand the American judicial system. You don't have to prove you didn't kill Clark. The police have to prove that you did."

"What if they can?" Katie asked anxiously.

"You let me handle that," Johnny said. He saw Al coming out the back door then and when Al nodded to him, Johnny held up his finger as if telling him he would be with him in just a moment. "Listen, you just take it easy for a while and leave everything to me. I'll get you out of this mess. You do believe that, don't you?"

"Sure," Katie answered. "I believe you can take care of the murder charge. But can you give my career back to me?"

"Don't worry about that either. When your fans learn that you are innocent, they'll be behind you one hundred percent," Johnny promised.

"If I thought they wouldn't be, I would kill myself," Katie said.

"No!" Johnny said sharply, grabbing his sister by the shoulders and shaking her. "Don't you talk like that. Don't you think like that. Ever. Do you hear me?"

"Johnny, you are hurting me," Katie protested.

Johnny loosened his grip, though he continued to hold her by her shoulders. He put one finger gently under her chin and lifted it so she would have to look up at him. The pain in his eyes was genuine. "Katie," he said softly. "Mama and Papa, our brothers, my wife, they are gone now...all gone. You and I have only each other. You must never talk like that. Promise me you won't even think of such a thing as suicide. It's a mortal sin, you know. For suicide, you go straight to hell."

Katie tried to laugh through the tears that had welled up in her eyes. "You are worried about mortal sin?"

"Yeah, sure. Look, anything else you do, you can be sorry. You can confess, you can ask for forgiveness. Suicide, you can't do all that. It's over. You know what I mean?"

"I...I didn't really mean I would kill myself," Katie said. "I was just trying to express how hard it would be if this caused me to lose my career."

"Honey, you won't lose it," Johnny said. "I promise you that. And haven't I always delivered on my promises? Always?"

"Yes," Katie agreed.

"I'll deliver on this one, too, you wait and see. Now I've got to talk to Al. We have some business to discuss. You'll be all right?"

"I'll be all right," Katie said. "You two go ahead, discuss your business."

Johnny kissed his sister on the forehead, then walked around to the other side of the pool to talk with his consigliere.

"What's up?" he asked.

"I just talked to our people back in New York," Al answered. "According to them, not only both brothers, but nearly half the Vaglichio Family has moved out here."

"Why?" Johnny asked.

"They're going into the movie business," Al said. "The way they figure it, we may have the distribution locked up, but without production, there is no distribution. They're going to try and get involved in the production end."

Johnny laughed. "What are you telling me, Al? That the Vaglichios are going to make movies?"

"No, I don't think so," Al replied. "But they are going to try and control those people who do make movies."

"I'll be damned. They are behind it, aren't they? They're the ones who set Katherine up."

"Can you think of a better way to control a movie than by killing the director and removing the star?" Al asked.

"Yeah, well, they aren't going to get away with it," Johnny insisted.

"I don't know what you have in mind, Johnny, but it's going to be very hard to prove the Vaglichios had anything to do with this."

"No problem, Al. The only one I have to prove it to is myself."

Across town, next to a flophouse hotel, a small sign read: *Jay Garland, Talent Agent, Entrance in rear.*

To reach the entrance one had to walk through a garbage-strewn alley then go down a flight of stairs under a fire escape to an unpainted wooden door. The door opened onto a long hallway that smelled of stale tobacco, mildewed wood, and urine. There were a half-dozen doors opening off the hallway. Four were to very low-rent apartments, one was to an astrologer's office with a sign that promised: *Advice in love and business* and one was to Jay Garland's office.

Inside his office, Jay Garland was attempting to toss playing cards into his upturned hat. He was halfway through the deck and had only missed twice when he was startled by a knock on the door. He looked up through the frosted glass and saw a man's shadow on the other side.

Jay put the hatful of cards under his desk, then sat up to try to look busy. He didn't know who his visitor was, but he was pretty sure it wasn't one of his clients complaining to him that he hadn't gotten them any work. They never bothered to knock. Neither did the bill collectors. Maybe this was somebody who actually did want to use his services.

"Yes, come in," he called.

The door opened and a dark-haired, dark-eyed man came in. Jay looked at everyone as if they were an eight-by-ten glossy, and his visitor, he decided, could actually be considered handsome...not leading role handsome, but leading villain handsome. With his dark pin-striped suit, he was openly defiant of the California dress code of light colors and open collars.

"Mr. Garland?" the man asked in a husky voice, sticking his hand out over Jay's desk. "My name is Mario Vaglichio."

"Good morning, Mr. Vaglichio," Jay replied holding out a limp hand. "What can I do for you?"

"I want to do business with you, Mr. Garland."

Jay chuckled. "So that's why you're dressed up like that. You think it's that easy? You think you can come in here looking like central casting sent you and I'm going to get you in the movies, is that it? Well, it's not that simple, Mr. Vaglichio. Acting is hard work and requires the strictest application of discipline, plus the—"

"I'm not interested in being in the movies," Mario interrupted, holding out his hand to stop Jay in the middle of what was obviously a practiced speech.

"Then what are you interested in?"

"I told you. I want to do business with you."

Jay broke into a relaxed smile. There were only two kinds of people who did business with him...those who wanted to be his clients, and those who wanted to hire his clients. He figured this must be the latter.

"Well, now, why didn't you say so?" he asked. He held his hand out toward a chair. "Have a seat, let's talk this over. Just what kind of talent are you looking for? I represent the best, you know. The very best. Who are you with? A movie production company? A theater? A night-club, perhaps?"

"My brother and I do own a few nightclubs," Mario replied. "But they are back in New York. And anyway, we wouldn't be interested in any of the bums you have as clients."

Jay's smile turned to a frown. "I'm not sure I appreciate you calling my clients bums," he said. "They are all professionals, and some of them have had starring roles—"

"Are you talking about Marla Peters?"

"Among others," Jay said.

"What is she now? Sixty? Seventy? I know all about Marla Peters. She hasn't been in a film since the war. And Derek Hudson, the other so-called star you have, can't stay sober long enough to complete a picture. You don't have anyone else who has ever done any more than a walk-on. In fact, you don't have anyone working for you but a bunch of bums and has-beens. Look at this office." Mario took it in with a sweep of his hand. "You think you would be doing business from an alley dump like this if you had something going for you?"

"This is just temporary," Jay said. "I'm looking for a more suitable office."

"Temporary, you say? You've been here for six years, Mr. Garland," Mario said.

"Who are you?" Jay asked. "And why do you know so much about me?" He was beginning to be a little frightened by his visitor.

"My brother and I have just moved out here from New York," Mario said. "We bought a movie star's house. Swimming pool, palm trees, tennis court. It was the house April Jackson and Tom Lane lived in before they were divorced. Do you know the place?"

"Jacklane, yes, of course I know the house," Jay said,

obviously impressed by someone who could afford such a house. "It's one of the nicest homes in Hollywood."

"It was also very expensive," Mario added. "That means we're going to have to do some business to make a little money, so we've decided to become your partners." Mario paused. "Your silent partners."

Jay shook his head. "No," he said. "I appreciate your offer, I really do. But I'm the kind of man who works best alone. I like to call my own shots, you see. Sometimes when a deal breaks, it breaks fast. You don't have time to consult with a partner...you have to make a decision right then."

"We've rented space on Sunset Boulevard," Mario said. "Do you know the Stalcup Building?"

"Yeah, sure I know it. That's a pretty expensive neighborhood, isn't it? How much does an office there cost?"

"I don't know."

Jay snorted. "I thought you just told me you rented an office there."

"I said we rented space there," Mario replied. "We have the entire fifth floor. You can move in tomorrow."

"I can move in tomorrow?"

"It should be pretty easy." Mario looked around Jay's office. "I can't believe you would want to move any of this furniture. You'll have to get all new stuff."

"And where am I going to get the money for all this? As you pointed out, the studios aren't exactly breaking down my doors for my clients."

"You don't worry about the money," Mario said. "We have all you will ever need and you will find that we can be quite generous with our friends."

Jay drummed his fingers on his desk for a long moment, then he smiled. "You know, it really would make my clients sit up and take notice if I started doing business from an office on Sunset Boulevard," he said.

"Forget about your clients," Mario said.

"Forget about them? What do you mean?"

"You are going to drop your clients. All of them."

"I couldn't do that. These people depend on me. It wouldn't be right. I can't just walk off and leave them."

"You feel a moral obligation to them?"

"Yes, of course I do."

"Do you feel a moral obligation to your furniture?"

"No."

"Your clients are like the furniture in this place...no more, no less. You're going to have to make up your mind, Mr. Garland. Now, which is greater—your sense of moral obligation or your ambition?"

"Mr. Vaglichio, I must tell you that you have me thoroughly confused," Jay said. "You come into my office and tell me you want to be partners with me. Yet you don't want anything to do with my office and now you tell me you don't want anything to do with my clients. Just what the hell do you want?"

Mario smiled. "Why, I want your soul, Mr. Garland."

"My...my what?" Jay gasped.

Mario laughed, then waved his hand. "Relax," he said. "Relax. What do you think, I'm the devil come to make a deal with you? It's all very simple really. My brother and I want to go into the agenting business. We have the money, but we need the name of a company that is already doing business."

"But why me?" Jay asked. "I mean, as long as we're talking here, we may as well lay all our cards on the table, don't you think? You were right when you said I represented nothing but a bunch of bums and has-beens. But the truth is, I'm pretty much of a bum and has-been myself."

"You put yourself in my hands, Mr. Garland, and you won't be a bum and a has-been for long. For example, suppose I told you that your first client in the new office would be Joan Leland? What would you think of that?"

"Joan Leland is a very talented actress," Jay said. "Perhaps one of the brightest new stars on the scene. But she is already represented by one of the most prestigious agencies in Hollywood. She is a client of Bailey and McDill Associates and there is no way she is about to leave them."

"But isn't it true that she was very upset about losing the role in *Aerodrome*?" Mario said. "It is my understanding that she was angry with Bailey and McDill Associates for not fighting for her."

"That was just the anger of the moment," Jay explained. "When she realized there was nothing they could do for her, she settled down."

"Call her," Mario said. "Offer her the part."

"What? I can't do that."

"Sure you can. Katherine Sangremano isn't going to be able to take the part. She's got all she can do to stay out of jail."

"Who?"

"Katie Starr."

"What did you call her?"

"Never mind," Mario said. 'The point is, would Joan Leland become our client if we could promise her the part?"

"If we could deliver on that promise, yes, I suppose she would," Jay said. "But if you're right, if Katie Starr is out of the picture, Galaxy will probably come back and offer Joan the role again, anyway. I mean, after all, she was their first choice."

"They won't offer her the role," Mario said.

"How can you be so sure?"

"My brother told me," Mario said. "He will not allow

Sid Friedman to offer Joan Leland the role unless she is represented by us."

"Did you say your brother won't allow it?"

"Yes."

"Who the hell is your brother?"

"My brother is a man who can make things happen, Mr. Garland. For you...or to you," he added, pointedly.

"Yeah, I see what you mean," Jay said nervously. He had not been directly threatened by this man, but for some reason, he was more frightened of him than he had ever been of anyone or anything. "Uh, you say I can move into my new office tomorrow?"

"Yes."

To hell with it, Jay thought. Why fight it? Like the old saying goes, if rape is inevitable, lie back and enjoy it. "All right, I'll do it. But I want to move today, now. Can we do that?"

"Of course, Mr. Garland, if you think you can get yourself moved that quickly."

"Hell, that's no problem. Like you said, there's no need to move any of this stuff. And if I'm going to be uptown, I'm going to need all new clothes, right?"

"But of course," Mario said. "We will see to it."

Jay smiled broadly. "Well then, the only thing I need to get me over to my new office is a cab."

Mario returned his smile. "You don't even need that, Mr. Garland. I have a car outside. If you'd like, I'll take you there."

"You've got a deal, partner," Jay said, sticking out his hand.

"And your clients?" Mario asked, motioning toward the filing cabinet full of resumes and portfolios. "The people to whom you feel a moral obligation?"

"To hell with them," Jay said coldly. "What have they ever done for me?"

CHAPTER 7

When Bill Carmack parked in front of the Beverly Hills police station, he was surprised to see an orange tree growing from the patch of grass that separated the sidewalk from the road. Of course, the patch of grass was itself unique to Bill, whose world as a child and an adult had consisted of nothing but concrete and brick.

Bill walked over to look at one of the oranges, then held it in his hand and sniffed it. The orange was as real as the palm trees that lined the streets. He smiled and stretched, then started toward the police station. The Beverly Hills police station was drastically different from the dreary precinct houses he was used to in New York. In New York, they were, quite often, cubbyholes in the corners of gray, dingy, brick buildings. Here, the police were housed in a landscaped, tan stucco building with a red tile roof. It was more like a house than a police station.

Once inside, however, the police station had a familiarity about it. The desk was manned by a bored-looking uniformed officer who was leafing through a magazine as he counted the hours of his duty, and this could have been any precinct in New York. Even the benches in the waiting room were the same.

"Yeah?" the desk sergeant said when Bill walked up to the bench. He didn't look up from his magazine.

"I'd like to speak with the department commander in homicide, please."

"You got a murder to report?" the desk sergeant asked, looking up now.

"No," Bill said. He showed the sergeant his badge. "I'm a federal agent from the Bureau of Investigation. I'm conducting an investigation that touches on the Deke Clark murder."

"Wait here a minute," the sergeant said. He went through a door, was gone for no more than a minute, then returned with someone dressed in mufti. The shoulder holstered pistol, however, gave ample evidence that the man in civilian dress was also a policeman.

"I'm Sergeant Blake Collins," the new policeman said. "May I help you, Mister...?"

"Carmack," Bill said. "Special Agent Bill Carmack, with the Bureau of Investigation." Again, Bill showed his badge. "I'd like to examine your files on the Deke Clark murder case, if I may."

"I suppose it would be all right," Collins said. "Sure, come on back."

Bill followed Collins down a long hallway, past several offices and bays filled with desks, some occupied, some not.

"This is my desk," Collins said, leading Bill into one of the smaller offices. He pointed to a chair. "Have a seat, I'll get the file. Coffee?"

"Yeah, thanks," Bill replied.

Collins pulled a folder from the file cabinet, then poured two cups of coffee and handed one of them to

Bill. "Why are the feds interested in a murder case?" Collins asked as he took a sip. "Seems to me that should be a matter for the local police."

"Murder is a matter for the local police," Bill answered. "And as far as I'm concerned, you fellows can have it. I'm not here to get into your business. I'm only interested in Communists."

"Communists?" Collins looked surprised.

"Yes," Bill said.

"Communists?" Collins said again. "You mean, like those people over in Russia?"

"Oh, they're not just in Russia, Sergeant Collins," Bill insisted.

"They're not?"

"No, sir. They're everywhere, trying to undermine the moral fabric of our country. They've infiltrated trade unions, schools, even the press. And now we have evidence that they are trying to penetrate the movie industry."

"I'll be damned. Well, I hadn't heard that," Sergeant Collins said.

"Of course you haven't. That's the way they work, you see," Bill went on. "They creep in quietly with a convert here and a convert there, until the next thing you know our most hallowed institutions are riddled with them."

"And you say this is going on all over the country?" the sergeant asked with some alarm.

"Yes."

"Why aren't we doing anything about it?"

Bill chuckled. "Well, we are, my friend, we are. Why do you think the Bureau sent me out here?"

"Did you come by yourself?"

"Yes," Bill said.

"That seems like a pretty big job for one man to handle."

"Oh, don't you worry about that," Bill said. "I'm well trained to ferret those people out." He put his finger to his forehead. "You see, the Communists work under a certain mindset, and if you understand that mindset, why, it's no big problem to locate them. That is, as long as you have the cooperation of the local police."

"Yeah, well, listen, you got that," Sergeant Collins promised. "I mean, anything you want to know, you just ask."

"Can I count on that?"

"Sure you can."

"The reason I ask is, sometimes these investigations go in rather twisting paths." Bill pointed to the file. "Now, you take this murder case, for example. I wouldn't be in the least bit surprised if the Communists weren't behind it. That means I might be asking you for a lot of information that you think I have no business knowing."

"You go ahead and ask. Whatever you want, I'll get for you," Collins said. "But you're wrong about the Communists being behind this. This case is as plain as the nose on your face."

"Is it?"

"Sure," Sergeant Collins replied. "Everyone knew that Deke Clark was balling Katie Starr. But he was married, see, and when Katie asked him to leave Tamara Welles and marry her, he wouldn't do it. So Katie got pissed off and"—Sergeant Collins made his hand into a gun—"bang! She puts a bullet in his brain. After that, it's all over but the shouting."

"Open-and-shut, huh?" Bill asked.

"Sure."

"Tell me, the two officers who found them. What made them go there in the first place?" Bill asked.

"I beg your pardon?"

"Officers, let's see, Arnie Stone and Jerry Farrell, I believe their names are," Bill said, checking the file. "What made them go up to Katie Starr's house?"

"Well, that's simple," Sergeant Collins replied. "Central dispatch sent them there."

"Central dispatch? Why?"

"If you'll look at the file, you'll see why. We got a call about a domestic disturbance. When Officer Stone called in on a routine check, we sent him out to Katie Starr's house."

"Who called in the domestic disturbance?"

"Uh, that we don't know," Sergeant Collins admitted.

"Have you checked with all the neighbors?"

"Yeah, sure we have," Collins replied defensively. "But none of them heard anything."

"If no one heard anything, then how could there have been a domestic disturbance?"

"Well, I...I don't know."

"Was it a man or a woman who called in the report?" Bill asked.

"We don't know."

"You don't know? You don't know whether it was a man or a woman?"

"Whoever it was talked in a low, husky whisper. It could have been either a man or a woman."

Bill hadn't been completely truthful with Sergeant Collins when he told him he was the only one working on the case. What he meant was that he was the only one working on the case who took the conventional way of identifying himself and perusing the police records. The other three had gone underground for their own investigative efforts.

Mike Kelly, for example, had gone straight to the movie set where *Aerodrome* was being shot. According to the advertisement, Galaxy Pictures had placed in *Variety*, the stunt coordinator for *Aerodrome* was looking for qualified aviators to fly airplanes for the aerial sequences. That was all Mike needed to know.

"Can you fly these crates?" the stunt coordinator asked him. The coordinator's real name was Bruce Hawkins, but he identified himself as Bruiser. He was holding a clipboard and he made no effort to take Mike's offered hand. Mike let his hand hang there for a moment, then he pulled it back.

"Yeah, I can fly them," he answered.

"I guess you were a war hero like all the rest of them?"

"I was in the war," Mike answered.

"Well, don't expect any special treatment because of that," Bruiser replied. "The war's over, even if you people don't know it. Okay, you've got the job."

"Don't you want to check me out first?"

"What the hell for? I don't fly, and I don't give a shit whether or not you can," Bruiser said.

"I don't understand."

"Look, if you can fly, that's fine. If you can't, that's fine too. You'll probably crash and kill yourself, but we'll have it on film, so it won't be a waste," Bruiser said cynically. "Either way it's no sweat off my ass. Now, do you want the job or not?"

"I want the job," Mike replied. "But I've got one question."

"What's that?"

"Is there even going to be a job? I mean, from everything I've heard and read, this picture might not even be made."

Bruiser looked at him suspiciously. "Why would you say something like that?"

"It's just that with the director dead and the star being

accused of his murder, I would think it might throw a pretty large monkey wrench into the gears. I mean, don't you think so?"

"Oh, they'll make the picture, don't you worry about that. There's already too much money invested not to. They'll just get another director and a new star, that's all. Friedman never really liked Deke Clark, anyway. And Katie Starr wasn't his first choice to play the lead. So when you stop to think about it, she might have done Friedman a big service by bumping off Deke Clark."

"What do you think? Did Katie Starr actually do it?" Mike asked.

"What do I look like to you, mister, the police department? Why you askin' so goddamn many questions about things that aren't any of your business? All you have to do is fly when I tell you. You don't worry about anything else that's going on around here. We've got people who are paid to worry about things like that...and you aren't one of 'em."

"I was just making a little conversation is all," Mike said.

"Yeah, well don't make it with me. You want to make conversation, you make it with one of the other fly-boys."

"When do I meet them? The other aviators, I mean."

"Friedman says we're going to start filming the flying sequences tomorrow," Bruiser answered. "They'll all be here then."

"Then I will be too." Mike looked toward the planes. "As a matter of curiosity, especially since I have a vested interest in the answer, are your planes in pretty good shape?"

"You'll have to take that up with Sam Fielding," Bruiser replied. "He's chief of all the aviators."

"Is he here now?"

"I don't know. If he is, he's down there somewhere."

"Okay if I go see him?"

"Yeah, I guess. But stay out of the way of the working people."

"Thanks," Mike said.

As Mike started toward the row of planes he saw a man in mechanic's overalls. "Excuse me, friend, is Sam Fielding around?" he asked.

"Fielding? No, he left for the day. He'll be here early tomorrow, though. We're supposed to start shooting then. Are you looking for a job?"

"I've already got one. I'll be working for Sam Fielding."

"You must one of the aviators."

"Yes."

"Well, if you show up early enough tomorrow, you'll get a chance to talk to him. Sam's an early bird."

"Okay, thanks. By the way, is it all right if I have a look around the planes?"

"Sure," the man in the coveralls answered. "Go ahead. You can't break 'em just by lookin' at 'em."

When Mike reached the flight line, he took a close look at the row of reconditioned biplanes. He laid his hand on one of the Nieuports. It was painted with the "Hat and Ring" insignia of the 94th American Aero Squadron. For just a moment as he stood there he felt a dizzying sense of *deja vu*. He had to hand it to the set designers. They had done their work well. This small California airport had been literally transformed into a World War aerodrome.

Mike hadn't been entirely frank with Bruiser. When the stunt coordinator asked if he had served in the war, what he was really asking was had Mike flown in the war. Mike had served in the war and he had seen plenty of aerodromes. But he hadn't actually been an aviator. He did, however, have an experience with an airplane just like this one, indeed he owed his life to the American who had been flying it at the time. Aided by the realism of the set, he found it easy to let his mind drift back to that day in France, so long ago, when he had lain, wounded and bleeding, in a little field in the American sector in the Argonne Forest.

Mike Kelly, lieutenant of infantry, American Expeditionary Force, and commander of the advanced listening post, tightened the bandage on his bleeding leg. It hurt terribly, and the thought that he might lose it weighed heavily upon him. He lay in a trench that was full of the dead of his little command, and fought the nauseating waves of pain that threatened to make him pass out.

It was important that Mike remain conscious because he had to warn the main element when the Germans started their expected attack. That was the whole purpose of his being here, some one thousand yards in advance of his own lines.

When the shelling stopped altogether, Mike pulled himself up to the parapet of the trench so he could look over toward the German lines. There, moving through the forest toward his position, he saw hundreds of dark gray shapes. The attack had begun!

Mike slipped back down into the trench and twisted the crank on the field phone to call headquarters. When he got no response, he twisted it again. It was a useless gesture, however, because the artillery fire had chewed the telephone lines to pieces. His phone was dead and he was completely cut off.

Mike searched among the bodies until he found the soldier who had the flare pistol. Taking it from the dead man's holster, he pointed it up and pulled the trigger. There was a *pop* then a hissing sound as the red flare arced high into the gray dawn sky. If he couldn't talk to his commander to tell him the size and direction of the attack, he could at least warn him that it was coming.

One of the German soldiers, seeing the source of the red flare, yelled something guttural and pointed at Mike. Several of the soldiers began firing at him. Mike slipped back down into the trench and covered up, listening to the drumming sound of the enemy's jackboots as they ran toward him. He realized that if he rose up and fired back at them, he would be killed. His only chance was to wait for them, then surrender.

The Germans interrogated Mike then turned him over to a handful of guards to be taken to the rear. He soon learned, however, that the guards had no intention of taking him to a prisoner-of-war camp. They planned to kill him!

A pilot of the American 94th Aero Squadron was flying some five hundred feet above the road when he saw Mike and his German guards moving to the rear. He swung his little biplane around in a large circle to line up with the road, then lowered the nose and swooped down to just a few feet above the ground. He flew directly at the little group of men, causing the four guards to dive into the ditches on either side of the road, three on one side, one on the other. That opened up some distance between the guards and their prisoner and gave the American pilot a clear shot at them. He touched the rudder bar just enough to line his guns up with the three Germans in the ditch to the right. He pulled the trigger and Mike watched as the bullets from the pilot's twin Lewis machine guns kicked up puffs of dust from the road, then laced across the Germans themselves. As the American aviator flashed by overhead the surviving German guard threw down his rifle and ran toward the relative safety of a nearby clump of trees.

The American pilot pulled the nose of his plane up

hard, throttled back the engine, then kicked the rudder bar to wrench it over into a hammerhead stall. This allowed him to go right back down over the same path he had just flown, though he was now going in the opposite direction. With the engine still at idle, he landed on the road itself, bouncing to a stop some ninety feet away from Mike. Mike smiled broadly as he hobbled toward the plane, moving as quickly as he could. The American pilot climbed out onto the lower wing and reached a hand down to help the American up.

"Taxi, mister?" he joked.

"Yeah. How about taking me to Times Square?" Mike replied over the noise of the idling engine.

"You've got it," the pilot answered. "Get in, quick!"

"Where?" Mike asked. He had reached the wing now and was confused by the fact that there was only one seat in the airplane.

"There," the pilot said, pointing to the seat. "Where do you think?"

"But what about you?"

"Don't you worry about me. I'm going to be sitting on your lap!" the pilot replied with a bubbling laugh.

Mike climbed into the seat, then the pilot got in on top of him. The weight of the pilot in his lap hurt Mike's leg, but he wasn't about to complain. He held on as the pilot gunned the engine, raced down the road, then lifted into the air just as a dozen or so German soldiers broke out of the tree line and began firing rifles at them. Mike could hear the bullets popping through the fabric but none of the bullets did any damage. Then he felt a sickening lurch in his stomach as the pilot stood the Nieuport on its tail for a steep climb away from the road.

"Oh shit!" Mike yelled. Involuntarily he wrapped his arms around his rescuer and squeezed hard as he held on for dear life.

"I know you're glad to see me, but don't squeeze so hard. I can't breathe!" the pilot said.

"Sorry," Mike replied, loosening his grip slightly. "I guess I got a little startled."

"A little?"

"A lot," Mike admitted.

The pilot laughed then and Mike began laughing as well. Both men laughed until they cried, laughing so hard that the sound could be heard, even over the roar of the engine. And there, in the skies over the German-lines in war-torn France, a friendship was born.

It wasn't until the two men met again after the war that Mike learned to fly, taking lessons from the very pilot who had plucked him from the clutches of the German death squad. That pilot, the one who had saved his life, taught him to fly and then went on a barnstorming tour across the country with him, was Johnny Sangremano.

While Bill was working the police department and Mike the set of *Aerodrome*, Joe took advantage of his unique talents to move into the Italian community to see what he could find out. Though he already looked Italian, there was a certain image he was trying to project, even within the Italian community. In order to achieve it, he had grown a pencil-thin mustache, combed his hair straight back, then slicked it down with a heavy application of hair oil.

What made Joe good at his job, however, wasn't just the subtle changes in his physical appearance. He also changed his entire demeanor. He walked with a challenging, swaggering gait, and he looked at people through insolent half-closed eyes.

As Joe stood on the street corner, he lit a cigarette by snapping the match head with his thumbnail. Then he blew out the fire, flipped the match away, then flagged down a taxi.

"Where to?" the driver asked as Joe slid into the back seat.

"Depends," Joe answered. "Where's the action in this town?"

"What kind of action you lookin' for?" the driver asked. "You wantin' a woman? If you do, I might be able to set you up. It's goin' to cost you, though, for the information and the woman."

"Hey!" Joe growled angrily. "What do I look like here? Someone who has to pay for it?"

"Okay, okay, don't get mad," the driver said, intimidated by Joe's outburst. "You never can tell about some guys. I mean some of 'em can make out like a champ anywhere they go, but they still like the whores, you know what I mean? It's like they get a kick out of it or somethin'."

"Well, I ain't like some guys," Joe said. "I want a woman, I'll get a woman. And I won't be needin' no help from you."

"I could maybe take you to a pool hall."

"Yeah, okay, a pool hall, that'll be good," Joe agreed. "And if it's my kind of people, all the better, if you know what I mean."

"Italian?"

"Yeah, of course I'm Italian. What do I look like to you, Chinese?"

The driver chuckled. "I know just the place."

There were palm trees, orange blossoms, and roses outside Letto's Pool Palace, but inside it could have been on Delancey Street in New York. The pool hall smelled of oregano, thyme, and garlic, the more so because the smells were wafted around by a dozen or more of the small oscillating fans that sat on stands mounted around the wall. A game was going on at a table in the back of the room and the two players were speaking in Italian.

Joe racked up the balls on the table just next to the one where the two were playing and began to shoot his game. He hit one ball then left it, purposely, so he could back around to the side of the table nearest the two players, the better to hear what they were talking about. When he did, he accidentally bumped into one of them.

"Hey!" the player said in Italian. "You got the whole place here. You have to use this table?"

"I'm sorry," Joe said, smiling politely and replying in English. "I'm Italian, but I don't speak the language."

"You don't speak Italian?" the man asked in English.

"No," Joe said. "I'm sorry. What were you saying?"

"I said why you using this table? You can have any table in here."

"I like the lie of the felt," Joe said, putting his hand down on the top of the table.

"The lie of the felt," the other man snorted. "What difference does it make?"

"Perhaps none to the average player," Joe said. "But it makes a lot of difference to someone like me."

"What? You mean you ain't even average?"

Joe smiled, then turned toward his table and lined up for a shot. He stroked the cue cleanly, there was a solid clack as the cue ball hit the others, then a scattering of balls to all the pockets. In one shot he had sunk more than half the balls and left the others lined up for easy shots.

"Damn," the man said in admiration. "I never seen anyone could do that. Where'd you learn to do that?"

"From my papa," Joe said, returning to the table to complete the run. "I've been playing pool since before I was tall enough to see over the edge of the table. It's how I make my living now."

"You a professional?"

Joe smiled. "In a matter of speaking," he replied. "I bet on my games."

"Who the hell can you get to bet against you?"

"Oh, I offer odds to make the game attractive," Joe said.

"What kind of odds?"

"Say you and I were to play eight ball," Joe said. "I'd let you choose one ball from the solids or stripes, your choice. All you have to do is knock that one ball down, then the eight ball. I, on the other hand, will have to take down all the rest of them. And if that isn't enough, I'll bet five dollars to your one dollar."

The man smiled. "Mister, you got yourself a game," he said.

"Guido," the man's partner said. "It's a sucker bet."

"The hell it is," Guido replied. "How can I lose? I've only got to knock down one ball."

Guido soon learned how he could lose, for even when Joe didn't run the table, he turned it over to Guido in such a way that it was practically impossible for Guido to knock his ball down. Three games and three dollars later, Guido let out a long string of Italian oaths.

"I told you," his partner said, also in Italian. He was leaning up against the table where they had been playing their own game. The balls were lying in exactly the same place so they could pick up the game again.

"Shut up with the 'I told you' shit," Guido growled.

"You're losing all your money."

"So what. The Vaglichios are looking for a few people. I can always go to work for them."

Joe perked up at the mention of the Vaglichios, but he gave no outward sign that he heard anything.

"You want to stay away from them, Guido. They're bad people."

"Why? Because they deal in booze? Hell, who don't deal in booze?"

"They're not lookin' for bootleggers or numbers runners, or anything like that," Guido's friend said. "They're lookin' for muscle."

"If they're willin' to pay, I'll do anything they want," Guido said. "Shit!" he said, switching to English, as Joe ran a fourth string. He took out another bill and handed it to him. "You're poison, mister. You know that?"

"Thank you so much," Joe said, taking the money. "Every contribution is appreciated." He looked at Guido's partner. "Would you like a game?"

"Not if you played naked and knocked the balls down with your cock," Guido's partner replied.

When Jason Vandervort stepped into the waiting room of Bailey and McDill Associates, there were three people ahead of him. One was a musician who held his instrument on his lap, one was a mother who kept a tight rein on her precocious daughter, and the third was a beautiful young woman who, every few moments or so, would take out her compact and check her makeup.

"Sign in," the woman at the reception desk said. "If you have a portfolio, leave it on the desk."

"Thank you," Jason said.

The woman looked up from her typewriter, then flashed him a friendly smile. "You're new, aren't you?" she asked.

"Yes," Jason said. "I just arrived in California."

"And you've come here to break into the movies."

"Yes."

The girl clucked her tongue and shook her head. "Would you take some well-meaning advice?"

"Sure."

"Go home," she said. "Go back to the girl you left in

Indiana, or wherever you came from. You are too nice looking a man to beat your brains out out here."

"Thanks," Jason replied. "But there is no girl in Indiana, and show business is in my blood."

The receptionist sighed. "All right, Mister"—she looked at his name—"Vandervort. Have a seat over there. I'll call you when it's time."

"Thank you," Jason said again.

The door to one of the inner offices opened and a man came out. Jason couldn't recall his name, but he had seen him in the movies many times, not as a star, but in major supporting roles. When he left, the receptionist took in the four portfolios that were lying on her desk. She came back out a moment later and smiled at the musician.

"You can go in now, Mr. Goodman," she said.

"Thank you," Goodman mumbled, grasping his instrument tightly. Jason wondered, in passing, just what the instrument was. The question was answered a moment later when he heard a clarinet being played. Whoever he was, he was really quite good.

When the mother and daughter went in a few minutes later, the mother carried a wooden square with her. The mystery of what that was, was solved when Jason heard the tapping of feet and knew that the little girl must be giving a demonstration of her dancing ability.

The beautiful young woman with the compact followed the mother and daughter in, but while the claranet player and the little girl had left smiling, the beautiful young woman left in tears.

"Okay, Mr. Vandervort. Mr. Pearson will see you now," the receptionist said.

"Mr. Pearson? I thought I would see Bailey or McDill," Jason replied.

"Heavens no," the receptionist said. "Mr. Bailey and Mr. McDill never handle auditions."

"Very well, then I suppose I'll see Mr. Pearson," Jason said.

"Oh good. He'll be so pleased," the receptionist replied sarcastically.

A slender man with prematurely thinning hair was looking through Jason's portfolio when he went inside. He waved his hand, indicating that Jason should sit down. Jason did so and remained quiet for a moment.

"Summer stock in New England," Pearson said. "A couple of small New York shows that I've never heard of, and some experience in college. That's not an overly impressive background, is it, Mr. Vandervort?"

"No, I guess not," Jason said. "Though I really do believe I am capable, and I would have had better credentials to show you if I had decided earlier that acting was really what I wanted to do."

"No doubt." Pearson closed the folder and looked at Jason. "Stand up, please, and turn around."

Jason did as he was asked.

"Are you, by any chance, related to the Vandervorts?"

"It shouldn't have any bearing on whether or not I get a role," Jason said.

"You went to school at Harvard, I see," Pearson said. "It would be easy to find out."

"All right," Jason admitted. "I am one of the Vandervorts."

"Why on earth would someone with your background want to be in films?" Pearson asked.

"It's just something I want to do," Jason said. "And I want to make it on my own," he added. "I don't want my father to buy any roles for me."

"Commendable, very commendable," Pearson replied. "But in a way your father may have just bought a role for you."

"What do you mean?" Jason asked.

"I mean, dear boy, that you just happen to be the right person, in the right place, at the right time." Pearson reached over to the corner of his desk and picked up a piece of paper. "We received a casting call for *Aerodrome*," he continued. "They need several young men to play aviators."

"That's no good. I can't fly," Jason said.

"Oh, you don't have to actually fly. They have stunt people to do that. All you have to do is stand around in an officer's uniform looking like a handsome, well-bred young man. In your case that means just be yourself. Are you interested?"

"Yes, very," Jason said.

"Good. See Nancy, she'll tell you where to go and what to do."

"Nancy?"

"Miss Bruening, the receptionist."

When Jason left Pearson's office, there were no more hopeful talents remaining in the waiting room. He walked over to the receptionist's desk. "I have a casting call for *Aerodrome*. Mr. Pearson said you would tell me where to go and what to do," he said.

"Well, you got the part," Miss Bruening said. "Congratulations."

"Oh no, I don't have the part yet," he said. "This is just a casting call."

Miss Bruening laughed. "Believe me, you do have the part. This isn't an open casting call," she said. "These are little plums that the studio sends out to a few selected agencies. It's all arranged so that no more people show up than there are roles."

"Oh," Jason said. "Well, in that case, this calls for a celebration. Could I interest you in dinner?"

"Hadn't you better wait until you get your first paycheck before you start spending it?" the receptionist asked.

"I have some money set aside," Jason replied. "It'll be all right."

CHAPTER 8

Sid Friedman stepped out of the shower and began patting himself dry with a thick, oversized towel. He put on his red silk pajamas, then slipped his feet into his slippers and went back into his bedroom.

"Hello, Mr. Friedman. Did you have a nice shower?" a man's voice asked from the shadows.

"What the hell?" Sid gasped. There, sitting on his bed, was a dark, powerfully built, frightening-looking man. "Who are you? How did you get in here?"

"My name is Luca," the man replied easily. "Luca Vaglichio. I believe you met my brother."

"How did you get in here?" Sid repeated.

"Simple enough, I walked in."

"I've got the house locked."

"Yeah, I noticed," Luca said, with no further explanation.

Sid started for the telephone. "I think you had better leave."

"That's not very hospitable of you."

Sid picked up the telephone. "I mean it. Leave right now, or I'll call the police."

"Oh, I wouldn't do that if I were you," Luca replied, holding out his hand to stop him. "Not unless you want to get into serious trouble."

Sid stopped "You...you are going to hurt me?"

"No, nothin' like that," Luca laughed. "The trouble I'm talkin' about is what would happen to you if the police find out that you are the one who hired us to take care of Deke Clark."

Sid replaced the receiver in its cradle. "What? What are you talking about?"

"Oh, I'm talking about murder, Mr. Friedman. You see, when you arrange to have a murder committed, you are just as guilty as the man who does the job."

"Are you out of your mind? I didn't arrange to have anyone murdered!"

"You do recall your conversation with my brother, don't you, Mr. Friedman? You told him you had a star you didn't want and a director you couldn't get along with. I believe you asked him to take care of the situation for you." Luca smiled broadly. "Well, we did."

"I...I did no such thing!" Sid said in a choked voice.

"Sure you did," Luca said.

"My God, what are you saying? Are you telling me you...you killed Deke Clark because you thought I wanted you to?"

"Didn't you?"

"No!"

"Oh, come now, Mr. Friedman. You don't think you will really be able to convince anyone that you are sad to see either one of them go."

"Well, maybe not, but that doesn't mean I would want anyone to do something like this."

Luca shrugged his shoulders. "Well, there you go. We're friends, you see, and friends try'n do things for each other. And sometimes they make a mistake. Perhaps we misunderstood. I guess in the future we're goin' to have to pay more attention to the little details, you know, just to make sure there ain't no more misunderstandings between us."

"The future? What are you talking about?" Sid asked. "There is no future as far as we're concerned." He pointed to the door of his bedroom. "I don't know how you got in here, but I want you out of here...now."

"Yeah, I got to be goin', anyway," Luca said, without making any move toward the door. "I'll be leavin' in a minute, but first, I got a favor to ask of you."

"A favor?" Sid choked. "What on earth makes you think I would do you a favor?"

"Well, you owe us one, don't you think? I mean, after what we did for you and all."

"After what you did for me?"

"You got no problems with your star or your director," Luca said.

"What's going on here? This isn't happening." Sid put his hand to the side of his head. "I've either gone mad, or I'm dreaming this."

"It's really quite a simple favor," Luca went on. "After all, the only thing we want you to do is use Joan Leland in your picture."

"I am going to use Joan Leland," Sid said. "As your brother pointed out, she was the one I wanted in the first place. My God, you didn't have to break into my house in order to get me to do this."

"I thought you might go along with it." Luca started to leave, but just before he got to the door, he turned back. "I'm glad we got this worked out. Tomorrow Jay Garland will call you to work out all the details."

"All the details?" Sid asked, confused by the direction the conversation was going. "All the details of what?"

"The details of your using Jay Garland's client Joan Leland."

'Jay Garland's client?" Sid laughed. "If you are going to break into someone's house with all these proposals, you ought to at least know what you're talking about. Joan is represented by Bailey and McDill, not Jay Garland. Who the hell is this Jay Garland, anyway? I don't think I've ever even heard of him. Oh, wait a minute, now that I think of it, I believe I have heard of him. He's the guy who represents Marla Peters, isn't he?"

"Not anymore," Luca said. "He has dropped his old client list and is building a new list. Joan Leland will be on his new list."

"Will be? You mean, she isn't represented by him yet?"

"Not yet."

"No, and she never will be," Sid insisted. "The Bailey and McDill agency is one of the most prestigious agencies in Hollywood. Why would Joan Leland abandon them?"

"Because she wants the role of Molly Tremaine in *Aerodrome* and she isn't going to get it unless she is represented by Jay Garland."

"You can't be serious when you say I can't hire Joan unless she is represented by Jay Garland. Why, he's nothing but a joke."

"We have become Mr. Garland's partners," Luca said. "Believe me, he ain't no joke no more."

"Well, it doesn't matter, anyway," Sid said. "I need a new actress, Joan is perfect for the part, and I work well with the Bailey and McDill agency. Why would I want to do a foolish thing like say I won't hire her unless she is represented by Jay Garland?"

"As an act of friendship, Mr. Friedman," Luca said. "Remember, you owe us."

Luca left the bedroom and closed the door behind him. Sid stood there for a moment longer, as if mesmerized by the whole thing. Then, in a moment of bravado brought on by Luca's departure, he walked over to the telephone. He was going to call the police.

"Oh, now, Mr. Friedman," Luca's voice said in the phone. "I hope you weren't thinking about calling the police. That wouldn't be considered a very friendly gesture, now, would it?"

With a little cry of alarm, Sid hung the phone up. Luca Vaglichio had anticipated his decision and picked up the phone downstairs!

———

The sun was just up when Mike Kelly reported to the converted airfield at the movie lot. It was buzzing with taxiing airplanes and revving engines. Mike looked around for the stunt coordinator he had spoken to the day before and saw him standing by a table with a man who was dressed in aviator clothing. He started over to them.

"Ah, you must be Kelly, the new man Bruiser was telling me about," the man said to Mike. "I'm Sam Fielding. I like a punctual man." Fielding stuck his hand out toward Mike. "Welcome to the Hollywood Air Corps."

"Thanks." Mike took Fielding's hand. "So what's going on today?"

"Oh, this is our big day," Fielding replied. "Our very first day of shooting. In fact, we've got a scene to shoot this morning and Mr. Friedman wants to do it before we lose the light. So how about it? Are you ready to go to work?"

"Sure, I guess so," Mike replied. "Do you have something in mind for me?"

"Why don't you fly the camera plane," Bruiser suggested.

"All right."

"Wait a minute, Bruiser," Fielding interrupted. "Kelly, have you ever flown a camera plane before?"

"No."

"Yeah, well, that's what I thought. Bruiser, I think it would be better if we let him fly either the German or the American plane. I can get Paul to fly the camera plane."

"Work it out any way you want," Bruiser said. "Just get everyone in the air. If we lose this light, Friedman is going to come down on me like stink on shit and if he comes down on me, I'm going to come down on you. You can count on it."

"We'll get your pictures," Fielding called to Bruiser as he walked away.

"He doesn't care too much for me," Mike said.

"Hell, what makes you think you're flying solo?" Sam responded with a chuckle. "He doesn't like anyone very much."

"Why not?"

"Who the hell knows? But it all works out okay, because people don't like him all that much either."

"Which plane you want me to take?" Mike asked.

"Take the Fokker," Fielding said. "By the way, don't think it was a knock against you that I had someone else fly the camera plane. It's just that I've never seen you fly before and the camera plane is the most important one up there. If the pictures aren't taken, everyone else is just wasting their time."

"I'm not insulted," Mike replied easily.

"Good man," Fielding said. "Okay, here's the scene. I'll be in the American plane, flying along nice and easy, when you come swooping down out of the sun. You'll make one pass at me, then I'll turn on you. We'll dogfight for a while, then you activate your smoke pot, flip over on your back, and dive toward the ground, trailing smoke."

"How far down?" Mike asked.

Fielding chuckled again. "As far down as you've got the guts to go,"

"What I mean is, do you have some sort of safety factor built in?"

Fielding laughed. "Safety factor? What do we need with a safety factor? We're invincible, didn't you know that?" He put on his own helmet. "Come on, Kelly, I believe I have your name on my dance card. There's your ship over there."

Mike started toward the little tri-wing Fokker. He was an accomplished pilot but he had never flown this particular type of airplane before, and when he hauled it off the ground a few minutes later, he very nearly pulled it around into a loop. The results of that would have been fatal, as he would not have had room to complete the maneuver.

Fortunately, he realized what he was doing in time to correct it, though his face was red as he imagined everyone on the ground watching, and laughing, at his less-than-professional takeoff.

Mike climbed to five thousand feet. From up here the illusion of being over a World War I battlefield was completely destroyed, for he could see orange groves, well-tended farmers' fields, and beautiful houses with landscaped lawns.

A Nieuport slipped up beside him and Mike saw Fielding giving him hand signals, telling him they were going to do a hundred-eighty-degree turn back across the field and that Mike should stay at altitude, while he and the camera plane dropped down. Mike was then to dive at him in a simulated attack. Mike nodded vigorously to show that he understood.

Fielding peeled out of the formation and dropped two thousand feet lower. Mike waited until the man was flying straight and level across the field, then he dived on him, sighting through the ring site in front of the windscreen. He got the airplane lined up perfectly in his guns —which, of course, were not loaded.

"Bang, bang, bang, bang, bang," he teased as the Fokker dived past the Nieuport. He was surprised at how fast he had come down and he suddenly realized that he had better pay more attention, so he hauled the Fokker out of the dive and started back up, only to see that the Nieuport had followed him down.

"Damn!" Mike said to himself. He was surprised at how quickly Fielding had been able to bring his plane around and get onto his tail. He decided Fielding was a very good pilot and felt relieved that this dogfight wasn't real. Fielding had obviously been in several aerial dogfights before. Mike had a feeling they had been real dogfights, against real German pilots.

Fielding flashed by Mike so fast, and so close, that the little Fokker was bounced around by the wake turbulence put out by the other airplane. Mike started climbing, to regain the advantage of altitude, and when he reached about four thousand feet, he turned back to make a second attack against Fielding.

Fielding had anticipated this maneuver and had already regained enough altitude himself to negate Mike's advantage. The two aircraft started toward each other, closing at a combined speed of three hundred miles per hour. Again Fielding flashed by so close to Mike, that it caused the little Fokker to bounce.

When Mike was certain that he wasn't going to lose

control of his airplane, he twisted around to locate Fielding and saw, with shock, that the other pilot had turned his plane on a dime and was now closing on his tail.

"I know you are supposed to shoot me down," Mike said aloud, to himself. "But I'm going to make you work for it."

Mike chopped the throttle and hauled back on the stick of the Fokker. The Nieuport stayed right on his tail. Mike watched his airspeed fall off until it dropped below flying speed. Then he fell over into a hammerhead stall, slipping back down past the pursuing American plane. For just a moment he had a good clear view of Fielding, and though the helmet and goggles actually covered most of his face, Mike could almost believe he saw, first, a look of surprise, then a look of admiration.

Mike pulled out of the stall, opened the throttle to full power, then wrenched around until he was lined up on the tail of the Nieuport.

"Ah-ha!" Mike shouted into the wind and was about to pull the trigger again when suddenly the airplane in front of him was gone. "What the hell?" he cried out. "Where did he go?" He twisted around in his cockpit, totally confused. Then, out of the corner of his eye, he caught the shadow of the Nieuport, coming out of a very tight inside loop. With that maneuver, Fielding was once again lined up on Mike's tail, and this time, no matter what Mike did, he was unable to shake him.

Finally, with a sigh of resignation, Mike reached down and pulled the handle to activate the smoke bomb and, with smoke streaming from his plane, rolled it over and started for the ground. To add a bit of authenticity to the staged crash he put the plane into a series of tight turns, almost a controlled spin. The result was a fifteen-hundred-foot corkscrew column of smoke. Mike came out of his maneuver at about five hundred feet, then turned and headed back for the airfield. A few minutes later all three planes—the camera plane included— touched down at approximately the same time, then taxied back to the revetments, where the mechanics were waiting to pull postflight inspections and make any repairs that might be necessary.

Fielding was out of his airplane and over to greet Mike as he climbed down. "Damn fine job!" he said enthusiastically. "You were really good up there."

"Good?" Mike replied. "I got shot down."

"You were supposed to get shot down," Fielding reminded him.

"I know, but I didn't want to make it so easy for you," Mike said. "I was trying to avoid it."

"And so you did," Fielding said. "At least as long as anyone ever did."

Mike laughed. "Then you have done this before," he said. "I mean for real."

"A few times."

"How many times?"

"Twenty-three while I was flying for the French," Fielding said. "Seventeen for the Americans. How about you?"

"I was in the war," Mike said. "But I didn't learn to fly until I came back home."

"Well, whoever taught you taught you well."

"Yes," Mike said, thinking of Johnny Sangremano. "He was a good teacher."

"Come on," Fielding said. "They are about to film a scene in the officers' club. They use people like you and me for the flying scenes and the long shots, but we're not pretty enough for the close-ups. For that they use only handsome men. Would you like to see who they have playing us?"

"Sure," Mike answered. "Why not?"

Mike and Fielding left the airplanes, already being crawled over by the mechanics, and walked over to the area where part of the film was actually being shot. Three cameras were set up around the set, numerous huge mirrors, positioned to catch the light, and several microphones, suspended from overhead booms, or hidden in key places. Sid Friedman was shouting through a megaphone to a small group of young men dressed as American army aviators.

One of the young men was Jason Vandervort. Neither Jason nor Mike acknowledged the other's presence.

"We can sit over here," Fielding whispered, pointing to a couple of chairs just out of the way.

A bell rang.

"Ready with sound, Mr. Friedman."

"Cameras?"

"Rolling, Mr. Friedman."

"Speed," someone said.

"Slate it," Sid ordered.

A young man stepped in front of the camera. He was carrying a little chalkboard, with a yellow-and- black-striped handle across the top. "*Aerodrome*, scene one, take one," he said, snapping the top down like a pair of scissors.

"Action!" Sid called.

When Mike returned that night to the house he and the other three men had rented, he was greeted with the smell of Joe Provenzano's spaghetti sauce. Steam was curling up from a big pot on the stove, and Bill, who was helping Joe, was about to start boiling the spaghetti.

"Now don't overcook it, Bill," Joe warned. "You always overcook the pasta."

"Damn," Bill said. "If we had it the way you like it,

we'd just pour it onto our plates right out of the package."

"Spaghetti has to be the right texture," Joe insisted.

"Mmm, smells good," Mike said.

"I was getting tired of hamburgers," Joe replied. "Where's Jason? Isn't he with you?"

"He'll be here soon," Mike answered. "We didn't come home together."

"Yeah," Joe agreed. "That's probably best."

As if on cue, Jason appeared at that moment. Although he had changed out of the uniform he was wearing on the set, traces of makeup remained on his face.

"You must tell me where you buy your rouge," Bill teased. "That shade looks particularly lovely on you."

The others laughed while Jason took a good-natured swing at him.

"Ah, it's ready," Joe said from the stove.

"Ready? I just dropped the noodles in for crying out loud," Bill complained.

"They're ready," Joe insisted, forking the noodles out into a large bowl. He transferred some to a plate, spooned on a little sauce, and handed it to Mike. A moment later, with everyone served, he joined them at the table. "Well, what do you think?" he asked.

"Delicious," Jason said. "And the pasta is done to perfection."

"All right, all right," Bill said. "I was wrong. But I never said I was the noodle expert around here."

"Does anyone have anything interesting to report?" Mike asked as they began to eat.

"I have something curious," Jason said. "I don't know if it means anything."

"Let's have it."

"Joan Leland is leaving Bailey and McDill Associates."

"Why?"

"I'm not really sure," Jason said. "I heard a few people talking about it. They were surprised—and angry. The ones who were talking said it was because she lost the part in *Aerodrome*. The funny thing is, according to what I hear down on the set, Joan Leland is coming back to the picture."

"Why would she quit Bailey and McDill now?" Bill asked.

"I don't know. That's why I mentioned it. It seems a little strange to me."

"It seems a little strange to me too," Mike said. "Keep your ears open, Jason. See what else you can find out."

"Okay."

"Bill? What about you? Anything yet?"

"I've looked through the police files on the Deke Clark murder case," Bill said. "I didn't run across anything we didn't already know."

"I don't have anything specific," Joe said as he expertly wound the pasta with his fork and spoon. "But the word is that the Vaglichios are looking for muscle."

"For muscle? What for?"

"I don't know," Joe answered. "I'll see what I can find out, but it's going to be tricky because if either Luca or Mario see me, they'll recognize me and our whole operation will be compromised."

"Hell, that's easy," Bill said. "Don't let them see you."

"That's a good idea," Joe said sarcastically. "I never thought of that."

"What about you, boss man? Did you learn anything today?"

Mike smiled. "The only thing I learned today is that I'm not nearly as hot a pilot as I thought I was."

When Joe returned to the pool hall the next day, he looked around for the two men he had befriended the day before.

"Seen Guido or Paulie today?" he asked as he began to rack the balls.

"Who's askin'?" one of the other players replied.

Joe put his hand on his hip then fixed his questioner with a belligerent stare. "Who's askin'? I'm askin'," he snarled. "Who the hell you think is askin', the pope? What'sa matter you?"

"He's okay," the proprietor said. "He and Guido and Paulie were playin' here yesterday."

"If you, Guido, and Paulie are such good friends, you wouldn't have to be asking," the player said in Italian.

"I don't speak Italian," Joe lied.

"What kind of Italian are you, you don't speak Italian?"

"I am an Italian who doesn't speak Italian," Joe answered.

"Okay, okay. So what do you want with Guido and Paulie?"

"Nothin'," Joe said. "I'm lookin' for a little game, that's all."

"You the hotshot player they were talkin' about yesterday?"

"That's him," the proprietor said.

The man smiled. "I'll give you a game," he said. He pulled a wad of money from his pocket, peeled off a hundred-dollar bill, and laid it on the side of the table. "Too rich for you?"

"No," Joe said, surprised at the size of the bet. He saw, immediately, that the others in the pool hall gave up their own games to come watch this one.

"Carlo, you'd better watch this one," one of them said

in Italian. "You can't play with him the way you do the others. He is too good."

"Then I will deal with him quickly," Carlo returned, also in Italian, as he made the break.

From the way Carlo played, and from what he could overhear from the conversation of the others, Joe realized that he had connected with the resident pool shark. Carlo made his living, and it was a good one, with his cue stick.

Joe had learned long ago that a pool hall was an excellent way to pick up a little information. That was because he was a good enough pool player to appear to be concentrating entirely on his game while he was, in fact, listening to the conversation of others. Today, however, he was having to concentrate more than normal on the game because Carlo really was good enough to beat him.

"Yeah, the Vaglichios got it all set up," one of the kibitzers said in Italian. "A bunch of wetbacks are bringin' in a boat load of heroin. It's supposed to be goin' to some black dealers, but it's going to be heisted."

Joe strained to filter the information out of the background noise and that broke his concentration so that he missed his shot. With a smile, Carlo took over and began methodically running the table.

"The way Guido tells it," the speaker was saying, still in Italian, "the Vaglichios are plannin' on movin' out here in a big way and they need a little operatin' capital."

"When is the heist supposed to take place?"

"Tonight," the speaker said. He looked up at the clock on the wall. "Hell, right now," he added.

When Carlo finally missed one, Joe got the cue stick back. By now he had overheard all the information there was to hear, so he could concentrate on his game. Like Carlo before him, he began running the table. Unlike Carlo, Joe didn't miss again.

"You're pretty good," Carlo said as Joe picked up his winnings.

"I get by," Joe replied.

"Yeah? Well, you more than get by. How'd you like to team up with me?"

"Doin' what?"

"Doin' what? Playin' pool, that's what. We could go all up an' down the coast, we could make a killin'."

Joe lit a cigarette, then stared at Carlo through the smoke for a long moment before he answered. "I don't know. I never worked with nobody else before. Let me think about it some."

"Yeah, you do that," Carlo said. "And think real good because you an' me...we could make us a lot of money workin' all the joints."

"Anybody else want a game?" Joe asked, racking the balls again. "How 'bout you, Carlo? You want a chance to get even?"

Carlo smiled and shook his head. "No," he said. "That's what makes me different from the suckers. The suckers, they always think they got a chance to come back on you. Me, I know better."

"Have it your way," Joe replied, just as glad that Carlo didn't want to play again.

Actually, Joe didn't want to play another game either. He now had some information that the others needed to know, but he couldn't just run out without arousing suspicion. Therefore, he stayed around the table for a few moments longer, tried again, unsuccessfully, to interest someone in a game, then replaced his cue stick, nodded good-bye, and left with the information.

LOS ANGELES BAY

The boat was anchored about a mile and a half offshore. Luca and Mario were both in the pilothouse with Casper Kincaid, the boat owner and captain. The pilothouse, like the entire boat, was dark. Mario looked down onto the deck and saw the huddled shadows of the six men, including Guido and Paulie, they had brought with them. Luca was standing at the window with a pair of binoculars, looking out across the water.

"You're sure they'll be comin' this way?" he asked Kincaid.

"This is the way they always come," the captain assured them. I know, because they used to use my boat. Then they found someone with an old boat who said he would do it cheaper." Kincaid had been chewing tobacco and he spat out a plug, hitting the spittoon, even in the dark, and making it ring. "They got no concept of loyalty, the damn Mexicans."

"Shh!" Luca said. "I see somethin' out there."

"It might just be a buoy."

"No, I don't think so," Luca said. He handed the glasses to Kincaid. "You're more experienced than I am. What do you think?"

Kincaid stared through the binoculars for a moment, then he smiled broadly and handed the glasses back. "That's them, all right," he said.

"Well, if we've seen them, we've got to expect that they've seen us too," Mario said.

"Not necessarily," Kincaid explained. "We're further out to sea than they are. We can see them in silhouette against the lights of the shore. There's nothin' behind us to show where we are." He grinned again and rubbed his hands together in eager anticipation. "No, sir, gents. If you ask me, we've got 'em right where we want 'em.

We'll be right alongside before they even suspect we are here."

"We better tell the others," Mario suggested.

"Yeah, I will," Luca offered. He walked across the pilothouse and opened the window so he could call down to the shadowed shapes who were waiting on the deck. "You fellas down there," he hissed. "We spotted the boat. It's comin', so get ready!"

"The boat is comin'? Good, I was gettin' a little bored sittin' here," Guido said.

"I bet I get the first Mex," Paulie challenged.

Kincaid started his engines, then began moving forward toward a spot where he would be able to intercept the dope-running boat.

"What kind of guns you think they'll have with them?" Luca asked.

"Like I told you," Kincaid replied. "When I was runnin' it for 'em, they never had more'n three or four people on board, and they was only armed with pistols."

"Good. At least we got 'em outmanned and outgunned," Luca said.

"The only problem is, if they think we're the law, they'll dump the stuff overboard," Mario said. "And if they do, all this will be for nothin'."

"Don't worry about that. We're goin' to hit 'em so fast they won't have time to dump it," Luca insisted. "Come on, let's you an' me get down to the deck."

"I'm right behind you," Mario replied.

"You guys hang on down there," Kincaid cautioned. "I'm goin' to have to run pretty fast to catch up with them."

"You just catch up with them," Luca said. "Don't you worry none about us."

By the time Luca and Mario were on deck, Kincaid had the boat moving at a pretty good clip. As a result of the boat's speed, it was throwing spray up over the sides and bouncing deeply as it plowed through the rolling waves.

"Ever'body," Luca ordered. "Stay down low. That way when they do see the boat, they won't see nobody on it and they won't think nothin' about it."

"They see us runnin' dark, they're goin' to get suspicious, aren't they?" one of the men asked.

"They might," Luca admitted. "But we can't show any lights because they'll run the minute they see something."

"There it is!" Guido said. "I can see it."

"Yeah, me too," Paulie agreed, pointing it out to the others.

"Ever'body get ready," Luca ordered. "Mario, you get on the spotlight. When we're close enough, turn it right on 'em."

"Right," Mario said, moving into position to operate the powerful spotlight that was mounted in the bow.

The outline of the Mexicans' boat gradually began to appear in the night before them. Mario waited until the boat was fully visible, then turned on the light and held it captured in his beam. The moment the Mexican boat was caught in the beam, its captain opened the throttle to full power to try to get away.

"Stay with him!" Luca shouted up to Kincaid. "Don't let him get away!"

"He's not goin' anywhere," Kincaid shouted back, increasing the power on his own boat.

The Mexicans started shooting, but as Kincaid had promised, they were armed only with pistols. Luca and Mario had taken the precaution of arming their men with submachine guns.

"Shoot 'em," Luca shouted. "Cut the sons of bithes down!"

The Vaglichio men started blasting away with their Thompsons, using the winking muzzle flashes of the Mexicans' guns as their target. One of the Mexicans grabbed his chest, then fell overboard. His body rolled once in the wake of the boat, then disappeared in the darkness of the night and the sea.

The shooting and the high-speed chase continued. The spotlight Mario was using was hit and exploded in a flash of sparks and a shower of broken bits of glass. Mario felt little nicks and cuts on his hands and arms, but he knew that it was just from the broken glass and therefore not serious.

Kincaid bore down hard on the Mexicans until his boat was dead even with theirs. One by one, the Mexicans went down under the superior gunfire until, finally, the single remaining Mexican threw down his gun and put up his hands. When that happened, the captain of the Mexican boat throttled back and threw up his hands as well. Kincaid had to chop his throttle to keep from overrunning the other boat. Now, with both engines no more than a quiet rumble, the two boats rocked side by side in the darkness.

The captain of the Mexican boat was American, and he peered up through the darkness at the boat that had just overtaken him. "Kincaid?" he called. "Kincaid, is that you?"

"Yeah," Kincaid answered. "It's me."

"I thought it was the police."

"You still got the stuff?" Luca shouted.

"What stuff?"

"Don't give me that 'what stuff' shit," Luca said angrily. "We'll just kill you where you stand and search the boat ourselves."

"It's in a couple of tool chests down in the engine hold," the captain replied quickly.

"You die for telling them!" the lone remaining Mexican shouted.

"No, he don't," Luca said easily. "You die." He squeezed off a quick burst from his submachine gun and the Mexican grabbed his stomach, then fell.

"Get over there," Luca ordered his men. "Throw that one and the others overboard, then bring the stuff to me."

Guido, Paulie, and another man stepped across the bobbing gap that separated the two boats. While two of the men tossed the bodies overboard the other went down into the engine hold.

"What...what happens to me?" the boat captain asked.

"What were they payin' you for this trip?" Luca asked.

"Five hundred bucks."

"Have you already been paid?"

"Half of it."

Mario pulled some money from his pocket. "Here's the other half," he said. "Nothin' happened out here tonight."

The captain smiled broadly then came down from the flying bridge and reached across the gap to take the money. It was two one-hundreds and a fifty. "Thanks," he said.

The tool chests were passed across to Mario. He set them down, opened them up, and looked at the little paper sacks inside. He stuck his knife into one of the bundles, then pulled it out with white powder on the blade. He touched it to his tongue, then nodded at Luca.

"Okay," Luca called up to Kincaid. "Let's get the hell out of here."

"Right," Kincaid said, opening the throttle and pulling away from the other boat. Their last view of the man who had captained the boat for the Mexicans was of him putting the money into his pocket, then climbing back onto the flying bridge as calmly as if he had just agreed to take on a fishing party.

"Now," Mario said to his brother as the two sat down in the cabin of the boat for the ride back, "We have a little operating money."

"Shit," Luca said. "This was too easy. This was like takin' candy from a baby. You sure you want to screw around with all this movie shit? We could do all right for ourselves just like this."

"Luca, this is just a drop in the bucket compared to what we can make," Mario said. "Besides, I don't know about you, but ridin' around on a boat in the middle of the night, gettin' my ass shot off, isn't my idea of a good way to make a livin'."

Luca laughed and punched his brother playfully on the shoulder. "You're just losin' the old touch, that's all. You're goin' soft in your old age."

"Trust me," Mario said. "Once we get our hooks into the movie business, you'll think messing around with dope and booze is peanuts."

"Okay, Mario, I'm lettin' you call the shots out here," Luca said. "What's next?"

"Next we make sure that Sangremano's sister is out for good," Mario said.

"The only way we're goin' to make sure she is out for good is to take care of Johnny. Otherwise he'll find some way to screw up the works."

"Are you saying we are going to have to kill him?" Mario asked.

"It's going to have to be done sooner or later," Luca replied.

"Yes, but we signed the treaty. If we violate it, we'll have all the Families down on us."

Luca smiled. "That was for New York," he said. "We're in California now."

BEVERLY HILLS, THE NEXT AFTERNOON

"Yes," Sergeant Collins answered in response to Bill's question. "As a matter of fact we did pull a Mexican's body out of the bay last night. How did you know that?"

"Something I overheard," Bill explained. "Who was he, do you know?"

"His name was Esteban Mendoza," Collins said. "He's small time. We've arrested him for selling dope a couple of times, that's all. You said it was something you overheard. What did you hear?"

"I heard that he and a few of his partners were bringing in a load of dope last night," Bill said. "But they were intercepted. According to the information I received, they were all killed and the dope was taken. Do the police have any information on anything about that?"

"No," Collins replied. "But then the people who were expecting the dope shipment aren't very likely to report it being taken," he added.

Bill chuckled. "No, I guess not."

"Who was it, did you hear?"

"If my information is right, the ones who attacked the Mexicans are the same people I'm after," Bill said.

"Communists?" Collins asked. "Are you telling me that Communists killed the Mexicans and took the dope?"

"Yes," Bill said.

"What the hell do Communists want with dope? I thought they were only interested in politics and stuff like that."

"That's true, but it costs a lot of money to mount a revolution," Bill explained. "And if they are wanting to overthrow the government anyway, it is certainly not going to bother them to violate the laws of the government, they are going to overthrow."

"Oh yeah, I guess so. I never really thought of that," Collins said.

"If you don't mind," Bill said, "I think I would like to read through all the arrest reports you have, dealing with dope. The people who took that stuff are going to have to unload it somewhere. Maybe if I look over the arrest reports, I'll find their biggest customer."

"That's a good idea," Collins agreed. "But you're probably goin' to have to go through half a dozen books. Come on, I'll help you carry them to your desk."

At that very moment, in the front of the police station, a young dark-haired woman was coming hesitantly through the door, clutching a scarf around her head. She stopped just inside the building and looked up at the high counter where the desk sergeant was writing in a book. After a long moment, the desk sergeant either saw, or sensed, her presence, and looked toward her.

"Can I help you?" he asked.

"*Sí,*"

"Do you need to talk to the police?"

"*Sí,*" she said again.

"Well, come on up closer," the desk sergeant said, motioning with his hand.

When the girl was very close, the desk sergeant could see the fear in her eyes. He didn't know if she was afraid because of something that had just happened, or if she was afraid because she was in the presence of a police officer. A lot of Mexicans were, he knew.

"Now, honey, what can I do for you?" he asked, making the tone of his voice gentle so as not to frighten her any more than she already was."

The girl began to speak something in rapid Spanish and the desk sergeant held up his hand to stop her.

"Hold it, hold it. Don't you speak any English?"

The girl shook her head no.

"Just a minute," the desk sergeant said. He pushed down on the button on his desk intercom box. "Roy? Roy, is Bustamante back there?"

"Uh, yeah, he's here," Roy said. "What's the matter, did he forget your trash cans again this morning?"

"No, nothing like that," the desk sergeant said. "Ask him to come up here, would you, please? I've got a little Mex gal who is scared to death about somethin' and she doesn't speak a word of English. I need Bustamante to talk to her for me."

"Yeah, okay, I'll send him right up," Roy's disembodied voice replied.

"Okay," the desk sergeant said to the frightened girl. He held up his hand. "Just wait here a minute."

A few moments later, Juan Bustamante, janitor and sometimes interpreter, came up to the front of the station. When he saw the young attractive Mexican girl, he straightened up and poked his shirttail down into his trousers. "*Qué?*" he said to her.

The girl began speaking rapidly, all the while making broad hand gestures. At one time she formed her hand into the shape of a gun.

"Hey, what is it?" the desk sergeant asked. "What's she talkin' about?"

"A murder, Señor Desk Sergeant," Bustamante answered. "She was the—how do you say with your eyes"—he pointed to his eyes—"to a murder."

"Eyewitness?"

"Eyewitness, *sí*. She was eyewitness."

"Who did she see murdered?"

"She does not know the person's name," Bustamante

said. "It happened behind the house next door to the house where she works."

The woman spoke again.

"She is a maid, Señor Desk Sergeant. In the place where she works she has a room on the second floor at the back of the house. From her window she can see the swimming pool next door."

The woman spoke again.

"She saw a man and woman having dinner," Busta-mante said.

The woman spoke again.

"They drank wine," he continued.

She spoke again, and this time she looked down at the floor and spoke in halting tones.

"She is most embarrassed to say they...I do not know how to say the word in English for what they did, except to use a very bad word, and I do not wish to use such a word in front of the señorita." He made a circle with the thumb and finger of one hand, then thrust the forefinger of the other in and out, several times.

"I understand," the desk sergeant said. "The man and woman had carnal knowledge."

"Sí, they had carnal knowledge."

"And then what happened?"

"The girl, her name is Señorita Rosita Chavez, did not wish to watch because it was... it brought shame."

"It was embarrassing?"

"Sí, it was embarrassing to her. So she looked away. Later she heard the sound of a gun and she looked over. She saw the woman shoot the man."

"Why hasn't she come to us before now?" the desk sergeant asked.

Bustamante asked the question and the girl answered in one short, cryptic sentence.

"She was afraid, señor. She is new to this country and

the woman who lives next door to her is a very wealthy person. She did not think it was the place of a peon to inform the police about the misdoings of a very wealthy person."

"Why is she doing it now?"

Bustamante asked, and when the girl answered, he nodded yes. "She asked her priest what she should do and the priest said she should come to the police."

"Tell her she did the right thing," the desk sergeant said.

"Say, Bill," Sergeant Collins said, coming over to the desk where Bill was busy reading through the arrest reports. "You wanted to be kept up-to-date on anything that happened with the Deke Clark murder?"

"Yeah," Bill answered, looking up from the books. "Have you got something?"

"We sure do," Collins said. "We've got it all locked up."

"Locked up?"

"Solved," Collins said. "The girl did it. I guess that proves that a woman scorned is someone you want to stay away from, whether she is a movie star or not."

"How do you know she did it?"

"We've got an eyewitness report," Sergeant Collins said. "The next-door maid saw everything."

CHAPTER 9

INDICTMENT HANDED DOWN FOR KATIE STARR

Special. *The Los Angeles County Prosecutor's Office announced today that an indictment for murder had been handed down against Katherine Sangremano, also known as Katie Starr.*

"There is ample evidence to support the charge that Miss Starr was involved in the murder of Deke Clark," Norton Potashnick replied, when questioned as to why the indictment had been handed down. Potashnick also said that due to the fame of the defendant as well as the intense public interest in the case, he would personally handle the prosecution duties for the state of California.

Deke Clark, the victim, and one of Hollywood's most successful directors, was, in fact, at work on Aerodrome when he was murdered. Mr. Clark was the husband of Tamara Welles, another well-known Hollywood personality.

The suspect, a well-known actress, was twice nominated for the Oscar and was this year's recipient of the Maxie Award. Ironically, she was playing the female lead in Aerodrome at the time of its director's death.

Aerodrome is being produced by Sid Friedman, who also

produced the current blockbuster Arabian Pleasures. When asked about his reaction to the indictment handed down against Katie Starr, he had this to say. "Katie Starr's friends at Galaxy Pictures, as well as her millions of fans across the country, are convinced that she is innocent of the crime. While we mourn the passing of Deke Clark, our slain comrade, we anxiously await the decision that will, no doubt, find Katie innocent of any wrongdoing."

When asked if Katie Starr's role of Molly Tremaine was secure, Sid Friedman reserved comment. In the meantime, rumors continue to fly that Galaxy Pictures is talking to Jay Garland, Joan Leland's new agent, about the role.

"I personally guarantee that when Aerodrome is released, Joan Leland will be playing the role of Molly Tremaine," Jay Garland reported. "And not only is she going to play the role, she is going to do it for more money than any actress has ever drawn for any starring role," he continued.

Bailey and McDill Associates, Joan Leland's longtime representative, refused to make a spokesman available for comment as to why Joan had, inexplicably, switched agencies.

SAN FRANCISCO

The law offices of Vaughan and Murchison smelled of leather and old books. The young woman behind the desk was hunched over her typewriter, erasing the mistake she had just made. She looked up when Johnny approached her desk, squinted at him, then, realizing that she wasn't wearing her glasses, picked them up and put them on.

"Excuse me," she said. "I'm nearsighted. I don't need the glasses to type or read, I just need them to see."

Johnny chuckled. "That seems like a good enough reason to wear them," he said. "Is Henry in?"

"Yes, he is," she said. "May I tell him who is asking for him?"

"Tell him tail number thirty-four," Johnny said.

"I beg your pardon?"

"Tail number thirty-four," Johnny said again. "He'll understand."

The young woman got up from her desk and started down the hallway toward the other offices. She was, Johnny decided, with or without her glasses, quite pretty.

"Johnny?" he heard a moment later. "Johnny, is that you?" He looked toward the hallway where the young woman had gone and saw a large bearded bear of a man coming toward him with his hand outstretched. "My god, it is you," the man said.

"Hello, Henry," Johnny said, taking the offered hand. "You're looking prosperous."

"You mean I'm looking fat, don't you?" Henry replied.

"Well, you have gotten grand," Johnny teased. "So how have you been since the war? Are you doing any flying?"

Henry patted himself on his rather large belly and laughed. "Are you kidding? I'm not sure I could even fit into the cockpit anymore. What about you? Are you flying any?"

"Oh, I do a bit of flying," Johnny said. "I have my own airplane now."

"Do you? Well, that must be fun."

The young woman who had gone to retrieve Henry Murchison hadn't left, and Henry, noticing that she was still here, teased her. "Really, Karen, sometimes you are just too obvious," he said.

"And you are too obtuse," Karen replied.

Henry laughed and put his arm around her shoulders.

"Johnny, this is my sister, Karen. Karen, this is Johnny Sangremano."

"This is Karen?" he said. "I remember you once showed me a picture of her, but she sure didn't look like this."

"I know," Henry teased. "She was an ugly little runt when she was a kid."

"Henry!" Karen gasped.

Henry laughed again. "I'll admit, you did grow up pretty," he conceded.

"Very pretty, if you ask me," Johnny said, and as Karen excused herself, he thought he saw a slight blush in her cheeks. The blush, in his opinion, made her even prettier.

"Come on back to my lair," Henry invited, and Johnny followed him down the long corridor and through an open door into his office.

"Do you recognize this?" Henry asked, pointing to a framed picture on the wall behind him. It was a head-on picture of two Nieuport Scouts on an airfield in France. There were two pilots standing in front of the planes, slouching in that insolent way all World War aviators had about them. The man on the left in the photograph was a younger, and much thinner, version of Henry Murchison. The man on the right was Johnny Sangremano.

"I not only recognize it, I remember the day it was taken," Johnny said. "You got yourself two victories that day, as I recall."

"Yeah," Henry, chuckling. "While you flew off to rescue some dumb doughboy who had gotten himself captured by the Germans. What was his name? O'Riley? Flynn?"

"Kelly."

"Kelly, yes. I knew he was an Irishman. I wonder

whatever happened to him. You ever hear from him again?"

"We kept in touch for a little while," Johnny said without elaborating. "We don't see much of each other anymore."

"Have a seat, Johnny, have a seat," Henry said. "Tell me, what can I do for you?"

"I need your services, Henry," Johnny replied. "I want to hire a lawyer."

"You need to do some business in California? What do you need, something incorporated?"

"I need a defense attorney for a murder trial," Johnny said.

Henry drew in a sharp breath, then he leaned back in his chair and stroked his beard as he looked at Johnny.

"I, uh...I thought you did most of your 'business' in New York," he said. "I mean, you are that Johnny Sangremano, aren't you?"

"You've heard about me?"

"Your name has made the papers a few times, even out here," Henry said.

Johnny sighed. "Yes," he said. "I am that Johnny Sangremano. But this isn't a New York case, and I am not the defendant. I need you for someone else. And she is innocent, Henry. I don't mind confessing that if I were hiring you for myself, that might not be true. But in this case it is."

"Who do you want me to defend?

"My sister, Katherine," Johnny said.

"Katherine? Yes, I remember her." Henry laughed. "In fact, didn't we once offer to trade sisters?"

"Yes," Johnny answered, also laughing at the remembrance.

"And you say Katherine is involved in a murder case? How did that happen?"

"I'm surprised you haven't read about it in the newspapers," Johnny said. "It's been on the front pages of practically every paper in the country."

Henry still looked blank.

"Katie Starr," Johnny said.

Henry gasped. "Katie Starr? You mean she is your sister?"

"Yes," Johnny said. "I thought you knew."

"No," Henry replied. "No, I didn't know. But yes, I have been reading about the case."

"Will you defend her, Henry?" Johnny asked.

"Johnny, I don't know," Henry answered. "Surely you can find someone better qualified than I. I haven't defended a criminal case since right after I graduated from law school and served a stint with the public defender's office. And none of them were capital cases."

"How did you do?"

"I won three and lost two," Henry said. "Hardly a sparkling recommendation."

Johnny chuckled. "At least it is a winning record," he said. "But what you did in the public defender's office doesn't matter. You are the one I want."

Henry drummed his fingers on the top of his desk for a moment or two. "The trial is where…down in Los Angeles?"

"Yes."

"When are you going back?"

"Tomorrow," Johnny replied.

"Give me until tomorrow to decide. I mean I have to really try and determine whether I might help or hurt her chances. It's at times like this that I think lawyers should have their own version of the Hippocratic oath, and it should begin the same way: 'First, do no harm.'"

"All right," Johnny said. "That's fair enough."

"In the meantime suppose I have my sister take you out to dinner tonight?"

"Huh-uh," Johnny said. "I take her out, she doesn't take me out. That's not the way Italians do things."

"Oh, don't be silly. This is the twentieth century and my sister is a modern woman."

Johnny smiled. "She is also a beautiful woman and it would be my pleasure to take her out...if she will go with me."

"Oh, don't worry about that. I'm sure she will be very glad to go."

Johnny stopped the rented car, then looked at the little sheet of paper on which Henry Murchison had written his sister's address. "This is the building where she lives," he said aloud. "Now all I have to do is find her apartment."

Karen's apartment was on the second floor. There was an elevator available, but Johnny took the carpeted stairway instead. There were four apartments on the second floor, but only one of them had flowers outside the door and Johnny smiled because he knew before he even checked the number that this would be her door. He twisted the little butterfly crank to ring the doorbell, and in a moment, so quickly in fact that he knew she must have been waiting for him, she opened the door.

"Oh my," Johnny said. "Don't you look beautiful."

Johnny wasn't just being nice. Karen was beautiful. She was wearing a white-beaded dress that clung closely to her slim, shapely form. An artful application of makeup had fulfilled the promise of beauty Johnny had noticed in the office earlier in the day.

"Thank you," Karen said as she locked the door behind her. She put her hand on Johnny's arm. "You're going to have to lead me," she said. "Remember, without my glasses, I'm as blind as a bat."

"Why don't you wear your glasses?" Johnny asked. "I think you look lovely in them."

"I think they make me look like an owl," Karen replied.

"Well, yes, but a lovely owl," Johnny suggested, to be rewarded by Karen's laugh.

"Do you have a taxi waiting?" she asked.

"No."

"Oh, you should have kept him. It's hard to get one down here."

Johnny chuckled. "I've rented a car."

Karen looked at him in surprise. "Isn't that a rather foolish extravagance?"

"Not when I'm trying to make an impression," Johnny said, holding the front door open for her. There, sitting at the curb, was a red Packard convertible.

"That's the car?" Karen gasped.

"Yes."

"My. When you want to make an impression, you go all out, don't you?"

"I want you to remember me," Johnny said.

"I don't think there's much danger I'll forget," Karen replied, slipping into the car as, once again, he held the door open for her.

"Do you like authentic Italian cooking?" Johnny asked as he got behind the wheel then put the car into gear and pulled away from the curb.

"I love Italian food," Karen replied.

"Good, because that's what I had planned for our dinner."

"Where are we going?" Karen asked. "We have several nice Italian restaurants in San Francisco, but I would be interested in knowing which one you thought was the most authentic."

"Why don't you just wait and see?" Johnny asked.

"By the way, I think it is safe to tell you now that I once had a terrible crush on you," Karen admitted.

"Did you?"

"Yes. Of course, I had nothing but Henry's pictures and description of you to go by, but you were my Prince Charming."

Johnny looked across the car and smiled at her. "And have I lived up to your expectations?"

Karen laughed. "Oh, I hardly think so. But then, who could live up to the expectations of a nine-year-old girl?" She looked around. "Where are we going?" she asked. "There are no Italian restaurants down here. As a matter of fact, there are no restaurants of any kind down here. This is just a residential neighborhood."

"I know," Johnny replied.

"But you said you were taking me to an Italian restaurant," she challenged.

"I said I was taking you to a place where you could get authentic Italian cooking," Johnny corrected. "I'm taking you to my uncle's house."

"Oh, that will be nice," Karen said. "Is your uncle a good cook?"

"I'll be doing the cooking. My uncle is dead," Johnny said. "We've kept his house because my sister often comes up here to stay."

"Is your sister there now?"

"No," Johnny said. "No one is there now. There will just be the two of us."

"No!"

Johnny looked over at Karen, a little surprised by her reaction. Then a shadow crossed his face and the smile left, to be replaced by a frown. He stuck his hand out to signal a turn and made a U-turn right in the middle of the road.

"What's the matter, Miss Murchison?" he asked dryly.

"Are you afraid to be alone with a mobster? Do you think they might be pulling your body out of San Francisco Bay in the morning?"

"No, it's just..." Karen started weakly, but she couldn't finish.

"It's just that you are frightened of me. Is that it?"

"No," Karen said. "Yes," she amended quickly, "but it's not what you think. I wouldn't want to go to a house, alone, with any man, whether he was a mobster or not."

"I'm sorry I popped off like that," Johnny said. "Of course you would feel that way." He sighed. "I should have explained the situation more carefully. You see, the truth is, I can't just go to a restaurant like everyone else."

"Why not?"

"They're too dangerous," Johnny said. "For me and for anyone who is with me."

"Dangerous?"

"A man in my...profession," he said, choosing the word carefully, "has to be on a constant lookout. I have many enemies, Karen. Many enemies."

"Oh," Karen said weakly. "I guess I've never really considered the nature of your, uh, profession. I mean, I've never known a mobster before."

"That's to your advantage," Johnny said. "Mobsters are not very nice people to know."

"But you are nice to know. And you are a mobster."

"Not by choice," Johnny defended. "It's a situation I inherited."

"Why don't you get out?"

"It's not as easy as all that," Johnny explained. "There are too many other people involved. However, I am moving toward legitimate businesses, and within another year or two the Sangremano Family will be completely finished with the booze, numbers, and anything else that is illegal."

"Oh, Johnny, I think that is wonderful," Karen said. "Listen, I was being foolish a while ago. I'd love to eat with you if you are still willing to have me."

Without answering her, Johnny put the car into another U-turn and started back in the other direction.

"Well, all right, but you're going to have to make up your mind," he teased. "We're going to have the police down on us for turning this street into a racetrack."

"That's all right. I'll get my brother to defend you," Karen said good-naturedly. "He's a pretty good lawyer, if I do say so myself."

"I hope so," Johnny replied. "My sister is going to need one. This is the street," he said, turning onto a wide, flower-and tree-lined avenue.

"Oh, this is a lovely neighborhood," Karen said.

Johnny's uncle's house was a beautiful old restored home. It was a large two-story house, with turrets, cupolas, dormers, and intricate lattice and trim work, true to the Victorian style of the 1880s when it was built.

"I love old homes," Karen said. "It would be nice to live in one like this someday."

"It's the dream of every Italian mama for her son to have a nice girl for a wife, a big family, and a house just like this," Johnny said.

"And you've never found such a person?"

"Oh yes, I found her," Johnny said.

Karen looked at Johnny in hurt surprise. "Do you mean to tell me that you are married? You should have told me before. What kind of girl do you think I am?"

"I think you are a very nice girl," Johnny answered easily. "And my wife is dead," he added without further explanation.

"Oh," Karen replied, mollified. "I shouldn't have snapped at you like that. I'm sorry for that, and I'm sorry about your wife."

"So am I," Johnny said. "She was a sweet kid." He smiled. "But that's been a while. I still have an emptiness in my heart, but at least the terrible hurt is gone."

Johnny parked the car in the curved driveway in front of the house, then escorted Karen inside. She commented on the beauty of the polished woods, and the elegance of the furniture. But she was most impressed by the kitchen.

"When my uncle died, the kitchen was about the size of an oversized closet," Johnny explained. "But what did he care? He had someone do his cooking for him. My sister, however, loves to cook, so when she took over the house, she had a big kitchen built."

"And you cook too?"

"Yes," Johnny said. "I guess it runs in the family. I find cooking relaxing. By the way, do you like veal *scaloppine*?"

"I'm sure I will," Karen answered. "I've never had it, but I do like veal."

"I thought we'd have a little veal *scaloppine* and some sautéed asparagus," Johnny said. He moved the ingredients over to the counter and began working with the thin strips of veal, seasoning it with oregano, garlic salt, and pepper. "Have you ever seen any of my sister's movies?" he asked as he began to heat oil and butter in a frying pan.

"Oh yes," Karen answered. "I'm a big fan of Katie Starr, although I didn't know she was your sister until this afternoon."

"Yeah, well, that's what happens when you change your name," Johnny said. "Of course, in Katherine's case, changing her name was probably a pretty good idea. It kept the public from knowing who she is, so she didn't have to overcome the stigma of being related to me. Unfortunately changing her name didn't hide her from my enemies."

"You keep talking about your enemies," Karen said. "Do you really have that many?"

"It's one of the hazards of my occupation," Johnny replied. He dredged the meat in flour, then added it to the pan. It made a loud, sizzling noise.

"And you think your enemies are also after your sister?"

"Well, they did manage to frame her for murder." He poured a cup of wine over the meat, then smiled at her. "By the way, I've just made you a criminal," he said.

"What? How? What are you talking about?"

Johnny held up the empty cup. "The wine I used in cooking," he said. "It wasn't cooking wine, it was real table wine. That's a violation of the law. It's a stupid law, but it's a violation nevertheless."

"I have a feeling it won't be with us much longer," Karen said.

Johnny chuckled. "That will put a lot of my associates out of business."

"And you?"

"Like I said, I'm trying to get out of the business, anyway," he answered. He added ham and cheese to the veal, then slipped it into the oven. "It won't be long now," he said.

The dinner was a success and Karen complimented Johnny on his culinary skills, admitting that she was somewhat daunted as she didn't consider herself a very good cook at all.

"Believe me, when a man looks at you, whether or not you can cook isn't the first thing to cross his mind."

"Oh? Then what is the first thing they think of?" Karen replied, raising one eyebrow.

Johnny looked at her in surprise, then saw that she was teasing him, and he laughed. "They probably wonder whether or not they can match wits with you. And the answer is no, they cannot."

"Mr. Sangremano—" Karen began, but Johnny held up his hand.

"Now that we have eaten together and you have totally destroyed me in a little verbal swordplay, don't you think you can call me Johnny?"

"Johnny," she amended. "If my brother takes the case...if he defends your sister, will he be in danger?"

Johnny looked at her and the smile left his face. "You get right to the point quickly, don't you?"

"Will he be in danger?" she asked again.

"I wish I could answer that, but I can't," he admitted.

"You mean, he may be in danger?"

"Yes. I would say that there is a very good possibility that he could be in danger."

"I see." Karen sighed. "Well, thank you for being honest about it."

Johnny reached up to touch Karen on the cheek. "Karen, I don't think I could be anything but honest with you," he replied.

Johnny's touch and gaze held Karen to him, much like a bright light will hold a small creature, caught in its beam. When he moved his lips toward her, she made no effort to back away. He kissed her, gently at first, then with more and more urgency. When the kiss was ended, she looked at him with an expression of surprise and innocent vulnerability. The surprise was not so much that he had kissed her, but that she had reacted so strongly.

"I'm sorry, I shouldn't have done that," Johnny apologized.

"I liked it," Karen replied.

"But you're Henry's sister."

"And a grown woman," she insisted. She took a half

step toward him and it was obvious that she wanted him to kiss her again.

"You are so beautiful," Johnny said. He backed away from her and smiled sadly. "It would be so easy now. You are so vulnerable and I..." He paused, then sighed. "I am too much the Sicilian gentleman. I cannot wear the mask, you see."

"The mask?"

"Yes, the mask. Nearly everyone wears a mask because they are afraid to let people see them as they really are. We are a world of clowns, in greasepaint. Don't you understand?"

"No," Karen replied. "I don't understand at all."

"I'll see if I can explain it," Johnny said. "Let's take the example of a beautiful young girl passing a middle-aged man and his wife. When she does so, they all put on masks."

Karen gave Johnny a confused smile. "What sort of masks?"

"The beautiful young girl pretends that she has no interest in making the man notice her, so she assumes the mask of boredom." Johnny passed his hand across his face, then assumed an expression of boredom.

Karen laughed.

"The husband," Johnny continued, "puts on the mask of innocence, because he does not want his wife to know he has seen and appreciated the beauty of the young girl." He moved his hand across his face again, then wore the look of angelic innocence.

"And what about the wife?" Karen asked. "Does she wear a mask as well?"

"Oh, but of course," Johnny said. "The wife doesn't want the beautiful young girl to know that she is jealous of her looks, so she wears the most concealing mask of them all, the mask of indifference."

"Before," Karen said, "when you told me you could not put on the mask with me. What mask would that have been?"

"At such times, I would have to be like the wife in my example and assume the mask of indifference. With you, I could not pretend indifference. I could not pretend that touching you, or kissing you, meant nothing. It would not merely be a game for me," he said.

"Because I am Henry's sister?"

"There is some truth to that," Johnny admitted. "You see, you represent a part of my past... a more innocent past, and I wouldn't want to do anything to destroy that. But there is more to it. I would feel this same way even if I had never met your brother."

"Why?"

Johnny put his hand on her cheek again. "I don't know," he answered. "Some things simply cannot be explained. Why I feel this way around you when I just met you, for example." He leaned toward her and she raised her lips to his, but, just before he kissed her, he pulled away with a groan. "No!" He put his hand on her arm. "Come on, I'm taking you home."

"But...but the evening is still early," Karen protested.

"Karen, please. Let me take you home now before something happens that we both regret."

"Oh," Karen said, realizing then what he was talking about. The idea frightened her, but it also thrilled her, and she shivered slightly in anticipation. "All right," she said. "If you think it best, we'll go."

A moment later, they were outside the house and Johnny was holding Karen's arm, guiding her carefully through the dark toward the car. He couldn't explain what it was that alerted him...whether he saw something, or heard something, or whether he just felt something that didn't seem right. Whatever it was, he felt the hackles rise on the back of his neck and he was pulling Karen down with him, drawing his gun even as a submachine gun opened up on them from behind the shrubbery at the far end of the drive.

"Get down!" he shouted, though his warning wasn't necessary since he was already dragging her down to the ground by force.

Large, irregular patterns of light erupted from the muzzles of two tommy guns as the two shooters moved the guns back and forth, spewing out bullets like they were spraying water hoses on the front lawn. Little sparks erupted in the night as spent and misdirected bullets slammed into the rocks, concrete, and even the Packard.

Johnny had his own pistol out now, and he began firing back, using the flame patterns from the tommy guns as his target.

A car screeched to a stop in front of the house and the two shooters ran toward it. Johnny hit one of them and saw him grab his leg.

"I'm hit!" the man shouted. The other shooter grabbed him and pulled him the last few feet into the car.

A third shooter was in the car and he started firing through the back window. His bullets hit the fuel tank of Johnny's rented Packard, causing it to go up in a brilliant flash of light and a great roar. Johnny threw himself over Karen to protect her as flaming bits of wreckage rained down all around them. When he looked up again a moment later, the shooters' car was gone and the Packard was a roaring inferno.

"Are you all right?" he asked.

"Yes," Karen answered, her voice muffled because he was still lying on top of her.

Johnny got up, then helped her to her feet. Her beautiful beaded dress was torn and smudged, and she looked at it and groaned.

"Never mind the dress," he said. "I'll get you another dress, I'll get you ten dresses. I just want to be sure that you are all right."

Karen wiped her hand against her dress, then she brushed a lock of hair back from her face. Like the dress, her face was smudged. "Is this an example of what you were talking about when you said you have enemies?"

"Yes," Johnny said. "Now you can see why I didn't want to take you to a restaurant."

"Would they really have done something like this in a restaurant?"

"Yes, I'm afraid so." He tried to put his arm around her, but she pulled away from him. "No," she said. "Don't touch me."

Johnny sighed and dropped his hand. "I don't blame you," he said.

"Oh, Johnny," Karen said. Though she had just backed away from him, she moved toward him and leaned her head against him. "I want you to hold me, I really do. But you..."

"I what?"

"You frighten me," she said.

Johnny sighed. "Listen," he said. "You got someplace you can stay tonight?"

"What do you mean? I have an apartment, you know where it is."

"Huh, uh," Johnny said, shaking his head. "You can't stay there."

"Why can't I stay there?"

"If Vaglichio's people knew where I was, they'll know where you are."

"So what? They're not my enemies."

"Yes, they are," Johnny said.

"Why would they be? I don't know them. I don't even know anything about them."

"They've seen you with me," Johnny said. "That makes them your enemies. I'm sorry," he added softly.

"You're sorry," she said. "So what do I do now?"

"I don't want you to be alone," he said. "What about Henry? Can you stay with him?"

"Well, yes, I suppose so."

"Good," Johnny said. "I'm going to take you there." He looked over toward the burning Packard. "As soon as I find a way," he added.

In the distance they could hear the wailing sirens of the police, responding to the many calls they had received from the residents of this affluent neighborhood, complaining that a war had broken out in the streets.

"Maybe the police will take us," Karen suggested.

"No," Johnny replied, shaking his head. "Come on, we've got to get out of here before the police arrive."

"Why?" Karen asked. "We didn't do anything. We don't have anything to hide."

"Karen, the last thing you need is to have your name linked with mine in something like this," Johnny said. "Trust me."

Karen hesitated for just a moment, then she nodded. "You're right," she said with a small smile. "I can just hear all the questions my friends would ask if there was a headline that read 'Karen Murchison involved with gangster.'"

Johnny chuckled. "I don't mean to be vain, sweetheart, but that's not how the headline would read."

"Oh? And how would it read?"

"'Johnny Sangremano involved with local girl,'" he said.

"Well, Mr. Sangremano, I must say you think rather highly of yourself," Karen teased.

"Will you, for chrissake, come on, and quit standing here arguing over who gets top billing?" Johnny urged in exasperation.

"Oh, yeah," Karen said. "I guess we had better get going."

Johnny led her through the backyard, down the alley, and into the street, a block away from his house. As luck would have it, he spied a passing taxi and managed to hail it with a loud whistle.

"Where to?" the driver asked.

As Johnny and Karen slipped into the backseat of the cab, she gave him her brother's address. The driver put up the flag, then shifted into gear and pulled away from the curb.

"Did you hear and see all the police cars a while ago?" the driver asked.

"No," Johnny said. "What happened?"

"Jeez, I don't have any idea," the driver replied. "All I know is I been seein' cops all over the place, comin' out here lickety-split." He chuckled. 'Truth is, that's why I come out here. I just wanted to see what was goin' on. You folks are lucky, I don't normally come out this way."

"Yeah," Johnny replied. "Well, I always said I'd rather be lucky than rich."

The driver laughed. "Rather be lucky than rich. That's a good one," he said. "I'm goin' to have to remember that."

Johnny had his arm up on the back of the seat and he felt Karen scoot up close to him. When he dropped his arm around her, she scooted even closer. He knew that it was probably a combination of fear and excitement, but that didn't lessen his appreciation of the moment.

CHAPTER 10

Once Johnny and Karen were in the light of Henry's house, Karen discovered that she had suffered a few minor cuts and scratches. These were the result of Johnny's pulling her down to the ground when the firing started. When Henry saw them, he got a basin of hot, soapy water and a washcloth and began cleaning them. When he asked what happened, they told him of the attack.

"They actually tried to kill you?" Henry asked. "My God, I can't believe it."

"Why not?" Johnny chuckled. "As I recall, there were a whole lot of people trying to kill us when we were in France."

"That was different," Henry said. "We were in a war."

"I'm in a war now," Johnny said. "The only difference is we don't wear uniforms and we don't salute flags."

"You run with a pretty rough crowd, don't you?"

"I suppose I do," Johnny admitted.

"My sister could've been killed."

"Yes, I know. I'm sorry."

"Sorry wouldn't have been worth much if she had

been killed." Henry finished treating her wounds and put the basin over on a table.

"Henry, why are you acting like this?" Karen asked. "Johnny saved my life."

"Yes, but don't you see? That wouldn't have been necessary if you hadn't been with him. Don't you realize you could have been killed?"

"I could step off the curb and be hit by a car and be just as dead," Karen said.

Henry looked at Karen for a moment, then at Johnny. Finally, he sighed. "You're right," he said. "Here I am yelling at you when I should be thanking you."

"No," Johnny said. "You're right. She wouldn't have been in danger if she hadn't been with me."

"Who do you think it was?" Henry asked.

"Oh, there's no doubt in my mind as to who it was," Johnny answered. "It was the Vaglichio Family."

"You think they followed you up here from Los Angeles?"

"Yes," Johnny said. "Well, maybe not either one of the Vaglichios themselves, but their men. Or what is more likely, a few men up here that he hired just for the job."

"And the Vaglichios are the people you think framed your sister?"

"I know they are," Johnny said.

"I must confess, Johnny, that you do travel in an interesting world." Henry rubbed his chin. "A much more interesting world than that of probates, contracts, articles of incorporation, and so forth. That's the world of law...at least the world of my law."

"Have you made up your mind yet whether you are going to defend Katherine?"

"Are you sure you can't find anyone better qualified for the job?" Henry asked.

Johnny laughed easily. "I'm sure I can find hundreds who are better qualified," he said. "But I want you."

"All right." Henry sighed. "If you want me, you've got me."

"Thanks," Johnny said, sticking out his hand.

"Listen," Henry added. "Where are you going to stay tonight?"

"Stay? Well, I'm not sure," Johnny said. "I guess I haven't thought about it, not since the trouble, anyway. I'll probably find a hotel room somewhere."

"No," Henry said, shaking his head. "Stay here. This is a big house with plenty of rooms."

"Okay, if you're sure you don't mind," Johnny said. He looked around. "This beats the last place we shared."

"I should hope so." Henry chuckled. "As I recall, our quarters at that French airfield had at one time been a barn."

"Ah, but it was a barn for sheep," Johnny reminded him, holding up a finger. "A sheep barn is much better than a cow or a horse barn."

Both men began laughing then and Henry laughed so hard that tears came to his eyes.

"What is so funny?" Karen demanded.

"Monsieur Mouchette," Henry said. "He was the owner of the farm, and he was so insistent that we understand how lucky we were to have a sheep barn rather than a cow barn or horse barn that he posted signs, detailing the difference."

"And Colonel Boyle made us attend a class on it," Johnny added.

"What are the differences?" Karen demanded.

"Who the hell knows?" Henry shrugged. "We used the posters for toilet paper."

"And we slept through all of Colonel Boyle's classes," Johnny added.

The two men exchanged stories until far in the night with Karen listening and laughing along with them. Finally, they said good night and retired to their rooms.

Karen couldn't sleep. She tossed and turned in her bed, but images and memories of the day kept intruding, keeping her wide-awake. Finally, in exasperation, she got out of bed and slipped on a silk dressing gown, then opened the French doors. She walked out onto the long balcony that ran across the back of the house and sat on the wide railing, leaning up against one of the support pillars. She pulled her knees up and when she did so, her gown fell back, exposing her legs. She wrapped her arms around them and rested her chin on her knees. The position was comfortable and the night breeze felt good.

A cluster of tall palm trees waved gently in the breeze and the fronds of one of them caught a moonbeam, scattering a burst of silver through the night. The fragrant scent of orange blossoms floated in from the nearby groves and the breeze caressed her skin as softly as the silk she was wearing.

"You can't sleep either, huh?"

Karen was surprised by the voice and she looked around to see Johnny standing in the shadows, leaning against the wall. "I didn't hear you come out," she said.

Johnny chuckled. "That's because I was already here," he replied. He moved over and stood beside her. "I had too much on my mind to sleep."

"I know what you mean," Karen replied. "I'm sure you are worried about your sister."

"Yes, but that isn't what was on my mind," Johnny said.

"Oh? What was?"

"This," Johnny said. He leaned down to kiss her, and this time Karen let the kiss go on much longer than she had before.

After the kiss, Johnny raised his head and spoke softly. "Do you know the term the bullfighters use, *momento de verdad*?"

"No," Karen murmured.

"It means 'moment of truth.' This is your moment of truth, Karen. If you want me to go away, tell me so now."

Karen smiled, then kissed him again, this time even more deeply than before. "I don't want you to go away," she said.

After the kiss, Johnny followed Karen back into her bedroom, then closed the doors. In addition to the moon and stars, he could see a winking red light high in the sky and could hear the distant drone of three engines as a plane winged its way to some faraway destination. He heard a soft rustle behind him, then looked around.

Karen had removed her silk gown and stood naked before him. Her skin reflected a subtle light, and the tuft of hair at the junction of her legs stood in bold relief against her alabaster body.

"You are sure of this?" he asked her.

"I'm sure," she said. "Hurry before I lose my nerve."

Johnny shed his clothes quickly, then moved to her, burying his face in her neck and kissing her smooth flesh.

Karen's arms went around Johnny's back and she ran her hands up and down his spine and shoulders.

"Why are we standing here like this, when we could be in bed?" Johnny asked.

"Why indeed?" Karen replied with an inviting smile.

CHAPTER 11

LOS ANGELES

"There is an all-out war brewing," Joe told the others during one of their periodic meetings. "First, the Vaglichios were looking for muscle, now Sangremano is."

"They aren't just using local muscle either, Mike," Bill said. "One of Sangremano's top lieutenants, Frankie Sarducci, is here. And he isn't the only one. I've spent some time down at the depot over the last few days, and there has been a steady stream of Vaglichio and Sangremano soldiers arriving from New York."

"What about that attempt against Sangremano last week?" Mike asked. "The one in San Francisco."

"SFPD says it was strictly local," Bill said. "The way the San Francisco police put it, the local hoods were afraid Sangremano was going to try and invade their territory."

"What kind of word are you hearing?" Mike asked Joe.

"It was Vaglichio," Joe replied. "No doubt about it."

"Yeah," Mike said. "That's pretty much what I thought."

"It seems strange for two New York Families to fight their war in California," Jason said.

"Not so strange when you stop and think about it," Mike reminded Jason. "Out here they are away from the other Families. There is no enforcement of the peace treaty between them."

"And that means they can do anything they want to each other without fear of reprisal from any of the other Families," Joe added.

"I think I see what you mean. You know, this could get very dangerous, very fast, couldn't it?" Jason asked.

"What do you mean, 'get dangerous?' It already is," Mike said.

———

On the wall in Jay Garland's new office hung a large framed photograph of him standing beside Charlie Chaplin. A large scrawl across the bottom of the picture read "To Jay Garland, a good friend and a good agent, best wishes, Charlie Chaplin." There was also an autographed photograph of Mary Pickford and Douglas Fairbanks. In truth, none of the autographs was authentic, and the only reason Jay and Charlie Chaplin were in the same photograph was because he once just happened to be standing beside the star at a racetrack.

The autographed picture of Joan Leland, however, was real. Jay Garland also had copies of Variety and the Los Angeles Times lying on the coffee table in front of the sofa of his office. The newspapers were not there by chance, nor was it a coincidence that both just happened to be open to the story about Joan Leland's surprise move from Bailey and McDill to Jay Garland.

Jay stood in his office, checking it with a critical eye, trying to determine its impact on potential clients. When he saw that Joan Leland's picture was crooked, he walked over and straightened it, then stepped back to check it again.

It was very important that the office make just the right impression because Jay was expecting someone this afternoon. Her name was Scylla Sinclair. She was an incredibly beautiful young woman who had been referred to Jay by a man named Peter Kolar. Jay and Kolar had been partners in a venture called Miss Arnold's School of Acting. It was actually a correspondence school, run out of the back of a grocery store. This morning, however, Scylla Sinclair, a young girl from Mayfield, Kentucky, had shown up at the grocery store, clutching her acceptance letter in her hand. She had mailed in her money and, not understanding that Miss Arnold's School of Acting was a correspondence course, had come to California to attend school and become a star.

Kolar, who owed Jay a little money, saw this as an opportunity to erase his debt through a little ingenious bartering.

"Hello, Jay," he had said when he called, earlier that morning. "Listen, you know the sawbuck I owe you? Well, now that you are there in your fancy office, I thought you might just forget it."

"You thought that, did you? And do you also think pigs can fly?"

Kolar had laughed. "Just kiddin' you, Jay, just kiddin' you," he said. "Actually I have every intention of paying you back. In fact, I can do it today if you would be interested in a little trade-off."

"A trade-off? What sort of trade-off?"

"I got a girl here," Kolar said. "She wants to be an actress in the worst way." He giggled. "And I mean the worst way. She said she was willin' to do anything to get into show business. If you want, I'll send her over to you."

"Is she used?" Jay asked.

"No, no, I ain't touched her, I swear," Kolar said. "I'm savin' her just for you. And she is fine, Jay. I mean she is really fine. I still got me a hard-on just from lookin' at her. Only, if you take me up on this, this squares us for the saw-buck. Now, what do you say?"

"Yeah, okay," Jay said. "Send her over."

"Done," Kolar said. "Only, Jay, go easy with her. I mean, she's a real rube from Kentucky."

"She's out of your hands now, Kolar," Jay said. "I've already bought her."

"Yeah," Kolar replied. "Yeah, I guess you're right."

That had been no more than a half-hour ago and Jay was looking forward to her arrival, especially if she was as beautiful as Kolar said.

A small knock sounded at the door and Jay called out, "Come in, for chrissake, this is an office, not a private apartment."

The door opened and a young girl stuck her head in. Her eyes were exceptionally large and dark, framed by long, delicate lashes. "I...I didn't know if I should come in or not," she said.

"Yeah, honey, that's what I'm here for," Jay said. "Come on in."

The girl was every bit as pretty as Kolar had promised, and Jay rubbed his hands in anticipation as he looked at her. "So, you want to be in the movies, do you?"

"Oh yes, sir," the girl said. "That's all I ever wanted."

"And your name is?"

"Scylla. Scylla Sinclair," she said.

"Scylla Sinclair."

"Do you like it?" she asked eagerly. "I made it up."

"Uh, yeah, it's nice."

"My real name is Maria D'Angelo."

"Yeah, well, we'll use the name you made up."

The girl smiled broadly as if she had just passed a test. "What do you want me to do?" she asked.

"What do you mean?"

"Mr. Kolar said that if I really wanted to get into the movies, I should do anything you ask me to."

"Uh, yeah. Yeah, that's right."

"Okay. So what do you want me to do?"

"Listen, honey, have you ever heard of the casting couch?"

"The casting couch? No, I don't think so."

As Jay looked at her the blood began to pound in his temples and a gnawing ache for her chewed at the pit of his stomach. By now his erection was so strong that it hurt, and he had to move behind the desk to keep her from seeing it. He didn't want to frighten her. At least not yet. "Do you want to be in the movies badly enough to go to the casting couch?" he asked.

"Yes."

Jay chuckled. "I thought you just told me you didn't know what it was."

"It doesn't matter. I'll do it."

"It means that a girl wants a part bad enough to sleep with a director for it."

"Sleep?"

"Well, not sleep, really. It's..."

"Fornication?" the girl asked.

Jay smiled...a small, evil smile. "Yeah, fornication, just like it talks about in the Bible," he said. "Have you ever done it?"

"Once," the girl admitted, blushing a fire-engine red. "It was out behind my daddy's barn, during the hay harvest. I was fourteen. That was four years ago. I've never done it since then."

"Why not? Didn't you enjoy making love?"

"Not particularly. Making love? Is that what it's called? That's a peculiar name for it. We didn't love each other. We were just doin' it to see what it was like."

"And what was it like?"

"It hurt."

"That was only because it was the first time," Jay said, feeling a little disappointed that she wasn't a virgin. "It will never hurt again. From now on it will feel really good. Haven't you ever wanted to do it again?"

"No."

"Well, that doesn't matter. The question is, would you do it again if you had to? Would you make love with a director to get into the movies?"

"What an odd question. Why would I have to?"

"Why would you have to?" Jay said. "Oh, you sweet, innocent child. Maybe you are not ready for this. Maybe you aren't cut out to be an actress."

"Yes! Yes, I am!" the girl said. "If... if I have to 'make love' as you call it, to a director to get into the movies, I'll do it."

"I must warn you, Maria, that most casting directors aren't handsome young men. Many of them are even older and less attractive than I. Could you, for example, make love with someone as unattractive as I am?"

Maria hung her head in silence for several seconds.

"Well, answer me, girl. Could you, or not?"

"I believe so," she finally said. "If that was the only way."

"Oh, it is the only way," Jay said. "Believe me, girl, it is the only way."

"Then I would do it," Maria said resolutely.

"Yes, you say that now. It is easy for you to stand there in front of me and tell me what you will do. But can you pass the test?"

"The test?"

"Yes. Suppose, for example, that I told you the only way I'll help you is if you let me make love to you right here, right now. Would you do it?"

Maria drew a quick, deep breath as if she were about to jump into a pool of ice-cold water. "Yes," she said. "If you really thought it was something that we must do, I would be willing."

"But you wouldn't want to?"

"No."

Jay smiled broadly. "Good, good," he said. "It is a measure of how bad you really want to be a star if you will make love to someone when you don't really want to do it. Maybe you don't have to. Maybe I was just testing you, to see if you really would," Jay said.

The girl sighed an obvious sigh of relief.

"On the other hand," Jay said, stroking his chin. Maria inhaled again, sharply. "On the other hand," Jay repeated, "you may have agreed just because you knew that I wouldn't really do anything. Well, my dear, this is a cruel business. And if you are going to be a client of mine, you must be prepared for anything. Therefore, I think it would be a good idea if I made you go through with it."

"I beg your pardon?"

"We're going to have sex, Maria D'Angelo."

"Oh," she gasped.

"It's not a new thing for you. You said you've done it before?"

"Yes," she said. "I've done it."

"Then, tell me."

"I beg your pardon?"

"Tell me."

"Tell you what?"

"I want you to tell me, and I want you to mean it. Say 'I want you to make love with me'.'"

"I want you to make love with me."

"Oh, you sweet, young, thing. I'm going to," Jay said. "We're going to do it until your brown eyes turn blue."

"Must...must we do this?"

"Yes. If you want me to help you, that is. Now, take off your clothes."

"All right. If you say so."

Slowly, and with shaking hands, Maria began to remove her clothes. "Have you someplace I can hang my clothes?" she asked.

At that precise moment, the door to Jay's office opened and Mario Vaglichio walked in. When he saw what was going on, he stopped in midstride and stared in shock and disgust. "What the hell is this?" he shouted. "What are you running here, a whorehouse?"

Maria screamed in fear and surprise, jumped up, and ran around behind the couch. Jay began hopping around, trying to cover himself with one hand while reaching for his clothes with the other.

"Mr. Vaglichio!" he said. "What are you doing here?"

"I'm the one asking the questions," Mario replied angrily. "Now, who told you you could bring whores down to the office?"

"I'm not a whore," the girl said from behind the couch. "I'm an actress."

"You aren't a whore, huh? Well, you sure as hell look

like one to me," Mario said. He saw her dress and he picked it up and handed it to her. "Get your clothes on."

Crying in fear and humiliation, the girl began to get dressed.

"Look here, you sonofabitch! You want to boff actresses, you do it on your own time in your own place, you hear me?" Mario growled. He looked at the girl. "And you," he said. "You ought to be ashamed of yourself. I had a daughter once. She was about your age when she got killed. If I had thought she was ever doing anything like this, I would have had her killed myself. What's your name, anyway?"

"Mar—"

"Scylla!" Jay said quickly. "Her name is Scylla Sinclair." Jay, who had his pants on, now, took Maria's clothes, then put his arm on her shoulder and guided her toward a door that led to another room. "You can get dressed in there, Scylla," he said.

Sniffing, and glad to be able to get a little privacy, Maria went without complaint.

"You can just leave by the other door," Jay called to her. "I'll get in touch." He closed the door behind her then reached for his shoes and socks. "You come into someone's place, you ought to at least knock," he whined.

"This isn't someone's place," Mario reminded him. "It belongs to my brother and me. You're just working here. Besides which, it isn't exactly like a bedroom somewhere. It's supposed to be an office. What kind of name is Sinclair?"

"I beg your pardon?" Jay reached for his shirt.

"The girl said her name was Sinclair," he said. "What kind of name is that? Is that English? Irish? She looked Italian to me."

"No, no, she wasn't Italian!" Jay said quickly, frightened that Mario might become overprotective if he thought she was. "She's Jewish."

"Jew?"

"Yeah. Scylla Sinclair is just her professional name. Her real name is Blum. Rhoda Blum."

Mario snorted. "I can see why she had to come up with another name."

"Listen, it wasn't what you think," Jay started.

"Don't lie to me," Mario said. "I can take a lot, but lies I don't take. How'd you get her to take off her clothes like that? You sure as hell aren't God's gift to women."

"She thought I could help get her a part in the movies," Jay said.

"And could you?"

"Well, I..." he began, but he was unable to finish.

"So what you are telling me is, you are taking advantage of her?"

"Well, yes. That's one of the extras of the business." Jay laughed and tried to make a joke of it. "Come on, Donnie, baby, sweetheart, now that you're in the business, it's time you learned a few tricks of the trade."

"What did you call me?"

"Donnie," Jay said. "Come on, you worried about the baby, about the sweetheart? That's just the way we talk out here."

"My name isn't Donnie."

"Okay, Don, then. I know that's your name. I've heard the others call you that."

"You don't call me don," Mario said, without bothering to explain that it was a title and not a name. "Only people with honor can call me don and you have no honor. I mean here you are, a Jew, and you were trying to take advantage of a young, innocent Jewish girl. What you were trying to do to your own kind is disgusting."

"Come on, Vaglichio," Jay replied. "I've found out a

few things about you and your brother. I know about your business dealings back in New York...the booze, the numbers, the whores. Who are you to tell me I'm disgusting and without honor?"

"My brother and I may do things that are against the law, but we don't do things that are without honor. Do you think one of us would ever take advantage of an Italian girl like that? I tell you the truth, Garland, if that little girl had been Italian, I don't know what I would've done." He held his finger out and waved it admonishingly. "Don't ever let me catch you doing this again," he said. "And especially, don't ever let me catch you doing somethin' like this with an Italian girl. You want to dishonor yourself, you go ahead, but not in a place my brother and I are paying for."

"Okay," Jay said. "I won't do anything like this again, I hope to die."

Mario laughed. "Funny you should say that. Because if you do do something like this again, you *will* die."

"I'm sorry," Jay said. "I'm really sorry. I won't do anything like this again, ever."

"Well, don't worry about it. It's over now. So let me tell you why I come down here. You're in the business, I want you to look over ever'one that's in the movie and let me know who I can buy."

"Buy?"

"Yes," Mario said. "Who can I buy? Who can I pay enough money to that his loyalty will be only to me, not to the movie people?"

"I'm still not following you."

"All right, I'll try to make it easy for you," Mario said. "I need an ace up my sleeve. I need someone on the inside of that movie...someone I can trust. In order to maintain complete control over the movie we're going to have to have the ability to destroy it at any time."

"Why would you want to do that?" Jay asked. "We've got our actress there now. What good would it do us to go to all this trouble to get her a role in the picture then destroy the picture?"

Mario laughed. "You think we went to all this trouble just to get Joan Leland in the picture?"

"Well? Didn't we?"

"She is a means to an end, Mr. Garland. Not the end itself. Now, who on this picture can I buy?"

"I don't know," Jay said. "It's going to be pretty hard. This is a major picture, you see, and everyone who is in it stands to benefit a lot more from a success than from having a flop."

"Pay whatever it costs," Mario said. "Just find someone I can trust."

"Yeah, okay, I'll do it," Jay promised. "I'll find someone.

Mario grunted, then started for the door. Just before he left, he turned back to Jay and pointed.

"You do anything like this again," he said, "I'm goin' to kill you myself."

Mario took the elevator downstairs, then started outside. He saw the girl over in the corner of the lobby, sobbing quietly.

"Rhoda," he said, starting toward her. When she saw him, she turned her back to him. "Don't be afraid of me," he said. "I'm not goin' to hurt you."

"I…I've never done anything like that before," the girl said. "I was so scared."

"I know, I know," Mario said. "He made you do it."

"He…he said it was the only way I could get into the movies," the girl sobbed.

"The really bad thing is, he can't get you into the movies, anyway," Mario said. "He was just telling you that so you would do what he wanted."

"But...but he's an agent, isn't he?"

"He's a bum," Mario said. "He's an agent because my brother and I made him an agent. Believe me, he can't do anything for you."

"I am so ashamed," the girl said. "I...I just got here today. If I had enough money, I would go home."

"You don't have enough money to go home?"

"I spent it all to get here," the girl said. "And to take the movie-star course."

"Here," Mario said, giving her five twenties. "Take this money and go home."

"I can't take this from you," she said, pushing the money back.

"Sure you can."

"Thank you," the girl said. "Thank you so much." She put the money in her purse. "I shouldn't have come here. I should have never left Kentucky."

"That's what I say. I mean, what's a nice Jewish girl like you want to be in the movies for, anyway?"

"Jewish?" the girl asked, looking up in surprise as she closed her purse. "I'm not Jewish, I'm Catholic. What makes you think I'm Jewish."

"You're Catholic? With a name like Rhoda Blum, you're Catholic?"

"Rhoda Blum? Wherever did you get that name? My name is Maria D'Angelo."

"Maria?" Mario said in a strained voice. "That's your real name? Maria? You are Italian?"

"*Sí, padrone.* My father came to Kentucky when he was a young man," the girl said, speaking Italian with a Sicilian accent.

"You are Sicilian?" Mario asked in a choked voice, also switching to Italian.

"*Sí.*"

"My daughter was named Maria," Mario said. He

looked back toward the elevator. "That sonofabitch," he muttered, switching back to English. "That sonofabitch! To try something like this with a Sicilian girl! He knew it. He knew it all along, that sonofabitch!"

Mario stuck his hand in his jacket pocket and wrapped his fingers around the butt of his pistol. With a singleness of purpose, he started back toward the elevator, where he jabbed impatiently at the elevator button.

Mario was so angry and upset about Jay lying to him about the girl that all he could think of was getting back up to the agent's office and settling things. He was so filled with rage that when the elevator doors opened, he didn't even notice that the elevator operator was a different man from the one who had brought him down, just a moment before.

"I'm going to kill the sonofabitch," Mario said under his breath as the elevator started up.

The elevator jerked to a sudden stop between floors.

"Hey!" Mario said. "What the hell is wrong with this thing?"

"Don't worry, sir, I'll take care of everything," the elevator operator said. His voice was a little muffled because his back was to Mario.

"Well, hurry up," Mario ordered.

The elevator operator turned around and faced Mario. There was an evil grin on his face and a sawed-off twelve-gauge, double-barrel shotgun in his hand. "You don't need to be in such a hurry to die, do you, Vaglichio?"

"Frankie Sarducci!" Mario gasped, recognizing Sangremano's lieutenant.

"You and your brother should hire better help," Frankie said. "They fired at Johnny from point-blank range the other night and they missed. I'm at point-blank range, too, and I won't miss," he added.

Frankie pulled the trigger and the flame pattern at the end of the sawed-off double barrels was wide enough to fill a third of the elevator car. The noise was so loud that it left Frankie's ears ringing and started a little trickle of blood flowing from his nose.

The front of Mario's chest looked like ground hamburger meat. There were two big splashes of blood on the elevator wall behind where he had been standing, then two smears down the wall to the floor. Mario was lying on the floor, his head held up at a grotesque angle by the elevator wall. His eyes were open and sightless, though even in their lusterless gaze there was still a hint of surprise and fear. The gun was halfway out of Mario's pocket and his hand was wrapped around it in a death grip.

Frankie, who had been wearing gloves to keep from leaving fingerprints, dropped the now-empty shotgun on Mario's inert body. Very calmly he started the elevator again and ran it all the way to the attic, ignoring the summoning bells from the floors he passed along the way.

"Hey!" someone called as the elevator passed by the fifth floor. There was a Doppler effect to the man's angry shout so that the first words were loud, but they grew weaker as the elevator passed on by. "I'M CALLING YOU, you son of a bitch!"

When Frankie reached the attic, he stepped out of the elevator, then reached back in and moved the handle to send it back down, full speed, to crash into the cellar, ten floors down. Once in the attic, he changed out of the elevator operator's uniform, then went out onto the roof and took the fire escape down. When he reached his car, parked just across the street from the Stalcup Building, he saw a couple of police cars and a fire truck arriving.

"What's going on over there?" he asked a group of

people who were standing near his car and staring intently at all the activity.

"I'm not really sure," one of them replied. "But the elevator may have fallen."

Frankie shivered. "What an awful way to go," he said as he slipped behind the wheel of his car.

CHAPTER 12

Luca Vaglichio was taking a nap when Ben Costaconti came into the shadowed bedroom to wake him up. Ben sat on the bed and put his hand on Luca's shoulder, shaking him gently.

"Don Vaglichio," Ben said.

Luca continued to snore.

"Luca," Ben said, shaking him more firmly. "Luca, wake up."

"Huh?" Luca said, opening his eyes. "What? What is it?" Ben stood up quickly. "Don Vaglichio, are you awake?"

Luca ran his hand through his hair, then across his eyes. "Yeah, yeah, I'm awake," he said. He sat up and swung his legs over the side of the bed. "What time is it? Did I oversleep?"

"No, Don Vaglichio."

"I didn't? They why did you wake me up?"

Ben hung his head and was quiet for a long moment. Finally, he spoke. "I have some bad news for you," he said. "Some very bad news."

"What is it?"

"It's your brother."

"Mario?"

Ben nodded.

"Is he dead?" Luca asked.

Again Ben nodded.

"When? How? Who?"

"It happened about an hour ago," Ben said. "He went down to see Jay Garland. Someone was in the elevator waiting for him as he was leaving. He was killed with a *lupara*."

"In the face?" Luca asked. "Did they shoot my brother in the face with a shotgun?"

"No, Don Vaglichio."

"Thank God for that," Luca said. "Where is he? Where is he now?"

"The police have the body down at the city morgue. They won't release it until it is identified by a family member."

Luca stood up and reached for his trousers. "All right," he said. "Have the car brought around. I'll go down now and identify him."

When Bill Carmack heard that Mario Vaglichio had been killed, he went down to the morgue to take a look at the body. The coroner pulled the sheet down past Mario's shoulders for Bill to see. There were two or three ugly blue holes just above the left nipple.

"Well, hello, Mario," Bill said under his breath. "I see coming three thousand miles didn't change things any. Here you are, lying on a cold slab full of buckshot, just like I always knew you'd wind up."

"You know this man?" the coroner asked.

"Yes," Bill said. "I've run across him a few times."

"Was he a friend?"

Bill chuckled and shook his head. "No, I don't think you could call him a friend."

"Yeah, well, somebody else must've felt that way too," the coroner said. "He sure pissed somebody off."

"I doubt it," Bill said, matter-of-factly.

The coroner looked at Bill in surprise. "What are you talking about? You see him lying there, don't you?"

"Yes, but this isn't anything unusual for the world this man lived in," Bill said. "A few shotgun pellets in the heart, liver, and lungs is just a mobster calling card."

Another man came into the back room and walked past the half-dozen tables that made up the morgue. All the other tables were empty.

"There's someone here," he said to the coroner. "He says he is the deceased's brother and he is here to identify and claim the body."

The coroner put the sheet back over Mario's head, then stepped away from the table. Bill did the same.

"Okay," the coroner said. "Show him in."

Bill watched as the bulky figure of Luca Vaglichio came into the room. He walked straight over to the table and pulled the sheet down. He stared at Mario for a long moment, then replaced the sheet.

"That's him," he said. "That's my brother."

"His name?"

"Mario Vincent Vaglichio," Luca said.

"And you are?"

"Luca Vaglichio," Bill said from where he was standing, over by the wall.

Not until Bill spoke did Luca realize he was here. Luca looked over at him, staring hard, trying to place him. Finally, he recognized him. "You," he said, pointing to Bill. "You're Carmack, aren't you? Officer Carmack?"

"Give the man a kewpie doll," Bill said sarcastically.

"What are you doing in California, Carmack? You are a little off your beat, ain't you?"

"I'm federal, remember?" Bill replied. "My beat is any

damn where I want it to be. But now that you bring it up, I might ask you the same question. What are you and your brother doing in California?"

"We came for the sun," Luca said. "You know it gets cold and wet back in New York in the wintertime. The climate is much better out here."

"You don't say," Bill replied. He looked intently, at Mario. "On the other hand, the climate didn't seem to agree with your brother all that much. Who killed him, Luca? Do you have any idea?"

"No."

"Do you have any idea why he was killed?"

"No."

"No idea at all?" Bill repeated. "He was killed with a *lupara*. Does that suggest anything to you? That is the weapon of choice among you Mafia people, isn't it?"

"Mafia? What is Mafia? I've never heard that word before. I'm afraid I don't know what you are talking about," Luca said.

"No, I'm sure you don't. I guess there's nothing at all unusual about someone in an elevator getting blown apart by a shotgun."

"Maybe it was a hunting accident."

"Of course it was," Bill said. "Just like the Mexicans who were dragged out of the bay the other night were all the victims of a boating accident."

"Could be," Luca said. "I don't know. I don't know nothin' 'bout no Mexicans."

"Or about a shipment of dope that was stolen that same night?"

"Someone stole some dope? From what I hear dope ain't legal," Luca said. "You can't really steal somethin' that ain't legal in the first place, can you?"

"You bring up an interesting legal point," Bill said. "If

I ever get you in a court of law, perhaps we'll discuss that very thing."

"You said if you ever," Luca said, smiling. "That's the magic word, lawman. 'Cause you see, I ain't ever goin' to do anything to let you get me in a courtroom. I'm livin' a clean life."

"Yeah." Bill looked again at the corpse. "So was your brother. And look what it got him."

"You got anything on me, Carmack?" Luca said. "'Cause if you do, let's have it. Otherwise, get the hell off my back."

"I've got nothing on you," Bill said. "For now," he added.

Luca smiled. "Yeah, well, that's just as I thought. If you got no objections then, I'll be going now."

"Yeah, go," Bill said. "And take your brother with you. His rotting corpse is beginning to stink up the place."

Luca's eyes flashed in anger and he took a step toward Bill, then he stopped. The frown on his face was replaced by a smile, but the anger did not leave his eyes. "Thank you for your concern about my brother," he said. "Maybe someday soon I'll get to return the favor. If not for your brother, then for one of those three friends who are always with you." Luca turned to the coroner, who had been watching the vitriolic exchange between the two men with complete fascination. "Can I take my brother now?"

"Yes," the coroner replied.

Luca looked over at Ben. "Get him," he said. "I'll be waiting in the car."

"I want to pay Johnny Sangremano back for this," Luca said in the car as they were driving back home.

"Are you sure you want to do that, Don Vaglichio?" Ben asked.

"What do you mean am I sure? Goddamnit, the sonofabitch just killed my brother! Of course I'm sure."

"Oh, I agree, we need to take care of Sangremano," Ben said. "But not just yet. Let's make him suffer for a while."

"Yeah? Well, I'm all for makin' the sonofabitch suffer," Luca said. "Just what kind of suffering did you have in mind?"

"For starters, we'll let his sister go to prison for murder,"

Ben said. "Then we'll take his movie business away from him. Then we'll take care of him."

"I hate to see the sonofabitch get away with killin' my brother...even for a little while," Luca said.

"Don Vaglichio, you know if Mario were here, he would agree with me," Ben said. "You know what a practical person he was. You'd be doing this for Mario."

Luca stroked his chin. "Yeah," he said. "Yeah, you're probably right. Okay, Ben, we'll try it your way for a while."

Jay Garland was standing out in by the fountain in the circular driveway of Jacklane, waiting for Luca when he returned home. He was holding his hat in front of him, turning it nervously, as he watched Luca and Ben get out of the big Cadillac.

Jay, who had no idea that Mario had been killed coming back up to his office to kill him, was very concerned about how Mario's demise, would affect him. Would he lose his plush new office space and his new client, Joan Leland? Would Luca hold him in any way responsible for Mario's death? After all, it did happen just outside his office. Surely not, Jay thought. Still, he didn't quite know how to handle these strange Italians who still insisted upon wearing dark pin-stripe suits, as if they were in New York in the middle of winter, rather than the light, colorful clothes more popular among Californians, native and transplants alike.

There was one positive thing about it as far as Jay was concerned. The incident happened so quickly that Mario would not have had time to share with his brother any of the details of the scene in the office between Jay and the little Italian girl.

"What are you doin' here?" Luca growled as he got out of the car. "Ain't you supposed to be tendin' to our business?"

"I just came out here to express my sympathy over the death of your brother," Jay said. "It was a terrible shame the way he was killed like that."

"Yeah," Luca grunted. "Well, things like that happen." He started into the house without bothering to invite Jay in but suddenly stopped on the front steps and looked back at Jay. "I'm curious," he said. "What was my brother doin' down at your office, anyway?"

"Oh," Jay said. "He wanted some information."

"What kind of information?"

Jay cleared his throat and looked around at the two or three men who were with Luca.

"What kind of information?" Luca asked again. "You can say in front of them. These men, I trust with my life."

"Your brother wanted to know who we could...get to on the movie set of *Aerodrome*. He wanted to know who we could persuade to be more loyal to us than he was to the production company."

"Yeah? Well, have you got that information?"

"Not exactly, but I have a good idea as to where we might start."

"Where?"

"With Bruce Hawkins."

"Never heard of him." Luca looked at Ben. "You ever hear of him?"

"Is he the one they call Bruiser? The stunt coordinator?" Ben asked.

"Yes, that's the one," Jay replied.

"The stunt coordinator? What good does it do us to have the stunt coordinator on our payroll?" Luca asked. "Mario talked to me about this, so I know what he was after. We need to be able to shut the thing down if we have to. How would this man Hawkins help us do that? I mean what do stuntmen do besides have a few fights, or fall down, or jump through windows or something?"

"It's more than just fights and falls," Jay said. "Bruiser is also in charge of the stunt pilots. And since the movie depends on the aerial scenes, he would be a very good man to have on our side."

"Mr. Garland may be right, Don Vaglichio," Ben said.

"If we could control the aerial sequences, we could control the entire movie."

"Yeah, all right," Luca said. "If you think it's a good idea." He looked back at Jay. "But you said you wasn't sure. What is it you ain't sure about?"

"I haven't approached Bruiser yet to see if we could, uh, buy his cooperation. But I think he might be susceptible. You see, he likes to play the ponies and he is in pretty deep with a few of the bookies around town. Some of the bookies, I understand, are getting a little impatient with him."

Luca turned to Ben. "Find out who he owes and make it good," he said. "Then go see this Bruiser and tell him to give his soul to God because his ass belongs to us."

"Wouldn't it be better if I dealt with Bruiser?" Jay asked. "I mean, this is my area of expertise." The purpose of this suggestion was to make himself as important to Luca as he could.

"You've done enough, thanks," Luca grunted.

"Yes, but there are certain subtleties about the business that you might not understand," Jay said. "Really, I think..." That was as far as he got because Luca went on inside without even responding.

Jay stood there for a moment longer. Finally, Ben looked back at him. "If you'll wait a few moments," he said, "I'll give you a ride back to your office."

"Yeah, thanks," Jay said, starting up the steps. "I've always wanted to look around this place, anyway."

"Just wait here, please," Ben said, and one of the other men stepped in front of him, staring at him impassively. "I'll only be a moment."

"Uh, yes," Jay said, seeing that his way inside the house was blocked. "Yeah, okay. I'll just wait out here for you, if you don't mind."

Jason Vandervort, wearing the uniform of an American aviator during the war, was standing next to the canteen truck, drinking a cup of coffee. The set was made up to resemble a pilots' "ready shack," and two lengthy scenes with all the extras had already been filmed. Now they were setting up for a close-up scene between two of the major characters.

Joan Leland, wearing a nurse's uniform, came over to the canteen truck, and Jason, smiling at her, moved quickly to draw a cup for her.

"Cream or sugar?" he asked.

"Both," Joan replied.

Jason prepared the coffee, then handed the cup to her.

"Thank you," she said. She took a sip of the coffee, then smiled at him over the rim. "Are you really part of the Vandervort family?" she asked.

Jason chuckled. "There have been times when my father has tried to deny it," he said. "But my mother insists that she has proof."

Joan laughed easily. "What I don't understand is, why are you out here, doing this?"

"Why is that so hard to understand?" Jason replied. "I'm just like everyone else. I want to be a movie star."

"If you really wanted to be a movie star, you could just make your own movie," Joan said. "I mean, your father is rich enough, isn't he?"

"Yes, I suppose he is. As far as that goes, I am, too, actually. My grandfather left me quite a bit of money, independent of my father's wealth. But what would be the fun of buying a role? It would mean much more to get it on my own, don't you think?"

"That's a very refreshing attitude," Joan said. "Especially when most people will get a role any way they can. Even the most famous and successful aren't above that kind of underhandedness."

"You're talking about Katie Starr?" Jason asked.

"Suppose I am?" Joan said. "It's no secret, is it?"

"No, I guess not."

"I mean, anyone who would use a mobster like Johnny Sangremano to frighten poor Sid into giving her the role, when he had already given it to me. It's just awful."

"Yes," Jason said. "Well, I suppose being in this movie is about the last thing on her mind now that she's trying to clear herself of a murder charge."

"I hope they put her under the jail," Joan said bitterly.

"Surely you don't think she really did it?"

"Why not? The police seem to think so."

"Yes, but as you said, she went to great lengths to get herself into this movie. Why would she then turn around and murder the director?"

"Who knows?" Joan said. "She was sleeping with him, maybe they had a lovers' quarrel."

"Miss Leland," someone called. "Miss Leland, they are going to shoot the flower scene now."

"Hmm," Joan said, finishing the coffee and handing the cup back to Jason. "Thanks for the coffee. I've got to go now."

"I enjoyed your company," Jason said, taking her cup and his back to the canteen truck.

As Jason was putting the cups back, he looked over toward the set where Joan's scene was about to be shot. It was called the flower scene because in it she was supposed to be giving inoculations to all the aviators and with each shot she also gave a flower. Jason leaned against the counter of the canteen truck to watch, when he saw a big black Cadillac pull up. Luca Vaglichio's consigliere, Ben Costaconti, got out of the car and began talking to Sid Friedman.

Jason wanted to get close enough to overhear what they were talking about, but he was afraid that Costaconti might recognize him, so he stayed over by the canteen, out of the way. Costaconti said a few words to Sid, Sid pointed to the flight line where all the airplanes were parked, and Costaconti nodded, then walked out toward the planes.

Jason looked toward the flight line and saw two airplanes circling around for a landing. Mike Kelly was flying one of the planes. If Costaconti happened to be out there when the two pilots climbed down from their planes, there was no way he could miss seeing—and recognizing—Mike Kelly.

Mike Kelly turned onto short final decent, keeping Sam Fielding's airplane in sight. Today's flying had been relatively easy, just a series of low passes by the camera.

Mike throttled back and the engine began to pop and snap as the hot exhaust gases cooked off some of the raw fuel that had worked its way, undetonated, through the entire engine intake and ignition system. This was the result of a fuel mixture that was a little too rich, but Fielding liked it that way. He felt that the overrich mixture caused the engines to run a little cooler and provided a little more power, even if it did increase fuel consumption.

"Who cares about how much gas we burn?" he liked to say. "The studio is paying for it. And in a job like this you never can tell when a little extra power is going to come in handy."

The wheels of Mike's Nieuport plopped down onto the sod strip just behind Fielding. In a normal landing Mike would also have let the tail skid drop and then would have taxied up quietly to the flight line. But he had already learned that this wasn't normal flying. Therefore, like Fielding in front of him, Mike maintained a highspeed taxi with the tail up. It was a delicate balance, keeping the control stick far enough forward to keep the airplane on the ground, yet not so far as to cause the plane to nose over. It was, in fact, more like, "ground contact" flying than taxiing.

Not until they were actually at the flight line did Fielding, and then Mike, slow down to a normal taxi speed. There, they dropped the tail and continued on to their parking places at a much more leisurely pace. Bruiser Hawkins was waiting there for them to go over the scene they had just shot and lay out the next sequence.

Line boys met the two airplanes, signaled for them to cut their engines, then hurried forward with chocks to put under the wheels. It wasn't until Mike took off his goggles that he saw one of the line boys speaking to a man in a dark suit and pointing toward Bruiser. The man in the dark suit started toward the stunt coordinator and as he got closer Mike could see that it was Ben Costaconti, consigliere to the Vaglichio Family. Or, Mike thought ominously, what was left of the Vaglichio Family.

It would not do for Ben Costaconti to see Mike, for the consigliere knew him, and that would blow his cover. Therefore, Mike found something to do at his airplane. Fortunately, his ploy was not too obvious because Sam, too, was busily at work on his own plane. Once Costaconti was gone, Mike and Sam walked over to talk to Bruiser.

"Who was that?" Sam asked.

"What's it to you?" Bruiser replied.

"Nothing, I guess. I just don't like strangers around where they have no business, is all."

"Look, Fielding, you worry about the flying, I'll take care of things on the ground."

"All right, if you say so."

"I still can't figure out why Bruiser is always in such a rotten mood," Mike asked as he and Sam walked away from the flight line.

"Well, you have to remember that the pilots make more than any of the other stuntmen in the picture," Sam said. "And Bruiser is a little jealous."

"But he's the stunt coordinator, isn't he? Surely he's making good money?"

"I suppose he is, but according to what I hear, he owes half the bookies in California. I guess something like that just keeps his switch spring-loaded to the piss-off position."

Mike laughed. "Yeah, I guess so," he agreed.

"Uh, by the way, some of the sound technicians brought a few cases of beer up from Mexico. You want to go knock down a few?" Sam invited.

"No, thanks," Mike said. "I think I'll just go watch them shoot for a while."

"Well, don't kick anything over. Friedman gets really upset whenever someone screws up one of his shots."

"I'll be careful," Mike promised.

Mike walked back up to the set. They were shooting the flower scene now and Jason was standing to one side with several other extras.

"So," Mike said, sauntering up to Jason as if he were meeting him for the first. "You must be one of the actors who play us on the ground."

"Well, you guys are okay in the air," Jason said. "You are far enough away that no one can see how ugly you are. When the camera comes in close, though, they want to see someone a little better looking. That's why they've got us."

The other extras laughed.

Jason stuck out his hand. "My name's Jason Vandervort."

"Mike Kelly," Mike replied. "Cigarette?"

"Thanks," Jason said, accepting the smoke. "Oh, but we'd better go over here. Mr. Friedman doesn't like us smoking too close to where they are shooting."

"Okay by me," Mike said easily.

The two men walked away several feet, then began speaking quietly.

"I guess you saw that Ben Costaconti was just here," Jason said.

"Yeah, I saw him."

"The question is, did he see you?"

"No, I don't think so. He was talking to Bruiser. What about you? Did he get a glimpse of you?"

"I don't know," Jason replied. "I was standing over by the canteen truck, so I just stayed where I was."

"I hope he didn't see us."

"I wonder what he wanted?" Jason said.

"Turns out Bruiser is a gambler and not a very good

one. He's got his markers scattered all over town and Luca Vaglichio just bought them all up."

"Vaglichio wants something from him," Jason said.

"It would appear so," Mike agreed. "The question is, what?"

"I don't know, but you can be sure it has something to do with the production of this film."

Mike looked around the set. "By the way, where is Friedman?"

"He just left," Jason said. "Don't you remember? Katie Starr's trial starts this afternoon."

"Yes, I remember," Mike said. "As a matter of fact, I plan to attend it."

"Mike, you're going to the trial?"

"Yes."

"Do you think that's a good idea? Sangremano is sure to see you, isn't he?"

"He may," Mike admitted.

"Then why are you going? You don't owe that sonofabitch anything, you know."

"I know," Mike said. "But I can't shake the feeling that there is more to this case than meets the eye. I think it is all connected, somehow."

"Johnny is the mafioso, not his sister," Jason reminded him. "And certainly not Deke Clark."

"No, but Vaglichio is," Mike said. "And with Katie Starr out of the picture, Joan Leland is in. Who is Joan Leland represented by?"

"Jay Garland," Jason said. "And Mario was killed just outside of Jay Garland's office."

"Exactly. That means there is a connection, through Garland, with Joan Leland and, consequently with this picture. And, of course, Costaconti was out here today to speak with Bruiser, no doubt to make some other connection. Now, do you still think there is no connection between Deke Clark's murder and the Mafia?"

"I see what you mean," Jason said. "But what if Sangremano sees you?"

"Oh, I intend for him to see me," Mike replied. "I'm going to walk right up and say hello to him. I don't mind if he knows I'm out here. I just don't plan to let him know that you and I have joined the movie business," he added, smiling broadly.

––––––––

"Did you get it taken care of?" Luca asked when Ben Costaconti returned from the movie set.

"Yes," Ben replied. "Mr. Bruce Hawkins is now in our debt."

"And he understands that?"

"Don Vaglichio, it is well over ten thousand dollars," Ben said. "There is no way he can't understand it."

Luca chuckled. "Good, good," he said. "It's always nice to have an ace up your sleeve."

"How would you like four aces up your sleeve?" Ben asked.

"Four aces? What do you mean?"

"Do you remember we saw Bill Carmack at the morgue?"

"Yeah, I remember that sonofabitch."

"I wondered then where the other three were, so I started looking."

"Any luck?"

Ben smiled. "Like I said, four aces." He started counting them off on his fingers. "Carmack is working at the Beverly Hills police station. He's made no bones about his identity, though he has those yokels down there convinced that he is out here looking for Communists."

"Communists, my ass," Luca said, laughing a low, wheezing laugh. "The dumb shits."

"Joe Provenzano is hanging out at Letto's Pool Palace. I overheard Guido and Paulie talking about a new pool shark, and when they described him, I knew who it had to be."

"What are we going to do about it?" Luca asked.

"I don't think we ought to do anything yet," Ben replied. "We know he's there, but so far he doesn't know that we know. This way we can keep an eye on him."

"What about the other two?" Luca asked. "Especially Kelly. That's the sonofabitch I really want to get rid of."

"They are working on the movie," Ben answered.

"Working on the movie? How?"

Ben chuckled. "Vandervort is an extra. He's playing the role of one of the pilots who hang around the ready shack. Kelly, on the other hand, really is a pilot. He's flying one of the planes in the picture."

"You're sure of this?"

"I'm very sure," Ben said. "I saw both of them while I was out there."

"Well," Luca said. "That is good information to know. Yes, sir. That is very good information to know."

LOS ANGELES

The defense had been provided with a private consultation room in the back of the courthouse. The room was like that used for board meetings and therefore had a long table, surrounded by straight-back, un-cushioned, un-upholstered chairs. There were only three windows and they opened onto a rather unattractive view of the alley. Also, as this room was routinely used for defendants, the windows were barred to discourage any ideas a defendant might have about bypassing the justice system.

The bailiff had shown Johnny, Henry, and Karen into the room a few moments earlier. Henry left to meet Katie and escort her back to the room so that now Johnny and Karen were alone. Johnny sat at the table and began drumming his fingers. Karen dropped the newspaper she had been carrying onto the table in front of Johnny. It was half folded, with the upper half up. One of the headlines in the paper read: NO NEW LEADS ON GANGLAND MURDER.

"They are calling it a gangland murder," Karen said.

Johnny glanced at the paper though he didn't read the story, then he looked up at Karen. "Who is?" he asked.

"I don't know," she replied. "The police, the newspaper, they."

"Whoever they is," Johnny said.

"Well?"

"Well what?"

"Is it?"

"I understand he was killed by a *lupara*," Johnny said.

"A what?"

"A shotgun."

"Yes, that's what the paper says."

"Then it probably was a gangland killing," he said. "If it was something personal, he would have been shot in the face."

"What? Why?"

"It's the final indignity," Johnny said. "Shoot someone in the face and their family can't have an open-casket service for them."

"How ghastly."

"It is intended to be."

"How can you sit there and talk about this so calmly."

"What am I supposed to do, Karen? Pretend that I'm all upset because Mario Vaglichio was killed? He killed both my brothers and he tried to kill me. I'm not sorry to see him go."

"You are not sorry to see him go. Does that mean you are happy?"

Johnny sighed and rubbed his hand across his chin. "Karen, do you want to ask me?"

"Ask you what?"

"Come on, you know what. If you want to ask me if I had anything to do with the killing of Mario Vaglichio, then come right out with it. Quit hinting around."

"All right. Did you kill Mario Vaglichio? Or have him killed?"

"No. Do you think I did?"

"Well, by your own admission it was a gangland killing," Karen said. "And, also by your own admission, you and the Vaglichios have long been enemies."

"It was a gangland killing, Karen," Johnny said. "And gangland is the operative word." He sighed. "Look. The Vaglichios came out here to California and suddenly started throwing their weight around. They didn't even bother to see if there might be someone else running things out here. They just came in like they owned the place. Only they didn't."

"What you are telling me is, there are gangsters out here, just like back in New York," Karen said.

"Yes," Johnny agreed. "Of course there are. Only out here they are smarter."

"Smarter? Why do you say that?"

"Because everyone has heard of all the New York and Chicago and Kansas City groups," Johnny said. "But the people out here have more sense. They keep their heads down and their names out of the newspapers."

"Why would someone like that want to kill Mario Vaglichio?"

"Karen, just because the people out here are smarter doesn't mean they aren't just as dangerous. In fact, they are even more dangerous because they are smart."

"Are you saying they killed Mario Vaglichio?"

"I'm not saying one way or the other," Johnny said. "I certainly wouldn't want to accuse someone who is smart and dangerous of committing murder."

"No, I guess not," Karen said. "Still, one can't help but wonder who did do it?"

"You asked me, Karen. And I don't mind answering it this one time," Johnny said. He held up his finger. "But after this never accuse me of anything again."

"I didn't actually accuse you," Karen protested. "I just asked, that's all."

"In this case asking is accusing," Johnny insisted.

"Well, you can't blame me for my suspicions. I mean you are a logical suspect; wouldn't you say?"

"Why would I be?"

"You are answering a question with a question," Karen complained. "But to answer your question, perhaps one reason you might be a logical suspect is because he tried to kill you the other night."

"Us," Johnny corrected. "He tried to kill us."

"All right, us."

"Since it was us, wouldn't that also make you a likely suspect?"

"I don't exactly travel in the same circles you do," Karen said.

"Exactly," Johnny agreed. "Because if you did, you would realize at once that I didn't do it. For example, do you remember a moment ago when I said something about shooting a person in the face when there was a personal motive in the killing?"

"Yes."

"Mario was not shot in the face."

Karen smiled. "Yes," she said. "Yes, that's right, isn't it? I mean, if you were avenging what happened to us the other night, he would have been shot right in the face, wouldn't he?"

"That's the way it is when it's personal," Johnny agreed.

"Oh, thank God," she said, breathing a huge sigh of relief. "You don't know what I've been going through, wondering if and thinking perhaps you were responsible for Vaglichio's death."

"Karen, right now the only thing on my mind is getting my sister cleared. There is no way I would do anything to discredit my sister, or to make your brother's job more difficult."

"I...I believe you," Karen said, smiling through her tears. "I believe you, and I won't question you again."

The door opened and Henry came in with Johnny's sister, Katie. Though she was neatly dressed and attractive, there was nothing about Katie's appearance to suggest that she was one of the nation's most popular movie personalities. Johnny knew that this was the way Henry wanted it.

"People may feel a lot of things for movie stars," he explained. "Admiration, respect, envy, maybe even love. But they don't feel sympathy for them. And from now until the time the trial is done, we want everyone's sympathy to be with Katherine. And by the way, it is Katherine, not Katie."

"How are you doing, Katherine?" Johnny asked, walking over to her and embracing her.

"I'm a little frightened," she admitted.

"Don't be frightened," he said. "Everything is going

to be all right. I promise you that. Everything is going to
be just fine."

CHAPTER 13

Any murder trial is spectacular and will draw a good crowd for that reason. If there is sex, or the hint of scandal, the interest in the case will be heightened. In the case of The People of California v. Katherine Sangremano, both the murder victim and the murder suspect had been found nude. That provided the sex. The murder victim was married, but not to the murder suspect. That provided the scandal.

Murder, sex, and scandal, would have been enough in itself to fill the courtroom, but added to all these attractions was the fact that the murder victim was one of the best known and most successful directors in Hollywood. And added to that was the fact that the murder suspect was one of Hollywood's best-loved motion-picture stars.

As a result of all these things, the courtroom was filled to absolute capacity. When all the seats were taken, several score more would-be observers of the American judicial system decided to wait in the hallway, content just to be close to the room where the most exciting trial of the year was about to take place.

When Mike Kelly reached the two huge, carved doors that led to the courtroom, he found that they had already been shut tight and were being closely guarded by two sheriff's deputies. "I have to get in there," he said.

"Sorry, mister, that's what everyone is saying," one of the deputies said. "There's no more room inside."

Mike showed them his badge. "It is important that I be in there," he said.

The guards looked at the badge, then at each other, then they shrugged their shoulders and one of them opened the door.

In addition to the spectators, there were at least two rows of newspaper reporters, not only from the immediate Los Angeles area but from all across the country. The reporters had spread out along the press benches with valises, tablets, etc. so that there could be room for another person if they would just make a few adjustments with all their paraphernalia.

"Why should I move?" one of the reporters replied when Mike asked him if he would please make room. "I don't see you wearin' a press badge."

"No," Mike replied, smiling broadly. "But I do have this badge. And if you don't move over and let me in, I'll just have you thrown out and I'll take your place."

Reluctantly, the reporter made room for Mike.

The fact that no cameras were allowed in the courtroom was not going to stop the newspapers across the country from running front-page pictures of the proceedings. Like the newspapers of a generation before, the front-page illustrations would be provided by quick-sketch artists.

Even though the trial had not yet begun, the artists were already very busy filling their sketch pads with pictures of the scene of the trial. It was a dramatic enough setting, even without the players on stage. On the west wall of the courtroom, for example, huge floor-to-ceiling windows opened out onto a beautifully landscaped lawn. The courthouse lawn was filled with huge, red hibiscus flowers and dominated by tall, waving palm trees. The most prominent feature inside the courtroom was the judge's bench. It was at the north end of the room and it was flanked by an American flag and a flag of the state of California. There was a large bas relief of the great seal of the state of California on the wall behind the bench.

Just to the judge's right was the witness box. To the judge's left was the bailiff's table and a table for the court clerk. Next came two larger tables...the defendant's table on the left as one looked forward and the prosecutor's table to the right.

"Here she is," Mike heard someone say. "Here is Katie Starr."

"Katie, why did you do it?" someone called. "Why did you kill him?"

"How are you going to plead, Katie?" another asked.

The bailiff cleared his throat. "If you people do not hold it down, the judge will order this courtroom cleared, and I will carry out that order," he warned.

Katie, who had answered none of the questions, took her seat at the defendant's table. Johnny, who was sitting just behind the railing that separated the legal part of the courtroom from the gallery, leaned forward and whispered something. Katie nodded and reached out to take his hand. He squeezed it, then she turned back to the front of the court. That little action, brother and sister holding hands across the railing, was poignant enough to fire the imagination of half the artists in the room and Mike saw that they quickly abandoned their current sketches and began working on this one.

Sitting just to Katie's right was her attorney, Henry Murchison. Henry had a tablet in front of him, along with several freshly sharpened pencils. Mike had never met Henry Murchison, though during the days he and Johnny were barnstorming together he had heard Johnny tell stories about the man who had been his closest friend among all the aviators he flew with during the war.

Many of the newspapers were surprised that Katie Starr had retained the services of a corporate lawyer like Henry Murchison rather than some well-known criminal lawyer. Mike wasn't surprised, though. He knew that someone like Johnny Sangremano would pay for loyalty and friendship, even if it was at the expense of skill and experience. Of course, in this case, the person who was ultimately paying the price was Johnny's sister. Mike couldn't help wondering whether Henry Murchison really was the best lawyer for her.

Katie was wearing a simple blue dress with a small ivory brooch that had belonged to her mother. Her hair was combed into bangs. What little makeup she wore was so pale as to be indiscernible.

Over at the prosecutor's table, Norton Potashnick sat with his assistant. Mike had not met the prosecutor, but he did know a little about him. The word was that Norton Potashnick was an extremely skilled attorney with a burning ambition. There had been rumors that if he got a conviction in this case, he would ride it, like a white horse, into the office of district attorney. Some said no, he would go all the way to the state attorney general's office, while others even hinted at a run for governor.

Like Henry, Norton had a tablet and pencils. He also had a briefcase full of notes and material.

"All rise!" the bailiff called.

There was a scrape of chairs and a rustle of skirts and pants as the gallery rose for the judge's entrance.

"The Superior Court of the Circuit Court, in and for the county of Los Angeles, is now in session, the Honorable Daniel S. Heckemeyer presiding," the court clerk intoned. "God save the United States, the state of California, and this honorable court."

Judge Heckemeyer, a robust man who looked even larger in his flowing black robes, strolled in quickly, then took his seat and struck the gavel twice. "Be seated," he said.

The gallery took their seats.

"The clerk will call the case."

"Your Honor, comes now before this court the case of California versus Katherine Sangremano. The charge is murder in the first degree."

"First degree?"

"First degree, Your Honor."

"Mr. Prosecutor, were there any negotiations on the possibility of a lesser charge?"

"No, Your Honor. The state is confident that it can sustain a charge of first degree," Norton Potashnick replied.

"Defense, was there no attempt to plea-bargain?"

"No plea bargain, Your Honor. Defense will enter a plea of not guilty."

"Very well," Judge Heckemeyer replied. "Mr. Potashnick, the state may present its case."

Except for a fringe of hair above his ears, Norton Potashnick was bald. Nevertheless, he had the habit, perhaps developed before he went bald, or, perhaps as a subconscious and futile denial of his baldness, of rubbing his hand across the top of his head as if he were brushing back his hair. He stood up and did this a couple of times before he began to speak.

"Your Honor, ladies and gentlemen of the jury," he began. "Of all crimes for which society holds individuals accountable, it deals most harshly with those persons who willfully deprive another human being of his life.

"This is as it should be, for of all crimes against man, murder is the most irrevocable. A thief may take a purse, but a purse may be replaced. An arsonist may burn a house, but a house may be rebuilt.

"But murder, ladies and gentlemen, is final and absolute. Once a murder is committed, the victim is gone forever. The victim's spouse, parents, children, siblings, and friends are thenceforth and forever denied the comfort of his presence or the joy of his company. And if that murder victim happens to be a man who, by his work, had a great and positive impact upon society, as in the case of Deke Clark, who was, as you all know, a brilliant director, then his murder is, indeed, a crime against all humanity."

Norton paused for a moment to let his last statement sink in, and during that pause, he again brushed back an imaginary wave of hair.

"The penalty for murder in the first degree is the forfeiture, by execution, of the murderer's own life. That is a most severe penalty...and it should be. Murder is also the most difficult charge to prove...and it should be. In fact, because of the difficulty in proving murder in the first degree, many prosecutors will accept a lesser plea in order to ensure a conviction."

Norton turned pointedly toward the judge.

"You may have heard the judge, at the opening of these proceedings, express some surprise that the prosecution had not opted for such a course. The state did not pursue such a course because the state is confident that it will be able to prove, beyond a shadow of a doubt, that Katie Starr willfully, and with malice and aforethought, committed murder upon the person of Deke Clark. Furthermore, she did this with the idea that her status as one of our country's most popular movie stars had bought for her a kind of immunity against the laws which govern the common person. We will prove that Katie Starr's life of privilege convinced her that she was much better than the common person and therefore considered herself above the law.

"We will establish motive, we will show opportunity, and we will present you with a picture of Katie Starr that is entirely consistent with that of a person who could, when provoked, fire a bullet into the brain of a man with whom she had, only moments before, been intimate. And we will do this, ladies and gentlemen of the jury, through the presentation of irrefutable physical evidence, and most damning at all, by the sworn testimony of an eyewitness. Your conclusion will be obvious and your duty clear. You will find the defendant guilty of murder in the first degree."

As Norton sat back down, his assistant reached over, very pointedly, and shook hands with him, congratulating him on his opening remarks. Mike saw that a few of the jurors had also noticed this and were visibly impressed by it. If he were the defendant in this case, he would be worried. Some of the jurors already had Katie convicted and the trial had not even begun.

"Does counselor for the defense wish to make his opening statement at this time?"

"Yes, Your Honor," Henry replied. He remained seated.

"Well, go ahead, Counselor, the floor is all yours," the judge said, and the sound of light laughter rippled across the room.

Henry cleared his throat and stood up. "Your Honor, before I begin with the opening statement, I would like to request that the court instruct the prosecution to refer to the defendant as Katherine Sangremano. Katie Starr is not her legal name, it is merely a stage name."

"Your Honor, she is known to the world as Katie Starr," Norton protested.

"Your Honor, how she is known to the world isn't important," Henry shot back. "It is not the world who will decide this case, it is the court. Katherine Sangremano is the one who is on trial for her life, not someone called Katie Starr. There is no Katie Starr. Katherine Sangremano plays the role of Katie Starr, just as she has played the role of Juliet, Queen Elizabeth, and Cleopatra. If the prosecution wishes to refer to her by an assumed name, why not choose one of those?"

Again the gallery laughed.

"Your Honor, can't you see what he is doing?" Norton protested. "He is trying to separate Katherine Sangremano the person from Katie Starr the movie star. It is the movie star we are trying here, not Katherine Sangremano."

"Is that so, Mr. Potashnick?" Judge Heckemeyer replied. He picked up a piece of paper. "Then why does the indictment read Katherine Sangremano?"

"Nevertheless, Your Honor, she is known as Katie Starr, and even refers to herself that way." He looked over at Henry. "She doesn't call herself Cleopatra, or Queen Elizabeth, or Katherine Sangremano."

Judge Heckemeyer looked at the paper for a moment, stroking his chin as he did so. Finally, he put it down. "The indictment is against Katherine Sangremano," he said. "And I am instructing you, Mr. Potashnick, to refer to her by that name."

"Thank you, Your Honor," Henry said.

I'll be damned, Mike thought. Score one for the corporate lawyer.

"Your Honor, ladies and gentlemen of the jury,"

Henry began. "At the conclusion of the prosecutor's opening statement, many of you saw him being congratulated by his assistant." Henry turned toward the prosecutor's table. "I too, congratulate you, Mr. Potashnick."

Henry clapped his hands, quietly.

"You see, ladies and gentlemen of the jury, my learned colleague is quite a distinguished orator and he gave a most brilliant opening statement. Of course, that's all part of the fireworks of a celebrated case like this...words that flow trippingly from the tongue, phrases which ring from the rafters, and an audience...oh yes, there must be an audience, enraptured by the speaker and hanging on every golden syllable.

"I'm afraid, however, that I won't be able to provide you with such a show. You see, I don't live in that world the way Mr. Potashnick does. The distinguished prosecutor is used to practicing law before an enraptured audience. I, on the other hand, am much more likely to be found looking for a precedent, poring over some musty book in a quiet library somewhere, trying to wrest justice from a difficult situation.

"However, that may not be too bad a background to bring to this case, because a difficult situation is exactly what we have here. Ladies and gentlemen, even the most perfunctory examination of the facts will show that this isn't at all the open-and-shut case the prosecutor would have you believe. There is, perhaps, opportunity, but there is no motive. There is fragmentary physical evidence, but none of it is conclusive. And there are no credible eyewitnesses. I say credible because the one eyewitness the prosecution does have, did not come forth until several days after the crime was committed.

"I need not remind you of the precept that one is presumed innocent until proven guilty, because that is one of the most sacred rights we Americans have. Also, I need not remind you that one cannot be found guilty if there is the shadow of a doubt as to that guilt. Because that, too, is a sacred right that all of us—bakers, dockworkers, office clerks, postmen, and yes, even movie stars —have.

"And so I ask you now to wipe any impression which may have been imprinted upon your mind by the brilliant and eloquent oratory of my esteemed adversary in his opening remarks. Consider not the eloquence but the evidence…not the fireworks but the facts. Then, when all the evidence is presented and all the testimony is heard, you will be able to decide this case on its merits. And on its merits, I feel confident that you will find Katherine Sangremano innocent of the charge of murder in the first degree."

After the opening statements of both lawyers, there was a bit of procedural business to take care of, then the judge adjourned for lunch. Many of the spectators, afraid they would lose their seats over the lunch period, refused to leave the courtroom. The bailiff allowed this until he saw a few opening sack lunches. Those who did so were hustled out immediately.

"Mike?"

Mike was about to leave the room when he heard Johnny call his name. He stopped, then turned toward the man who had, at one time, been his closest friend.

"Hello, Johnny," he said.

"Mike, it was good of you to come."

Mike shrugged his shoulders.

"Would you eat lunch with us?" Johnny invited.

"All right," Mike agreed, and he turned away from the public exit to follow Johnny back through the courtroom and out one of the back doors.

"Henry made arrangements to have lunch brought

into the defense conference room," Johnny said. "I would very much like for you to meet him."

"After all the tall tales you told about Henry Murchison, I want to meet him," Mike replied with an easy smile.

Henry, Katie, and Karen were sitting at one end of the conference table when Johnny arrived with Mike. A waiter was spreading out food for them.

"Set an extra place," Johnny said. "We have company."

"Mike." Katie smiled, greeting him. "It's good to see you again."

"Hello, Katherine," Mike said, taking Katie's hand.

"And this is Karen Murchison," Johnny said. "She is Henry's sister and is assisting him with the case."

"Miss Murchison," Mike greeted.

"And you saw Henry working this morning," Johnny said. "Henry, this is Special Agent Mike Kelly, of the Bureau of Investigation."

"Federal?" Henry asked.

"Yes."

"He's been after me for a long time," Johnny said.

"I still am," Mike said. "And I'm going to get you."

"Not during lunch, I hope," Johnny replied. "I mean, look, we have cold roast beef, potato salad, deviled eggs, sliced tomatoes. We can at least have a truce during lunch, can't we?"

Despite himself, Mike laughed. "We'll have a truce during lunch," he agreed.

"Johnny, I don't know if this is such a good idea," Henry said. He looked at Mike. "Actually I don't know if it is a good idea for you, either Mr. Kelly. I mean, how would it look to your superiors if they knew you were having lunch with Johnny Sangremano?"

"It would look like I was doing my job," Mike said.

"Johnny, this is not a good idea at all, and I strongly suggest—" Henry started, but Johnny waved him off.

"Come on, Henry, don't be such a fuddy-duddy," Johnny said. "One thing about having a friend as your enemy is that he is always honest with you. You think I don't know that Mike is going to listen to every word said here to see if he can use it against me? Hell, what's new about that? We've been going through this little dance for quite a few years now. We both know how to play the game. Mike, pass the horseradish."

Mike laughed and pushed the jar across the table to Johnny, who began making copious use of it.

"I figured you were here in California," Johnny said. "I heard that Carmack was working with the police force." He chuckled. "I understand he is supposed to be looking for Communists."

"That's right."

"Well, I hope he finds them. I might be a mobster, but I am an American mobster and I don't appreciate anyone trying to overthrow the government. So if there is anything I can do to help, you just let me know. Now, let's see. Carmack is here and you are here…what about Joe Provenzano and Jason Vandervort? Are they here also?"

"Johnny, you know I can't tell you that," Mike replied, putting mustard on his own sandwich.

"Yeah, I know," Johnny replied. "But you can't fault me for asking."

"By the way, Counselor," Mike said to Henry. "I want to congratulate you on your opening move…getting the court to refer to the defendant as Katherine Sangremano rather than Katie Starr."

"Thanks," Henry said, obviously pleased by Mike's praise.

"Katherine, you don't have to answer of course, as I'm

sure your counselor would advise you, but don't you remember anything of that night?"

Katherine looked at Henry and Henry nodded once, granting his assent.

"I remember having dinner with Deke on the table beside the pool," she said. "We talked. I don't remember anything after that until I found myself sitting on the diving board, looking over at Deke. By then he was already dead. The police came soon after that."

"How long was that?"

Henry held up his hand. "I'd rather she not say anything else," he said. "You understand."

"All right," Mike said.

"Mike, the Vaglichios are responsible for this," Johnny said. "They killed Deke. There is absolutely no doubt in my mind."

"Which one of them, Johnny? Luca or Mario?" Mike asked pointedly.

"What difference does it make? They are two peas in a pod, anyway."

"You mean they were two peas in a pod, don't you?" Mike replied. "In case you missed it, Mario is dead."

"Yeah, yeah, I heard about that," Johnny said. "I can't honestly say that I'm sorry."

"But of course you know nothing about it?"

"No, nothing."

"Mr. Kelly, if you don't mind, I would like to keep all our energy focused on Miss Sangremano's case," Henry said. "Your curiosity about the Vaglichio incident, whether it is professional or personal, is best served somewhere else."

"All right, Counselor," Mike said, raising his hand. "Your point is well taken. I'll let it drop, for now."

"Yeah, let's change the subject to something more interesting," Johnny said and smiled brightly. "Listen, have either one of you fellas been out to the set of *Aero-drome*? I hear they have nearly as many airplanes out there as we used in the entire war. Nieuports, Spads, Fokkers. Wouldn't it be fun for the three of us to go out there and get one apiece and just tool around the sky for a while?"

"Oh, heavens," Henry complained. "I haven't flown in years."

"What about you, Mike? You're keeping your hand in, aren't you?"

"Oh, do you fly, too, Mr. Kelly?" Karen asked, speaking for the first time since they were introduced. "Were you with these two during the war?"

"No," Mike said. "That is, yes, I fly, but no, I wasn't with them during the war. I learned after the war."

"He was a good student," Johnny said.

"Johnny taught you to fly?" Karen asked.

"That's right," Mike answered, noticing with interest that Karen had called him Johnny, not Mr. Sangremano. He couldn't help but smile. Johnny's charm with the ladies had been established long ago. "Johnny taught me everything I know."

"Ah yes," Johnny said, holding up his finger to illustrate his point. "But I didn't teach him everything I know, and that's the important thing."

There was a knock on the door and a man stuck his head in. "Court reconvenes in five minutes," he announced.

"Thank you," Henry replied.

"Henry, what will happen this afternoon?" Johnny asked.

"This afternoon the prosecution will began presenting its evidence," Henry answered

The first witness for the prosecution was Officer Arnie Stone.

"What time did you receive the report of domestic disturbance?" Norton asked.

"It was about five minutes until midnight," Arnie answered. "I know because my partner said if it had been just a few minutes later, it wouldn't have been our case."

"And where was the domestic disturbance?"

"It was at Katie Starr's house."

"Objection," Henry said quickly. "The court has instructed that the name Katie Starr not be used."

"Sustained," the judge replied. He looked at Norton. "Counselor, please instruct your witnesses to refer to the defendant as Katherine Sangremano."

"I beg your pardon, Your Honor, it was unintentional."

"Continue."

"When we got there, we found Miss Starr...that is, Miss Sangremano, standing over Deke Clark's body, holding a gun. We immediately drew our own weapons and pointed them at her, and ordered her to put her gun down. She did so, then I sent my partner into the house to call the station and report the murder."

"Miss Sangremano was nude when you arrived?"

"Yes."

"And Deke Clark?"

"Yeah, he was naked...that is, nude too," Officer Stone said.

"What happened next?"

"I asked her if she killed him. She said she didn't know whether she had or not."

"She didn't deny it?"

"She said she didn't think so, but she didn't know."

"I see. And then what happened."

"Well, I looked at the lounge chairs alongside the pool and found one that seemed to have semen stains."

"Your Honor, let the record show that item number,

uh, seven, I believe..." Norton put his glasses on and looked at his tablet for a second, then nodded his head. "Yes, item number seven is the lab report indicating that the stains were, in fact, semen stains."

"So directed."

"Officer Stone, was the defendant out of your sight for any period of time while you were there?"

"Only for a few moments, while she went to the bathroom."

"Where was the bathroom?"

"There was one right there in the pool house, right next to the pool. It's really a nice place back there, you should see it. Swimming pool, tennis court, pool house, it's pretty ritzy."

"In other words, not your common backyard?" Norton suggested.

"No, sir!"

"Objection," Henry said quickly. "Not relevant."

"Sustained."

"Officer Stone, while Miss Sangremano was in the bathroom, would it have been possible for her to wash her hands?"

"Yes."

"So if she had any powder residue as the result of having just fired a pistol, she could have washed it off?"

"I, uh, suppose she could have," Officer Stone said. "That was my fault, I shouldn't have let her go. She told me she had to throw up."

"No further questions."

Henry got up and walked halfway toward the witness box, then he stopped. He put his hands together in the attitude of prayer and chucked himself under the chin in a sort of nervous gesture before he spoke. "Did she throw up?"

"Yes."

"How do you know?"

"I heard her," Arnie said. "And later, when Detective Murphy opened the door, she was standing over the toilet bowl where there was evidence that she had thrown up."

"What happened to that evidence?"

Arnie looked confused. "I beg your pardon?"

"The evidence that she threw up. What happened to it?"

"Well, I... I flushed it down the toilet," he said.

"Did it not occur to you that if she had been in a comatose state as she claimed that it might have been because of something she ingested?"

"No, I didn't think about it," Arnie admitted.

Henry started toward the defense table, stopped, and turned back toward the witness. "Officer Stone, do you believe Katherine Sangremano killed Deke Clark?"

"Objection!" Norton said quickly. "That's for the jury to decide."

Henry smiled broadly. He didn't know why, but he just had a hunch that Officer Stone might not believe his client was guilty and the fact that the prosecutor was protesting the question now was proof that his hunch was right.

"Your Honor, Officer Stone is a witness for the prosecution...an expert witness, if you will. He is a police officer who has been involved with several murder cases and, like all good police officers, can develop an intuitive feel for a case. The prosecutor obviously has people on his team who feel that Miss Sangremano is guilty, or we wouldn't be trying this case. Since Officer Stone is a part of this prosecution team, and was, in fact, the first one on the scene, I would be interested in knowing what he thinks."

Judge Heckemeyer leaned back in his chair and

crossed his arms across his chest for a moment. "All right," he finally said. "You may answer the question."

"No," Arnie said. When he saw that the judge didn't quite understand what he was saying, he amended it quickly. "I mean no, Your Honor, I don't think she is guilty."

"Why not?" Henry asked.

"When I got there, she was standing over him, holding the gun. I don't believe she would have shot him and then just stood there until we arrived. That would have been several minutes, maybe longer. It just doesn't make sense. Why would she have done that?"

"Why indeed, Officer Stone? No further questions, Your Honor, subject, with your permission, to the right of recall," Henry said.

"So directed. Redirect?"

Norton raised his hand as if he were about to ask something else, then he nodded and dropped his hand back to the table. "No redirect."

After Officer Stone came the homicide detectives and the lab technicians. The court learned that the .25-caliber bullet that killed Deke Clark was fired from the very gun Katherine Sangremano had been holding when Officer Stone and his partner arrived on the scene. Furthermore, purchase records proved that the gun belonged to Katherine Sangremano.

The final witness before adjourning for the day was Dr. Emil Urban, a pathologist. "Death was due to an insult to the brain caused by the traumatic intrusion of a lead bullet, approximately three ounces in weight. This brought on a massive hemorrhage which caused the brain to swell beyond the confines of the cranium, shutting off the brain stem," Dr. Urban reported in a dry monotone. "Other than the injury, the victim showed no apparent organ damage or life-threatening diseases or illnesses. He was of normal weight and height and was, in all respects, very healthy for a man of his age.

"An examination of the contents of his stomach showed that digestion was well under way for the meal he had consumed...principally eggs and cheese, which would be consistent with the quiche he was reported to have eaten."

"Thank you, Doctor. Your witness, Mr. Murchison."

"Doctor," Henry said, without getting up from his table. "In the report you filed here I see that there were other things in his stomach besides the eggs and cheese."

"There was bread," the doctor said. "And wine. And traces of various nostrums."

"Various nostrums? You mean medications? I thought you said Mr. Clark was a healthy man."

"Healthy, yes. but also vain. It is my understanding that he was very concerned about falling hair," the doctor said. "He was constantly trying remedies and we found traces of such things as tincture of cantharides, spirits of rosemary, laudanum, and gum camphor."

"All this to stop falling hair?" Henry asked.

"Well, none of it actually works," the doctor replied, rubbing his own bald head. "If it did, I would use it."

The gallery laughed.

"Thank you, Doctor," Henry said. "I have no further questions, again subject to recall."

"Redirect, Mr. Prosecutor?" the judge asked.

"No redirect, Your Honor."

"Very well, then court stands adjourned until nine o'clock tomorrow morning."

————

That evening Johnny was in his parlor with his head back and his eyes closed, listening to a Caruso recording. He had asked Henry how he thought the trial was going, but the lawyer told him it was much too early to tell. Johnny thought things were going well; everything Henry had done today seemed persuasive to him. But then he was, admittedly, prejudiced on behalf of his sister.

The problem was, Johnny had no experience with courts and didn't really trust them. It was much easier to settle things yourself. Johnny had a history of settling things for himself, so it was no surprise when first Karen, and then Mike Kelly, accused him of having a hand in Mario Vaglichio's killing. He had denied it to both of them, but he didn't think either one of them believed him.

They would have believed him if they understood the significance of how Mario Vaglichio was killed. It was strictly business. That was why he had been shot in the chest. If Johnny had killed Mario, he would have shot the sonofabitch in the face.

"Godfather?"

Johnny opened his eyes and saw someone standing in the hallway door. The light was coming from behind so that his visitor was in shadow, but Johnny knew that it was Al Provenzano.

Johnny reached over to the record player and lifted the needle. "Come in, Al," he said.

"I'm sorry to disturb your tranquility," Al apologized.

"Don't be silly. You know that you, of all people, have my ear at any time," Johnny said. "What is it?"

"I have some disturbing news," Al said.

"About my sister?" Johnny asked anxiously, sitting up straighter.

"No, no, nothing like that," Al said, concerned that he had alarmed his boss. "It's about Frankie Sarducci."

"What about him?"

"I have just learned that Frankie is the one who killed Mario."

"Oh, damn," Johnny said. He sighed and pinched the bridge of his nose for a long, silent moment before speaking again. "I know it was a thing of honor for him. He was trying to avenge the attack against me up in San Francisco. But this was a hell of a time to do it...right in the middle of Katherine's trial. What on earth made him do it without my sanction, anyway?"

"I wish it had been an act of honor, Godfather, but it was not," Al said quietly. "He killed Mario for another reason."

Johnny looked at Al in surprise. "What do you mean? What other reason could there be?"

"Money," Al said. "The coloreds paid him to do it."

"Al, maybe you had better tell me what's going on."

"It seems that the Vaglichios knocked over a drug shipment that was coming in. A bunch of Mexicans were bringing the stuff up for a bunch of colored dope pushers. The Vaglichios hit the boat out in the bay, killed all the Mexicans, and took the dope. Dope that the coloreds had already paid for. They found out about it, found out who did it, and put out the word that they wanted the Vaglichios killed."

"And you're telling me that Frankie did their dirty work for them?"

"Yes," Al said. "Actually, I suppose he thought he was being pretty smart about the whole thing. He figured you were going to order the Vaglichios killed sooner or later, anyway, so he thought he would just move the schedule up. He was getting paid by the coloreds to kill Mario, but in his mind and in his heart he was killing Mario as an act of vengeance for you."

"Al, enemy or no, Mario was Sicilian. Not only that,

he was a made man. No non-Sicilian can order a Sicilian killed."

"What do you want to do about it?" Al asked.

Johnny rubbed his chin. "I don't know."

"You know what needs to be done," Al said. "What the code says must be done."

"Yes, I know, I know," Johnny said, waving his hand impatiently. "I should have him killed."

Al was silent.

"I can't do that, Al," Johnny finally said. "Frankie's been with the Family too long. I can't order him killed."

"What are you going to do?"

Johnny sighed. "I'm going to cut him loose."

"That's the same thing as killing him," Al said.

"No, it isn't."

"He'll never be trusted again. And he won't have the protection of the Family if the Vaglichios decide to take revenge against him."

"He can go somewhere," Johnny said. "He can change his name, start a new life."

"You don't really expect him to do that, do you?"

"Why not?" Johnny replied. "My God, Al, if you only knew how many times I have wished I could do that very thing."

"I have read that kings sometimes feel that way," Al said.

Johnny chuckled. "Well, I wouldn't exactly call myself a king. But I can understand why they might feel that way. Where is Frankie now?"

"I don't know," Al said. "He's around, somewhere."

"Does he know that we know?"

"I don't think so."

"As soon as you see him again, tell him that we know," Johnny said. "And tell him of my decision."

"He'll want to see you. He'll want to plead his case."

"No," Johnny said, shaking his head no. "I don't want to see him. Not now, not ever."

"Very well, Godfather." Al stood and walked over to the record player, turned it on, and put the needle back down. "I'll leave you with the Great One."

Johnny leaned back in the darkness, listening to Caruso sing. Al wouldn't understand it, perhaps no one would, but he would give anything if he could change places with Frankie now. He would love to go somewhere, change his name, and start a new life.

CHAPTER 14

"Your Honor, the state calls Miss Rosita Chavez to the witness stand," Norton Potashnick said at the beginning of the second day of the trial.

"Rosita Chavez," the bailiff called.

A young, very attractive, dark-haired, dark-eyed woman came to the witness stand. A Bible was put under her left hand, and she raised her right.

"Do you swear to tell the truth, the whole truth, and nothing but the truth, so help you God?"

"Sí,"

"This is it," Henry whispered to Katie. "This is their star witness…their entire case hinges upon her testimony."

"Who is she?" Katie asked. "I've never seen her before."

"She is a maid for the Willoughbys. Do you know the Willoughbys?"

"Yes, I know them. They are very nice people, my next-door neighbors."

"The fact that they are your next-door neighbors gives the maid's testimony some degree of credibility. The police have examined her room and have verified that from the window there is an excellent view of the side of your pool nearest the pool house."

"That's where I keep the lounge chairs," Katie said.

"Yes."

"Your Honor," Norton explained, after Rosita was sworn in, "as the witness speaks no English, I will be doing all my questioning through an interpreter."

"Have you informed the defense of such an intention so that they may get their own interpreter."

"I have, Your Honor."

Judge Heckemeyer looked over at Henry. "Do you have an interpreter?"

"I do, Your Honor," Henry said. "My interpreter will be Miss Karen Murchison."

"Murchison?"

"My sister, Your Honor. But she is also an employee of Vaughan and Murchison, where her duties include translation work."

"Very well, if you are satisfied, the court is satisfied. You may proceed, Mr. Potashnick."

Norton established the girl's identity, her place of employment, its proximity to Katie's backyard, and why she was in position to look out over the pool.

"And now, if you would, please tell the court, in your own words, what happened on the night in question."

Through the interpreter, the girl began to speak.

"I polished the silver for Mrs. Willoughby. When I finished, I went to my room. I was not yet sleepy, so I sat at the window, looking out. The moon was very bright and the night was beautiful and I thought I am very lucky to be here and have such a wonderful place to work and to live.

"I looked next door and saw a man and woman taking their meal at a table by the swimming pool. She was so beautiful and he was so handsome and the setting was so lovely and romantic that I was moved by the scene."

"Is that woman present now?" Norton asked.

"*Sí*," the girl answered. There was no need to translate that one-syllable answer, so the interpreter remained silent.

"Would you point that woman out to the court, please?"

Rosita waited until the question was framed in Spanish, then she pointed toward the defendant's table, directly at Katie.

"Let the record show that the witness pointed toward Katherine Sangremano. Miss Sangremano, would you stand, please?"

Katie looked at Henry and he nodded, so she stood.

"Is that the one?" Norton asked.

"*Sí*,"

"Please, go on."

"After the meal the man and woman began to kiss. They would kiss and drink wine, and kiss some more, then drink more wine. Then they removed their clothes and began to engage in an act of fornication." Though the girl's voice was hesitant and embarrassed sounding, the interpreter translated in a very clinical monotone. "I looked away then because I was too embarrassed to watch any further."

"Did you ever look back at any time that evening?"

"*Sí*,"

"Please explain the circumstances to the court."

"I heard a loud noise, like the sound of a gun being fired. I looked back into the yard and saw the woman standing over the man. She was holding a gun, like this." Rosita demonstrated by holding her arm down and forming her hand into the shape of a gun. "Very near the man's head."

"What did she do then?"

"She put the gun down on the man's chest, wiped her hands like this"—she wiped her hand on her chest—"then glanced around as if looking to see if anyone saw her. I was very frightened that she might look into my window and discover that I was watching, so I moved away from the window so she could not see me."

"Did you look back later?"

"No."

"Why not?"

"I was afraid."

"Why did you wait so long before you came to the police with your story?"

"To live in such a house, Miss Sangremano must be a very wealthy woman. I am a very poor woman. In my country the police do not believe the stories of the poor when they report bad things about the very wealthy. I was afraid it might be that way here also."

"You have not made this story up, have you? You aren't telling this story because you are jealous of Miss Sangremano's wealth?"

"No! I am telling the truth," Rosita insisted.

"Thank you," Norton said. "Your witness, Mr. Murchison."

"Miss Chavez, you said the man and woman committed an act of fornication?"

"*Sí*." Rosita cast her eyes down.

"Was it forced?"

"She does not understand the question," Karen said after passing the question on.

"This act of fornication, did the man force himself upon the woman? Was there a struggle?"

"There was no struggle."

"Then you might say that it was an act of love?"

"*Sí*,"

"Don't you think it a little odd that in one minute they would be making love and in the very next minute she would shoot him?"

"Objection, Your Honor, calls for a conclusion."

"Sustained."

"Did you hear any sounds of disagreement? Were there any loud words spoken? Any argument or fighting going on?"

"No."

"You said they were drinking wine. How much wine did they drink?"

"I do not know."

"Do you think they may have drunk enough for someone to pass out?"

"Objection. Calls for a conclusion."

"Your Honor, I submit that a reasonable adult can judge whether or not a person is drinking excessively."

"But excessive to one person is moderate to another," Norton insisted.

"Objection sustained. Witness need not answer the question," Judge Heckemeyer said.

"How long a time passed from the time you last saw them in their lovers' embrace until you heard the gunshot?" Henry asked, changing his tactic.

"About one half-hour."

"And you did not look at all during that half-hour?"

"No."

"If you were not enjoying the scenery through your window, how did you engage yourself during that half-hour? What did you do?"

When Karen translated the question the girl gasped aloud, mumbled something, then covered her face with her hands.

"She asked how did you know?" Karen repeated.

"How did I know what?" Henry asked, puzzled by the strange response to his question.

"Objection, Your Honor," Norton shouted quickly.

"On what grounds, Counselor?" Judge Heckemeyer asked.

"The question is irrelevant."

"No," the judge said. "I am inclined to give the defense some latitude here. You may continue."

Henry wasn't sure where this was going, but he realized that he had struck some sort of nerve. "Miss Chavez, how did you spend that half-hour?" he asked again.

The girl, keeping her face covered, said the answer very quietly.

Karen asked for clarification; then, when she was sure she knew what the girl said, she looked toward her brother. "Masturbation," she said.

There was a tittering of nervous laughter in the courtroom, but Judge Heckemeyer brought his gavel down sharply and cut it off.

"Counselor, do you wish to pursue this line of questioning further? I will allow it, but you must establish, quickly, where it is going."

"No, Your Honor. Subject to recall, I have no further questions," Henry said.

"Redirect?"

Norton stood up. "Miss Chavez, you did not actually see the gun being fired, is that right?"

"Sí,"

"How quickly after you heard the gunshot did you look to see what happened?"

"Immediately. I looked right away."

"Do you think it would have been possible for anyone else to have shot Mr. Clark, other than the woman you saw holding the gun?"

"Objection, Your Honor," Henry said. "Calls for a conclusion on the part of the witness."

"Overruled. It's a reasonable question. Witness may answer."

"I do not believe it was possible for anyone else to have fired the gun," Rosita answered.

"Thank you. No further questions."

"Witness may step down. Court is adjourned until two o'clock this afternoon."

"I don't know," Henry said to the others in the defense conference room. As he had done yesterday, Mike joined Johnny, Katherine, Henry, and Karen. "I don't mind telling you, the maid's testimony this morning was pretty damning. It hurt us badly."

"Can't you do something to discredit her?" Johnny asked.

"I don't see what it would be," Henry answered. "She obviously has no vested interest in the testimony. According to the police report she didn't even know who Katherine was. She is new to this country, she has seen very few movies, and she had no idea Katherine was a movie star."

"But she did know Katherine was wealthy. I mean she made a big point about Katherine being wealthy and she being poor. Maybe it's an act of jealousy. Maybe she's trying to put the rich woman in her place," Johnny suggested.

"No," Henry insisted. "If we take that tactic, it is sure to backfire on us. Anyway, I don't think that's the case. I think she actually saw...or at least she thinks she saw, what she reported."

"Then what you are saying is that you believe my sister killed Deke Clark," Johnny said a little sharply.

"Johnny, he didn't say that," Karen said. "You aren't being fair."

"Well, what did he say?"

"Johnny." Katie spoke up quickly. "Johnny, I don't know that I didn't kill him. I don't think I did, I certainly had no reason to. But I can't say what I did do while I was out."

"That's what interests me," Mike said. "Have you ever passed out like that before?"

"No. I'm not what you would call a heavy drinker."

"Maybe it isn't how much you were drinking, but what you were drinking. With Prohibition in effect it's not like you can go down to a store and buy a good bottle of wine." Mike smiled. "I know, because I've spent a good part of the last few years helping to enforce it. Don't you think it is possible that you got some very bad liquor?"

"No. Deke brought the bottle. He managed to bring some very good wine back from France the last time he was there."

"Did you drink the entire bottle?"

"I can answer that," Henry said. "Actually there wasn't that much wine drunk at all. In fact, there is a little over half a bottle of it left."

"Where is it now?"

"In the evidence room at the police station."

"It might be worth looking at."

There was a knock on the door then and Karen answered it. Sid Friedman was standing on the other side.

"Hello," Sid said. "If you don't think it too awkward, may I come in?"

Karen looked toward Katie, who nodded. "Come on in, Sid," Katie said.

"Thanks," Sid said. When he saw Mike, he looked surprised. "Say, what are you doing down here? I know you, don't I? Aren't you flying for me? Yeah, you're one of my stunt pilots, aren't you?"

Mike looked over at Johnny and saw him smiling. Aware that his cover was blown, Mike nodded. "Yes, sir, I am flying for you," he said. "But Bruiser and Sam gave me a couple of days off. I have a personal interest in this case."

"I might ask you the same question, Sid. What are you doing here?" Katie wanted to know. "Don't you have a movie to do?"

"As a matter of fact I do. But I wanted to stop by and wish you the best of luck," Sid said. "Katie, you know we're pulling for you...every one of us. If there is anything you need, anything at all, you've got my support."

"Yes, I could see how much support I was going to get from you when you replaced me in the movie," Katie said dryly.

"I'm sorry about that," Sid said. "But Katie, you understand this business as well as anyone. You know how much money we have tied up in *Aerodrome*. I had no choice, I had to go ahead with the filming. And I have to tell you, I would have gone ahead and used Joan whether Mr. Vaglichio came to see me or not."

"Wait a minute! What did you say? Vaglichio came to see you?" Johnny asked.

"Yes. That's why I'm here now. I have something I need to tell you. I know I should have told you before, but I was too frightened. However, after the testimony I heard in court this morning, I can't help but be more confused than I am frightened."

"What is it that you find so confusing?" Henry asked.

"Shortly after Deke was killed, Luca Vaglichio came to see me." Sid shivered. "I had just finished with my bath, and when I came back to my bedroom, there he was, sitting on my bed, in my bedroom, just like he owned the place. I know that the house was locked up tighter than a drum, so I have no idea how he got there. What I do know is that it was about the most frightening thing that ever happened to me."

"He was waiting for you in your bedroom?" Karen asked. Involuntarily she shivered.

"Yes."

"What was he doing there? What did he want?" Henry asked.

"I can answer that," Johnny said. "Vaglichio is trying to get his hand into the motion-picture business. That's what you meant about replacing my sister whether Vaglichio wanted you to or not?"

"Yes. But like I said, under the circumstances, I would have been forced to replace her, anyway, regardless of any consequences with the distribution," he added, looking pointedly at Johnny. "But it was the way Vaglichio asked me that frightened me."

"I can see that," Henry said. "Having someone suddenly appear in your bedroom could be quite disconcerting."

"It was more than that," Sid said. "It was what he said to me. You see, he told me that he killed Deke Clark. What's more, he said that he did it because I had asked him to, and he said if I didn't cooperate with him, he would see to it that I was implicated in the crime."

"My God, Sid, did you ask him to kill poor Deke?" Katie asked.

"Heavens no!" Sid replied quickly. "And I don't even know where he got that idea. All I told him was that I had a star I didn't want and a director I couldn't get along with."

"That's all somebody like Vaglichio would have needed," Mike suggested.

"Well, that's it then, isn't it?" Katie said brightly, looking at Henry. "I mean, if Sid goes on the stand and testifies about all this, won't that get me off?"

"I'm afraid not," Henry replied, shaking his head.

"But why not? That's the same as a confession, isn't it?"

"It's not even close," Henry said. "And it won't be unless Vaglichio takes the stand himself and makes a full confession. If I put Mr. Friedman on and he started testifying to what he just told us, he would be gagged immediately and his testimony thrown out of court as hearsay."

"Yes, well, I don't want to testify, anyway," Sid said, waving his hand. "The only reason I told you this at all was because I thought it might help in some way. But I'm sure not going to go out in the public and say something like that. Not with a man like Vaglichio running around free."

"But you have to," Katie started. "It's our only chan—" She was interrupted by Johnny.

"No," he said. "Henry's right, it wouldn't do any good. Besides which, Vaglichio didn't do it."

"What?" Katie said. "What do you mean he didn't do it? You heard Sid. Vaglichio told him that he did do it."

"That's exactly why I know he didn't do it," Johnny said. "If he had done it, he would never have told an outsider about it. He was just using that to frighten old Sid here, and evidently he did a pretty good job." Johnny sighed. "No, I know now that he didn't kill Deke Clark, just as he knows by now that I didn't kill Mario."

"But Johnny, you've been saying all along that Vaglichio did do it," Katie protested.

"Yeah, I know," Johnny said. "And until this minute I thought he did."

"Well, that puts us back to square one," Henry said.

"It also brings up a very difficult question. If Vaglichio didn't kill Deke Clark, who did?" Henry asked.

Johnny took Katie's hands in his, raised them to his lips, and kissed them gently. Then he looked deep into his sister's eyes. "It had to be you, Katherine."

"No!" Katie said as tears sprang quickly to her eyes.

"It had to be you," Johnny said. "You heard what the girl said this morning. She saw you standing over Deke's body, holding a gun."

"But why would I have done such a thing?" Katie wailed. "Don't you understand? I loved him, Johnny. You don't know how much I loved him."

"You also say that you can't remember anything that happened that night."

"That's true, I don't remember anything, but I swear I would have remembered that. I don't care how out of it I was; I wouldn't forget doing something like that...especially if it was to someone I loved."

"Henry, what about temporary insanity?" Johnny asked. "Can we plead that?"

"That's a last-ditch kind of plea," Henry answered. "You usually don't bring anything like that up unless there is nothing else left."

"Yes, but in Katie's case, it's not just clutching at straws. It may be true," Karen said. "I mean, she doesn't remember anything since the wine. There has to be some reason for that."

"Wait a minute," Mike said. "Henry, do you recall yesterday, when the doctor read the contents of Deke's stomach?"

"Yes, of course. I called his attention to them. They were in the autopsy report."

"Have you got that report with you?"

"I think so," Henry said, digging through his briefcase. "Yes, here it is."

"Could I see it, please?" Mike asked, reaching for the report.

"Mike, what is it?" Johnny asked. "Have you got an idea?"

"I don't know," Mike replied. "I might. I know there was something in that report that didn't sound right, and it's been nagging at me ever since."

Mike took the list and began reading aloud: "Tincture of cantharides, spirits of rosemary, laudanum, and gum camphor." He looked up. "When the doctor mentioned all these 'nostrums' yesterday, he just included laudanum along with the other things, the harmless things like rosemary and gum camphor. What he didn't say was the amount of laudanum they found. But look at this," he said. "Deke Clark had enough laudanum in him to stun a horse."

"What is laudanum?" Karen asked.

"It is a very old pain remedy," Sid said. "It comes from the same stuff that morphine is made from."

"It is very rare now, because morphine is much more potent," Mike said.

"Isn't that the same thing heroin comes from?" Karen asked.

"Yes," Mike answered. "And of course heroin is even more potent. Katherine, you knew Deke as well as anyone. Did he use heroin?"

"No," Katie insisted.

"You're sure?"

"I'm positive."

"Anyway, they found laudanum in his body not heroin," Johnny said.

"Some people use laudanum because it is less potent and they don't want to get hooked on heroin," Sid said quietly. "Of course, it is very difficult to come by now. Hardly no one processes it because from the same amount of extract that you can make a little laudanum, you can make a lot of heroin. That makes laudanum even more expensive than heroin."

"You seem to be speaking with some authority on this, Mr. Friedman. Do you know anyone who uses laudanum in such a way?" Henry asked.

Sid nodded.

"Who?"

"I have used it," he admitted. "I don't anymore."

"Did Deke ever use it?" Henry asked.

"No, never," Sid replied. "In fact he used to get very angry with—" he stopped in midsentence.

"With who? With you?"

Sid shook his head. "No. With Tamara," he said. He sighed. "Tamara still uses it. As a matter of fact, Tamara is the one who got me started on the stuff."

"That would explain where the laudanum came from," Henry said. "But it doesn't explain how Deke got it into his body...especially so much of it."

"If you'll let me, I might be able to find out the answer to that," Mike offered.

"Mike?" Johnny said. "I know there is more to your getting involved than old friendship. But, for whatever reason, I thank you for your help."

AT A POOL HALL ON THE OTHER SIDE OF TOWN

"Hello, Joe," Guido said as he approached the pool table where Joe Provenzano was playing a game, alone, since he could no longer get anyone to play against him. "You're not makin' any money at the table, are you?"

"You've been reading my mail," Joe answered laconically.

"Well, you can't live on your reputation. So how would you like the chance to make a few bucks?"

"I don't know," Joe said, looking up. "It depends on whether or not it's worth my while. How much are you talking about?"

"Five hundred dollars," Guido said.

Joe whistled softly. "Yeah, I'd say that's worth my time. Who do I have to kill?" he teased.

"You're some kidder, ain't you?" Guido laughed. "Come on, it won't take no time at all."

"All right," Joe agreed. He stroked the cue one last time, knocking nearly half the remaining balls down. Then he put the cue in the rack and followed Guido out the back door. A blue Chevrolet was parked in the alley and Guido's friend Paulie was leaning against it with his arms folded across his chest.

"Get in the front," Guido invited. "Paulie can ride in the back."

"Actually I'd rather ride in back," Joe said. "I get carsick when I ride in front." This wasn't true, but Joe often used the excuse, because when he rode in the backseat, no one could get behind him.

"Yeah, okay, you want to ride in the backseat, be my guest. Paulie, you get up front."

"Fine by me," Paulie mumbled.

Guido and Paulie spoke quite a bit of Italian while they were on their way to wherever it was they were going. Joe listened in on the conversation, but all they talked about was food they had eaten, women they had known, and parties they had been to. If Joe hadn't known better, he would almost believe they were making small talk just for his benefit. But that couldn't be true because they didn't know he could speak Italian.

"Here it is," Guido finally said, turning down an alley

way between two large warehouses. "It's in the back of the building here."

"What is it?" Joe asked. "We pullin' a heist?"

"We'll tell you what you need to know when you need to know it," Guido answered. 'Trust me, it's better all around if not too many people know what's goin' on."

"Yeah," Joe said. "Yeah, I guess you're right. There's less chance of things going wrong that way."

"You're a smart man, Joe."

Guido pulled up to a garage door and honked the horn, a loud *oogah* sound that echoed back from the wall of the building. A moment later, the door started going up, pulled open by a rattling chain and pulley.

"Good," Guido said. "They're here." He put the car in gear and drove it through the open door. The door came down behind them. Guido stopped the engine, then got out of the car. "Come on, we may as well all get out and stretch a bit," he offered.

The man who had opened then closed the big warehouse door came over to them. "Is this him?" he grunted.

"Yeah," Guido answered. "This is him."

"I'll be back," the man said.

Joe suddenly began to feel uneasy. It wasn't anything he could put his finger on, but there was something wrong here. Then he saw three people coming out of the shadows toward them. One of them was the man who had opened the door. He and another man were guarding the third, who, Joe noticed with some surprise, was in handcuffs. When they got closer, Joe saw that the man in handcuffs was Frankie Sarducci, one of Johnny Sangremano's lieutenants.

"You know this man?" Guido asked Joe.

"No," Joe lied.

"How 'bout you?" the man who had opened the door asked of Sarducci. "Do you know this man?"

Sarducci said nothing.

"Well, seein' as you don't know him, let me tell you about him," Guido said. "His name is Sarducci. Frankie Sarducci. He's a paisano, right? Only this paisano, he don't know from nothin'. He don't know, for example, how to tell the difference between his own people and the coloreds."

Paulie laughed. "Hey, Guido, you know what I think? I think he changed his luck. Yeah, I think he was gettin' hisself a little black poontang. That right, Sarducci? You gettin' yourself some of that?"

"What he did, see, was he took money from the coloreds to kill a made man," Guido went on. "Now, you know what that means, don't you?"

"I'm not sure," Joe replied.

"Well, hell, it means he's got to die," Guido said. "And you're goin' to get your chance to make your bones right here, because you're goin' to kill him."

"No," Joe answered. "I'm not."

"What do you mean you're not? Here's your big chance."

"I'm not a made man," Joe said. "I've got no right to do this."

"Well, you might call this your initiation," Guido said. He took out his gun and handed it to Joe.

Joe took the gun and looked at it, then he looked at, Sarducci. Sweat was pouring down Sarducci's face and he was grimacing in fear, but he said nothing. Joe found that unusual because he knew that Sarducci not only knew who he was but also knew what he was.

"Come on, Joe. Are you with us or against us?" Guido asked. "You got to make up your mind right now."

Joe realized at that moment that this was all a setup. They might use him to kill Sarducci, but they were going to kill him. "All right, I'll take care of it," he said. "But before I do, I want to hear his confession."

Guido laughed. "You want to do what?"

"I want to hear his confession," Joe said again. "If I'm going to kill another Sicilian, I'm going to at least give him a chance to confess his sins."

"Shit," Guido said. "Who knew we would get us some kind of a religious nut? All right, you want to listen to his confession, you listen to him. You heard the man, Sarducci. Start confessing."

"No, not here," Joe said. He pointed to a spot about fifteen yards away. "We'll go over there," he said. "He has the right to a private confession."

"Yeah, all right, go ahead," Guido said, relenting. "Okay, Sarducci, only I hope you ain't sinned a whole lot in your life, 'cause you ain't got long to confess."

"Thank you," Sarducci said.

Joe herded Sarducci over to the spot he had pointed out. "Get down on your knees with your back to them," he said quietly. Then he added, "Thanks for not telling them who I am."

"Hell, they already know who you are. All they want from me is for me to tell 'em they're right," Sarducci replied. "But I don't plan to give the bastards the satisfaction."

"That's what I thought," Joe said. "Hold your hands out in front of you. I'm going to try and shoot the handcuffs in two. If I do, there's a gun in an ankle holster on my right leg. Get it, then turn around and start firing."

"What are you two mumblin' about over there?" Guido called.

"He's confessing, I'm praying," Joe called back.

"He's prayin'," Guido said to the others, then he laughed, a low, evil laugh.

Sarducci stuck his hands out in front of him and Joe

bent over as if listening. With his movements masked from the others, he was able to put the barrel of the gun right on the centerpiece of the handcuffs. He fired. The handcuffs popped in two and Sarducci grabbed the gun from Joe's ankle holster, then rolled over and started shooting toward Guido and the others.

Joe dived to the floor, already firing. His first shot brought Guido down, then he turned toward Paulie. There were four of them against Joe and Sarducci, but Joe and Sarducci had the benefit of surprise and the advantage of lying down. The warehouse echoed with the sound of gunfire as they exchanged shots until, finally, all four were down.

"Yeah!" Sarducci said. "Yeah, we got 'em. We got ever' goddamn one of the bastards!" He and Joe stood up and walked toward the four bodies. All four were dead.

Joe turned his gun toward Sarducci. "I'll have to have my gun back now, Frankie."

"Yeah, well, what if I don't want to give it to you?"

"You have no choice. I'm pointing this gun right at you."

"You might be out of bullets."

"I might be. You are," Joe said.

"How do you know?"

Joe chuckled. "You're using an automatic. Look at the chamber."

Sarducci looked down and saw that the slide was back and the chamber was open, indicating that the last bullet had been fired.

Sarducci sighed. "Shit," he said. "Well, some days chicken, some days feathers." He handed the gun over.

"Get in the car," Joe said. "You drive."

"Don't you think we ought to open the door first?" Sarducci asked.

"Go ahead."

Sarducci walked over to the chain and pulled on it until the door was up. Then he came back and slid behind the wheel of the Chevrolet. Joe got in beside him and, with a wave of his pistol, indicated that they should get going.

When they first drove from the shadows of the warehouse and into the bright sunshine outside, both men were temporarily blinded by the sun. By the time their eyes were adjusted, they saw a car bearing down on them, fast.

"What the hell?" Sarducci said. "What is that crazy sonofabitch doin'?"

"They're after us!" Joe shouted, noticing at the last minute that every window of the oncoming car was bristling with guns. "Get down!"

The guns opened up and bullets began smashing into the Chevrolet—through the radiator, into the engine block, through the tires, and through the side windows and the windshield. Sarducci lost control of the car and the right two wheels ran up a loading ramp, tipping the car over, further and further until it flipped upside down. It slid for several feet along the alley, chewing up the treated-cloth top and spewing out a long shower of sparks from the friction of metal against the concrete. The sparks ignited the gasoline and the car went up in a fiery whoosh.

Joe felt a searing in his lungs as he inhaled the fire.

Then he felt nothing.

Mike, Bill, and Jason were in the front office of the city morgue. Johnny was also there.

"Poor Al," Johnny said. "He's back there trying to identify both bodies, Frankie because he worked with us and Joe because he is a blood relative."

"There are four other bodies back there besides Joe and Frankie," Mike said. "And they were working for

Vaglichio. What's going on, Johnny? Have you brought your war out here?"

"I swear to you, I'm not trying to make a war against Vaglichio," Johnny replied. He pointed toward the back. "Sarducci killed Mario on his own."

"Then you admit that your man did kill Mario Vaglichio?"

"Yes, I do admit that," Johnny said. "But Sarducci did not have my sanction. It turns out that the Vaglichios hijacked a shipment of dope and the people who were supposed to get it hired Sarducci to get even for them."

"I thought Sarducci was working for you."

"He was until that happened," Johnny said. "When I found out about it, I cut him loose."

"And signed his death warrant?"

"No, he signed his own death warrant by waiting to get himself killed," Johnny replied. "If he had taken the next train out of here, he would've been okay."

Al came back into the room then. He closed the door and leaned back against the wall for a long moment, holding a handkerchief to his nose and mouth.

"Al? Al, you all right?" Johnny asked.

"Yeah," Al finally said. He put his handkerchief away and shook his head. His eyes were red-rimmed and shiny with tears. "My God, you should've seen them, Johnny. Both Joe and Frankie were burned so bad that, the truth is I couldn't tell which one was which. I'm not looking forward to telling their families about this."

"It won't be necessary to tell Joe's family," Mike said. "He worked for me, I'll tell them."

"No," Al said sharply. Then he softened. "Look, Kelly, I know Joe was your friend. And I know he was a federal lawman. But he was family. And I'm family. And among our people, family is important. I'll tell them. Believe me, they'll take it a lot better from me."

"Listen to him, Mike. He's telling the truth," Johnny said.

Mike looked at Bill and Jason, and quietly, they nodded their heads in agreement. "All right," he finally agreed. "You tell the family."

"Look, if you'd like, you can come to the funeral," Al offered.

"No," Mike said. "What you saw in there, and what you'll be taking back to New York, isn't Joe. Joe is here, with us." he put his hand over his heart. "We'll have our own memorial service for him."

"Al," Johnny said. "I'm still tied up with my sister's trial. You'll see to everything? Get them on a train back to New York?"

"Yes, of course."

"And Frankie's family," Johnny said. "Take care of them, too, just as if he were still one of us."

"I'll see to everything, padrone."

"Mike, Bill, Jason, I'm truly very sorry about Joe," Johnny said. "I know you are deeply grieved."

"You know," Bill said, as the three of them got into their car to drive away. "I can almost believe that Johnny is sorry."

"Yeah," Jason said. "I can see why the two of you were once such good friends."

"Yeah," Mike growled. "Well, let's not lose sight of reality, though, shall we? Joe is dead because of people like Johnny Sangremano. And Joe was not only a better friend, he was a much better man. I haven't changed my mind one whit. I still intend to put both Johnny Sangremano and Luca Vaglichio away."

"We're with you, Mike," Bill said.

"My resolve is still strong," Jason assured him.

"Good," Mike said. "I'm glad to hear that we are still all together on this."

"What about the trial?" Bill asked. "Do you still want us to help with the defense?"

"Yes," Mike answered.

"Why?" Jason asked.

"I'm not sure why. Maybe it's because my involvement with this case has let me get a few important glimpses into the Mafia. Maybe it's because I really do think Katherine Sangremano is innocent and I just want to see justice served. Or maybe..." Mike let the sentence dangle.

"What?" Bill asked.

"Maybe it's because I know I'm going to get Johnny sooner or later, and before I do, I want to do something for him in memory of the friendship we once had."

"It doesn't matter," Jason said.

"What do you mean?"

Jason smiled. "If you want to help Katherine Sangremano, we'll give it everything we've got. And it doesn't matter why," he said. "As far as I'm concerned, it's reason enough just because you want to do it."

"Damn right," Bill seconded.

"I thank you," Mike said. "I thank both of you."

"Drop me off at the police station," Bill said. "I'm going to have to get into the evidence room. I've got some work to do."

CHAPTER 15

"Your Honor, defense would like to recall Dr. Emil Urban to the witness stand," Henry said when the defense started presenting its case.

Dr. Urban was brought back to the stand and reminded that he was still under oath.

"Dr. Urban, when you testified about the contents in the deceased's stomach, you mentioned several nostrums, as you called them, which were used to treat hair loss. Do you recall that?"

"I do," Dr. Urban replied.

"One of the nostrums you mentioned was laudanum. Is that correct?"

"It is."

"Dr. Urban, have you ever heard of laudanum being used as a treatment for hair loss?"

"Well, no," Dr. Urban replied. "But then, there is no known treatment for hair loss."

"But there are recommended treatments, are there not, whether effective or not? For example, I have here a book entitled Health Knowledge published in London, England, and copyrighted in 1919 by Domestic Health

Society, Incorporated. It is often used as a physicians' reference, I am told. Are you familiar with it?"

"I am," Dr. Urban answered.

"Let me read to you the recommended internal treatments for falling hair." Henry opened the book to a marked page, cleared his throat, and began to read. "Tincture of cantharides, rose water, aromatic vinegar, spirits of rosemary, oil of sweet almonds, aqua ammonia, gum camphor, bay rum, glycerine, and fluid extract of jaborandi. Nowhere does it mention laudanum."

"Perhaps it was something Mr. Clark was trying on his own," Dr. Urban suggested.

"As a doctor, you are aware of the effects of laudanum, are you not?"

"Yes, of course."

"Suppose I told you that we have analyzed the bottle of wine Mr. Clark and Miss Sangremano were drinking that night and discovered it to be fifty-percent laudanum and fifty-percent wine? What do you suppose the effect of that would be?"

"Objection!" Norton called. "That is speculative."

"Overruled," Judge Heckemeyer answered. "The witness is a physician and should be qualified to answer the question."

"What would the effect be, Dr. Urban, of ingesting a normal wineglass-sized drink, that consisted of one-half wine and one-half laudanum?"

"Intoxication," Dr. Urban replied.

"Intoxication to what level?"

"Well, that would depend on the tolerance factor," Dr. Urban hedged. "If they were regular users of laudanum...I mean, the way some people smoke opium, or use heroin, then it would take a great deal to affect them."

"I have the medical records of both Deke Clark and

Katherine Sangremano," Henry said. "There is no known record of either of them ever having used the drug. I have signed affidavits from several friends and co-workers, all of whom swear that neither Deke Clark nor Katherine Sangremano were users."

"If they weren't users, how did it get in the wine bottle?" Dr. Urban asked.

"You have posed a most interesting question, Dr. Urban," Henry replied. "One that we will examine later. But back to my original question. What would be the level of intoxication for people like Deke Clark and Katherine Sangremano, if they had not built up a tolerance to the drug, and if they consumed a drink-sized mixture of fifty percent laudanum and fifty percent wine?"

"It would be rather high," Dr. Urban admitted.

"Could it induce a stuporous state?"

"Yes."

"Could the wine-laudanum mixture have induced a stupor so deep that while they were both passed out a third party could have come onto the scene, shot Deke Clark, then left, without Katherine knowing anything about it?"

"Objection, Your Honor. That is strictly conjecture!"

"Your Honor, I'm not asking the witness if he thinks that is what happened," Henry replied quickly. "I am merely asking him if, in his medical opinion, the stupor induced would be deep enough for such a thing to have happened. He is, by the prosecutor's own validation, a medical expert."

"Objection is overruled. You may answer the question."

"Yes," Dr. Urban said. "Medically that would be possible."

"No further questions."

Norton Potashnick was on his feet before Henry even sat down. "Dr. Urban, as defense has already stipulated as to your medical expertise, I would like to ask you if we would have any way of knowing whether or not Katherine Sangremano was herself the victim of laudanum intoxication on the night in question?"

Dr. Urban smiled. "Not without a medical examination conducted at the time," he said.

"And to your knowledge no such medical examination was conducted?"

"No, sir."

"So given the possibility that Deke Clark was in a laudanum-induced state of stupor, there is no way to verify that Katherine Sangremano was suffering the same malady, is there?"

"There is no way that I know of, no, sir."

"If Miss Sangremano had administered the drug to induce a stupor in Deke Clark, would that have made it easier for her to shoot him?"

"Objection, Your Honor. Calls for conclusion."

"Your Honor, my question is no different than that posed by the defense a few moments earlier. I'm not asking Dr. Urban if he believed that she administered the drug. I am only asking if she had administered the drug, would the resultant stupor have made it easier for her to shoot him. That is a medical question."

"Objection overruled," Judge Heckemeyer said. "With the stipulation that the answer not exceed those specific guidelines."

"You may answer the question, Doctor," Potashnick said.

Dr. Urban cleared his throat, then said loudly and clearly. "Yes, it is quite possible that if Miss Sangremano did administer the—"

"Your Honor, I object to the words quite possible and

request you instruct the witness to use the words medically possible" Henry challenged.

"Sustained," said Judge Heckemeyer. "Witness is so instructed."

"It is medically possible that if Miss Sangremano did administer the laudanum, it would have put Deke Clark into a stupor, thus making it easier for her to shoot him."

"Objection, Your Honor. The witness's answer exceeded your guidelines."

"Sustained. Strike the part of the answer thus making it easier for her to shoot him."

"I have no further questions, Doctor. You may step down," Norton said, returning to his own seat.

Henry popped up again. "Your Honor, defense would like to recall Miss Rosita Chavez to the stand, please," Henry said.

Rosita was brought back to the stand and reminded that she, too, was still under oath.

"Miss Chavez," Henry began. "You stated that you saw both Miss Sangremano and Mr. Clark drinking wine, did you not?"

"Yes."

"Did you see the wine poured?"

"Yes. The man poured the wine for both of them."

"Were both drinking from the same bottle?"

"Yes."

"Now, this is very important, Miss Chavez," Henry said. "Did the woman actually drink it? Or did she just hold the glass while the man did the drinking?"

"She drank the wine too," Rosita said. "I remember because they hooked their arms together, like this." She made a gesture, holding her arm out as if linked with another arm. "I thought at the time that would be a good way to drink wine with someone you love."

"Thank you, Miss Chavez," Henry said. He started

toward the table; then, as if suddenly remembering something he turned back toward her so quickly that Rosita, who was just beginning to stand, let out a little gasp of alarm. "Wait a minute!" he said. "I do have one more question. During your previous testimony you said something about the woman putting the gun down and wiping her hands..." Henry turned to the clerk. "Could you read back that part of her previous testimony, please?"

The clerk looked through her notes, then read back in a monotone voice: "'She put the gun down on the man's chest, wiped her hands like this, then glanced around as if looking to see if anyone saw her. I was very frightened that she might look into my window and discover that I was watching, so I moved away from the window so she could not see me.'"

"Yes," Henry said. "That's what I'm looking for. Miss Chavez, you said she wiped her hands. What did she wipe her hands on?"

"Her blouse."

"Her blouse? You mean she was wearing a dress?"

"Not a dress. A blouse and pants. It was black silk. It was very pretty."

"But didn't you say she was naked?"

"Yes, before. But when she shot the gun, she was wearing pants and a shirt."

"Are you sure she was wearing clothes? When you saw her earlier, she was naked. But you are telling me that for some reason she put on clothes for the shooting, then she took them off again."

"I do not know if she took them off again. I did not see her after that."

"The policemen both stated that she was naked when they found her. Don't you find it very unusual that she would be naked, get dressed, shoot Mr. Clark, then get naked again before the policemen arrived?"

"Objection, Your Honor," Norton called.

"Sustained."

"It was a rhetorical question, Your Honor; I didn't actually expect the witness to answer. I don't think anyone could answer such a poser," Henry said. "I have no further questions of this witness."

"Mr. Potashnick, do you have any questions?"

"Miss Chavez, could you describe the clothes she wore in more detail?"

"The pants and shirt were made of black silk. They were thin, and very beautiful."

"Was it something someone would wear on the street?"

"I do not think so."

"Were they more like pajamas?"

"Perhaps they were pajamas."

"You stated it was one half-hour from the time you saw her naked until you saw her with the gun. In your opinion would that have been enough time for her to have put on the pajamas?"

"Yes."

"Thank you, Miss Chavez. I have no further questions."

"Your Honor, defense would now like to recall Police Officer Arnold Stone."

Officer Stone returned to the stand.

"Officer Stone, you testified that Katherine Sangremano was nude when you found her, is that correct?"

"Naked as a jaybird," Officer Stone said, and the spectators laughed.

"Did you find her clothes lying about anywhere?"

"Oh yes, sir. Her clothes and his too."

"What was she wearing?"

"Nothing."

"I'm sorry, let me rephrase the question. What were the clothes you found for her?"

"Oh, it was a real pretty thing," Officer Stone said. "It was red dress with"—he put his hands to his shirt—"what do you call those sparkly things? The little beady like things that catch the light?"

"Sequins?"

"Yes, sequins. It was a red dress with sequins up here and frills, like tassels, hanging from the skirt."

"What about a black silk shirt and trousers? Perhaps something like lounging pajamas? Did you find anything like that?"

"No, sir, we didn't find anything like that."

"What did Deke Clark's clothes look like?"

"Tan trousers and jacket and a yellow shirt," Officer Stone said.

"Were they the kind of clothes one might mistake for black silk? If Miss Sangremano had been wearing them, for instance."

Officer Stone laughed. "No, sir. There's no way you could mistake his clothes for black silk."

"Thank you, Officer. No further questions."

"Mr. Potashnick?"

"No questions, Your Honor."

"Your Honor, defense would like to recall Officer Tibbals, the police dispatcher, to the stand."

Officer Tibbals had also testified earlier, so it was not necessary to swear him in.

"Officer Tibbals, you took the call on the domestic disturbance, is that correct?" Henry asked.

"Yes."

"It was a woman's voice?"

"Yes."

"You testified earlier that you did not know whose

voice it was. Do you have any idea whose voice it wasn't?"

"Objection, Your Honor. That question is too vague."

"Sustained. Clarify your question, Counselor."

"You are not an eyewitness, Officer Tibbals, but you are what we might call an ear witness. You get several telephone calls per day, do you not?"

"Probably a hundred," Tibbals replied.

"Do you have any repeat callers? People who, for one reason or another, call the police on the slightest pretext?"

"Dozens of them."

"Can you recognize them when they call?"

Tibbals laughed. "Yeah, I know who they are. Even if they change their names, they don't fool me. I've heard their voices too many times."

"I imagine you have become quite expert at recognizing voices over the phone."

"I suppose so," Tibbals said proudly. "But then, that sort of goes with a job like mine."

"The person who called in the domestic disturbance that took Officer Stone and Officer Farrell to Miss Sangremano's residence that night, had you ever heard it before?"

"No."

"You are convinced then, that it wasn't one of your 'repeat' callers?"

"No, none of them. I'm sure of it."

"Officer Tibbals, have you ever seen any of Miss Sangremano's movies? Bear in mind that she is known, professionally, as Katie Starr."

"Yes, I've seen her movies. I've seen just about all of them."

"She has a rather distinctive voice, does she not? One that you would recognize right away?"

"Yes."

"Was it her voice you heard that night?"

"Objection!"

"Overruled."

"Think carefully, Officer Tibbals."

"I don't have to think about it," Tibbals said. "It wasn't her."

"No further questions," Henry said.

The next witness Henry called to the stand was Mrs. Deke Clark. Unlike Katie, who had been dressing "against" her status as movie star, Mrs. Deke Clark, or Tamara Welles, was playing her status to the hilt, with elaborately coiffed platinum hair, artificial eyelashes, and a deep crimson slash of lipstick.

"Do you prefer Mrs. Clark or Miss Welles?" Henry began.

"Professionally I'm Tamara Welles. I think I prefer that," Tamara said.

"Then I shall call you Miss Welles," Henry said, smiling pleasantly. He began his questioning routinely, asking her about her husband's personal habits, whether or not he was very often late in returning home, whether or not she had become alarmed on the night in question when he didn't return home.

She answered that he was often late because of the requirements of his work. For that reason, she wasn't too worried when he didn't come home early.

"Did you love your husband?"

"We had a good marriage."

"Did you love him?"

"Objection, Your Honor. She already answered that question."

"She said she had a good marriage. She didn't say whether or not she loved him," Henry responded. "It is germane to my case."

"Witness will answer."

"We got along well," Tamara tried.

"Did you love him?" Henry asked again. He took a step closer and spoke more quietly. "I could push this whole line of questioning into something much more personal and embarrassing," he suggested. "You don't really want me to do that, do you?"

"No," Tamara replied just as quietly.

"Then answer my question, please. Did you love Deke Clark?"

"No, I can't say that I actually loved him...or that he loved me. But as I say, we did have a good marriage, under the circumstances."

"Miss Welles, did you know that your husband was having an affair with Katherine Sangremano?"

"Yes," Tamara said. "I was quite aware of that. And Deke knew that I was aware."

"And yet you still say that you had a good marriage?"

"I am...a tolerant woman," Tamara explained. "I allowed him his occasional peccadillo."

"I see. And was Deke Clark equally tolerant of you?"

"Objection. The question is irrelevant."

"Your Honor, Miss Welles is a critical witness in this case. Her relationship with her husband must be clearly established."

"Sustained. You may continue, Counselor."

"Was your husband tolerant of you?" Henry asked.

"He was...understanding," Tamara said.

"Understanding. Yes, perhaps that is a better word. Well, we'll leave it that way for the time being. Now, Miss Welles, if you would, tell me about the wine Deke and Katherine consumed that night."

"The wine? What do I know of the wine?"

"It was the wine that Deke Clark took along on his, uh, assignation, with Katherine Sangremano. I have to assume that he brought it from your home."

"I don't know anything about it," Tamara said. "It is illegal to possess wine."

"You know nothing about the wine? If I got a warrant and had your house searched, I wouldn't find any wine?"

"You couldn't do that, could you? I mean search my home?"

"Oh, I could if I could convince the court that I believe it would provide evidence to support the case for the defense. And I could convince the court, Miss Welles, believe me. Do you want me to request a warrant and a search?"

"No," Tamara said. "No, that won't be necessary. The wine you are talking about may have been some wine that we...that is, that my husband brought back from France on our last trip over."

"Yes, thank you, that would corroborate Miss Sangremano's statement as to its origin. But now the big question is, where did the laudanum come from?"

"The laudanum?"

"The wine was laced with laudanum, Miss Welles. Where did the laudanum come from?"

"I...I don't know."

"You do know about laudanum, don't you, Miss Welles?"

"I know what it is, yes."

"In fact, Miss Welles, couldn't we take it a little further than that? Isn't it true that you use laudanum?"

"Well, perhaps I do," Tamara said defensively. "Sometimes. For pain. Anyway, as far as I'm concerned, it's better than morphine or heroin. It's much less addictive and much less potent. There's very little possibility that anyone would actually become addicted to laudanum."

"You claim that it is neither potent nor addictive. And yet you are a regular user, are you not?"

"I suppose so."

"Have you ever tried to increase its potency by mixing it with wine?"

"No!"

"Is it not possible, Miss Welles, that you made yourself a little wine-and-laudanum highball, then forgot about it and let that bottle get away from you?"

"No," Tamara said again. She put her hand to her forehead. "I told you. I don't use it like that."

"Ever?"

"Never."

"Then how did the laudanum, which you admit to using, get into the wine that you also admit to having?"

"I don't know," she said quietly, so quietly that the clerk asked her to please repeat the answer.

"I don't know," Tamara said again, louder this time.

"Miss Welles, let me suggest a scenario here," Henry said. "Let me suggest that you knew your husband was going to take that wine down to Katherine's house, so you purposely laced it with laudanum."

"No," Tamara said.

"You laced it with laudanum, Miss Welles, then you waited long enough for the laudanum to take effect. You then went to Katherine's house and found them nude and passed out, perhaps even in each other's arms."

"No," she said again.

"You went into Katherine's house and got the gun you knew she kept there, came back outside, put the barrel of the pistol between your husband's eyes, and pulled the trigger. You didn't have any trouble, of course, because Mr. Clark was out cold, as a result of laudanum intoxication."

"No!" Tamara said. "I didn't do it, I tell you!"

"It wasn't Miss Sangremano Miss Chavez saw standing over the body, holding the gun, was it, Miss Welles? It was you. You knocked them both out with a wine-and-laudanum cocktail, shot your husband, then telephoned the police to report a domestic disturbance."

"It was not me! You're talking crazy!"

"Miss Welles, suppose I got that search warrant, not to look for wine, but to look for those black silk pajamas that Miss Chavez saw. Would we find those pajamas in your house?"

"No, I...I mean, what if you did find those pajamas in my house, that wouldn't prove anything, would it?"

"Oh, it would prove a great deal," Henry said. "It would prove—"

"Leave her alone!" a woman's voice suddenly screamed from the gallery. "Leave her alone, I tell you! She didn't do it!"

There were gasps of surprise from the spectators.

"Order in the court," Judge Heckemeyer said, banging his gavel against the desk. "Order in this court or I will have the room cleared!"

Finally, order was restored and everyone grew quiet. The woman who had shouted out was still standing.

"Bailiff, bring that woman up here," Judge Heckemeyer ordered.

The bailiff went back into the gallery to put his hand on the woman's upper arm then bring her as far forward as the railing.

"Young woman, what is your name?"

"My name is Alex Jensen," the woman answered.

"What do you mean disturbing my court like that? Can you give me one reason why I should not hold you in contempt?"

"I'm just trying to see justice done, Your Honor," Alex replied.

"And where, pray tell, has justice gown awry?" Judge Heckemeyer asked.

Alex pointed toward Henry. "This man is trying to

make you believe that Tamara murdered her husband. She didn't do it. She isn't capable of doing such a thing."

"That is a determination for the jury to make, Miss Jensen. Now, I'm ordering you to return to your seat and make no further outcry."

The bailiff started to take Alex back to her seat, but she twisted out of his grip and faced the judge again. "I know she didn't do it, Your Honor, because I did!"

"Alex, no!" Tamara said. "You don't know what you're saying!"

"Don't you understand, Tamara?" Alex said, her voice breaking. "I love you. I couldn't stand to have him around you. You wouldn't divorce him...you were too concerned about how a divorce would look, what it would do to your career if...if people found out about you. Oh, if only you had the courage to overcome your fears...to overcome your secret shame and leave Deke, once and for all. But you wouldn't, or perhaps you couldn't, do it. So I took care of it for you. Deke can never come between us again."

"Miss Jensen, are you confessing to this court that you, and not Miss Sangremano, killed Deke Clark?"

"Yes. I laced the wine with laudanum, and I went down there and shot him." Alex looked at the judge. "So do you see, Your Honor, it's me you want, not Tamara? Leave her alone. Please, all of you," she added, looking around the court. "Leave her alone."

"Your Honor, I move for dismissal of all charges against my client," Henry said.

"Prosecution concurs," Norton said quickly.

"Granted," Judge Heckemeyer said with a loud rap of his gavel. "Bailiff, place this woman under arrest."

KATIE STARR BACK IN *AERODROME*!

In a dramatic turn of events, Sid Friedman announced today that Katie Starr would be returning to the starring role in the Galaxy Pictures in production <u>Aerodrome</u>.

"With her courageous court battle behind her and her innocence clearly established, Katie Starr has won the love and admiration of fans from all across America," Friedman told this reporter. "It would be foolish not to bow to the wishes of her adoring public. It was always Galaxy's intention to return her to the screen in a starring role as quickly as possible, and <u>Aerodrome</u> is the natural choice."

When asked about Joan Leland, who had replaced Miss Starr in the movie, the director indicated that Miss Leland would be retained in the picture, and in the role for which she had signed, that of Molly Tremaine.

"However, the importance of the role of Molly Tremaine has been reduced in importance," Friedman explained. "A new character has been written into the story. This new character, Allison Cairns, is now the female lead of the movie.

"It is, of course, no secret," Friedman went on, "that I was never happy with Katie Starr in the role of Molly Tremaine. That was in no way intended to indicate a lack of confidence in Katie's ability as an actress. Indeed I feel as I have always felt, that Katie Starr is one of the finest performers in our profession. However, I never believed that the Molly Tremaine role took full advantage of her considerable range. The new character, Allison Cairns, does."

In the story, Allison Cairns is a young girl from New York who goes to France to look for her fiancé, an aviator whose airplane does not come back from a dawn patrol. Though the character does exist in the book, it has been greatly expanded in the new screenplay, according to Friedman, in order to accommodate the public's demand that Katie Starr be reinstated in the movie, and in order to provide Miss Starr with a character of sufficient scope and dimension to utilize her many talents.

"Goddamnit! We had a contract with Galaxy Pictures," Luca said angrily, slapping the newspaper down on Jay Garland's desk.

"And we still do," Jay replied. "The contract has not been breached."

"What do you mean it hasn't been breached? Katie Starr is back in the picture, isn't she? And she is the star, isn't she?"

"That's true," Jay agreed. "But Joan is still in the movie, she is still playing the role of Molly Tremaine, and most importantly she is still receiving the same amount of money. Like I told you, they have not violated one letter of the contract."

Luca twisted the newspaper up into a tight roll, then began pacing back and forth in front of Jay's desk, slapping the newspaper against the palm of his hand. He spun around and pointed his finger at Jay.

"Sangremano is behind this, that sonofabitch," he muttered.

"Listen, I don't know what you are so upset about," Jay said. "I told you, we've still got a good contract. They've still got to pay us every penny they promised or we can take them right to court."

Luca looked over at Jay through eyes that were narrow and cold. Jay had never been looked at like that by anyone, and he shivered involuntarily.

"Get out," Luca said quietly.

"I beg your pardon?"

"Get out of here," Luca repeated. "I'm closin' down."

"You're...you're closing my office?"

"I'm closin' everything," Luca said. "Your office, the movie, everything."

"No! No, you can't do that! We have an agreement! I gave up my business for this."

"Do you want to give up your life for it?" Luca asked coldly.

"No," Jay said. "No, uh, okay. Okay, you're right. They did do us dirty. Maybe we had—"

"There ain't no 'we'," Luca said. "You are out of it."

"Uh, yeah, sure. Yeah, okay. Whatever you say, Mr. Vaglichio," Jay said. He started for the file cabinet. "I'll just collect my things and go."

"You've got no things to collect," Luca said. "Just go."

Jay felt a sinking sensation in the pit of his stomach. There was fifteen hundred dollars in a brown envelope at the rear of the top drawer of the file cabinet. He had, very cleverly, skimmed it off the top of the expense account the Vaglichios had set up for him. Without that envelope, he had nothing but the clothes on his back and the money in his pocket. The money in his pocket amounted to six dollars and thirty cents.

CHAPTER 16

When Bruiser Hawkins finished working on the two airplanes, he left the flight line and walked back into the maintenance hangar to pour himself a cup of coffee. His hands were shaking so badly that he had to put the cup down on one of the workbenches and hold the coffeepot with both hands in order to pour it without spilling.

He wrapped his hands around the cup of coffee and walked over to the door of the hangar to look out on the airplanes that were lined up in one long row. Most were still in the heavy shadow of early-morning light, but the two Nieuports he had been working on this morning were on this end and more clearly visible.

Bruiser felt a hollow sensation in the pit of his stomach and a weakness in the back of his knees. He had never done anything quite like this before. He had never done anything to deliberately sabotage a picture. It wasn't anything he would have ever believed himself capable of, but they say that everyone has his price and Luca Vaglichio had met Bruiser's.

The large brown envelope that Luca Vaglichio gave

Bruiser yesterday had contained all of his IOUs as well as ten thousand dollars in cash. All Bruiser had to do in return was make a small adjustment on one of the airplanes.

He thought about not doing it. He had the IOUs and the money; he could just keep his payoff and do nothing. It wasn't something he thought about very long, though. He knew, without being told, that Luca Vaglichio was not the kind of man you double-crossed.

Bruiser heard a car approaching and when he looked around, he saw that it was Sam Fielding arriving for work. Sam was nearly always the first one on the set each morning, but Bruiser managed had to arrive first enough times to avoid arousing suspicion today.

"Good morning," Sam said pleasantly as he got out of his car. "Oh, the coffee looks good. Any of it left?"

"Help yourself," Bruiser said. "I made a fresh pot."

"You?" Sam asked with an exaggerated gasp. "The stunt coordinator stooping to make coffee? My, my, what is this world coming to?" He walked over and poured himself a cup. "You know, I was thinking as I was lying in bed at about four this morning," he went on, "if I could just figure out some way to hook up one of those little bags like they have in hospitals, I could just start the coffee running into my veins as soon as I got in from partying. Then a couple of hours later I'd be bright-eyed, bushy-tailed, and ready to start all over again."

Bruiser laughed.

"Soon as I finish my coffee," Sam said, "I'd better get over to the ready shack and see what the shooting schedule is this morning."

"Don't bother," Bruiser replied. "I already got it for you." He picked up a clipboard from one of the tables and handed it to Sam.

"Gee, thanks, that saves me a trip over," Sam said,

taking the board and looking at the schedule. "I see I'm supposed to strafe the flight line this morning. How do you want to work it?"

"The only thing we'll get this morning are the aerial sequences," Bruiser explained. "Two of you will swoop down and fly over the parked airplanes, shooting your guns. Later we'll set charges in half a dozen or so of the planes on the ground, blow them up, then edit the two segments together. It'll look like your guns are blowing up there." Bruiser pointed to the two Nieuports. "For film continuity you'll have to use those two planes. That's the same two we had in the previous segment."

"Okay. I'll need another pilot. I'd better see who I can get hold of this morning."

"I left word for Kelly to be here early," Bruiser said. "He took a few days off for the trial, he may as well start earning his money."

"Okay by me," Sam said. "He's a good pilot. I like using him."

"Go ahead and get the scene started without me," Bruiser said. "I have to run back into the studio this morning and make sure the Paris bistro set is ready for the big fight scene."

"Yeah, sure, go ahead, I'll take care of things here," Sam replied.

Bruiser started toward his car.

"Bruiser?" Sam called.

"Yeah?"

"What's wrong?"

"Wrong? Nothing's wrong," Bruiser replied, startled by the question. "Why do you ask?"

Sam chuckled. "No particular reason, I guess. It's just that you made coffee, you laughed at my joke, you got the shooting schedule down here for me, and you took care of getting the second pilot. Now, what I want to know is, why are you treating me so well?"

I'm just trying to do my job, that's all," Bruiser said.

"Yeah? Well, if you don't watch it, you're going to wind up actually making friends with someone. Then what would you do?"

"You're full of it, Fielding," Bruiser growled. Sam's laughter chased him to the car.

It was almost an hour before they were actually ready to shoot the scene. By that time, the light was good, the crew was ready, and the cameras were in position. Sam and Mike walked out to the two Nieuports to do a walk-around inspection just before takeoff.

As Mike was moving the elevator up and down on his Nieuport, he saw a tiny crack beginning to develop on the elevator bellcrank.

"Sam?" Mike called.

Sam was twenty feet away, conducting a preflight inspection on his own plane. He looked back over his shoulder. "Yeah?"

"You want to come over here and have a look at this?"

"What is it?" Sam asked, coming toward him. "You find something?"

"Yes, I'm afraid so." Mike pointed to the crack. "That doesn't look too good."

Sam looked at it closely. "Um, no, it definitely does not," he said. "If that thing breaks, you'll have no elevator control. We'd better get it replaced."

"Why don't I just get another plane?"

"You can't. We have to use these two in order to match up with some of the earlier sequences," Sam said. He stroked his chin for a moment while he thought about it. "I tell you what we could do, though. Why don't you get the Fokker and we'll do another dogfight scene while they're fixing this one?"

"Okay by me," Mike said, smiling. "That's more fun, anyway. I'll go get the Fokker ready."

"I'll tell the camera plane to get in the air," Sam said.

Today was to be Katie's first day of shooting, so she had invited Johnny, Henry, and Karen to come down to the location with her. Henry and Karen, who would be returning to San Francisco this afternoon, readily accepted the invitation; neither of them had ever seen a movie being shot before, and they thought it would be a wonderful experience. In addition, Johnny told Henry how much like a real aerodrome this particular location was and Henry thought he would like to get a look around, just for old time's sake.

A Nieuport and a Fokker were taking off just as Katie and her guests arrived on the set and both airplanes passed over the car, their engines roaring loudly as they clawed for altitude.

"Look at that, an Allied plane and a German plane taking off together," Henry said. He laughed. "Now that's something we didn't see."

"Well, no, but how about the rest of it?" Johnny asked. "Looks pretty real, doesn't it?"

"Amazingly so," Henry agreed.

When Jason Vandervort saw the car arrive, he walked over to greet them. "Congratulations on winning your case, Miss Starr," he said.

"Thank you," Katie replied.

"You're still here, Vandervort?" Johnny asked. "I figured you and Mike would be gone, now that your little secret is out."

"There are about three more scenes that I have to be in," Jason said, "or else they would have to reshoot all the earlier scenes. Mr. Friedman was good enough to give me this part, so I don't want to cause him any inconvenience. As soon as those other scenes are done, I'll leave."

"Where will you go?"

Jason smiled. "Come on, Mr. Sangremano, you don't really think I'm going to give you my itinerary, do you?"

Johnny chuckled. "I guess not. What about Mike? Is he still here?"

"You just missed him. He's up there in the Fokker," Jason said, pointing to the tri-wing airplane that was now about a thousand feet high. "He's going to fly for them for the rest of the day, then he'll quit tomorrow."

"Is that so? Well, maybe when he quits, I'll take his place," Johnny suggested. "How about it, Henry? You want to go back to war?"

"Not even for the movies," Henry replied.

"Johnny, if you and Henry will excuse me, I need to get down to makeup," Katie said.

"Sure, go ahead. We'll just stay around here and watch for a while."

"Karen, would you like to come with me?" Katie invited.

"I'd love to," Karen replied enthusiastically.

Another car came through the gate then.

"Who's this coming?" Johnny asked Jason.

Jason looked over toward the car. "Oh, that's Bruiser Hawkins. He's the stunt coordinator." He chuckled. "If you really are serious about flying, he's the one you'd have to see."

Bruiser got out of his car, slammed the door behind him, then walked over with a puzzled expression on his face. "What's going on here, Vandervort, do you know?" he asked. "Why aren't they filming?"

"They are. The camera plane is already up there. Mike and Sam just took off."

"What's the camera plane doing up? We don't need the camera plane to film the strafing sequence," Bruiser said.

"Oh, I think there's been a change."

"A change? What sort of change? I don't know about any change."

"I know; Sam changed it after you left this morning. It seems that Mike found something wrong with the plane he was going to fly," Jason said. "So while they're making the repair Sam and Mike are going to shoot an aerial battle sequence."

"They're going to shoot a dogfight sequence?" Bruiser asked in a choked voice. "What planes are they using?"

"Well, Sam is in a Nieuport and Mike is flying the Fokker," Jason said. "Why, what's wrong?"

"Which Nieuport? Which Nieuport is Sam using?" Bruiser asked, nearly shouting the words.

"He's in the same one he was going to fly for the strafing sequence."

"Oh my God!" Bruiser moaned, turning ashen faced. He turned around and leaned against the hood of his car. "Oh my God. This wasn't supposed to happen. I didn't plan for this to happen."

"What is it, Bruiser?" Jason asked. "This is more than just a change in schedule. What has you so nervous?"

When Bruiser looked back at Jason, his eyes were wide and his face was covered with perspiration. "The two Nieuports," he said. "This morning I...I loaded their guns with incendiary ammunition. With real incendiary ammunition."

"What? Why would you do that?" Jason gasped.

"They were supposed to shoot up the flight line," he said. "Mr. Vaglichio..."

"Vaglichio?" Johnny said sharply. "What does Vaglichio have to do with it?"

"Vaglichio paid me to stir up enough trouble to shut down the picture. I thought if Fielding and Kelly shot up the flight line—I mean really shot it up—and damaged enough expensive airplanes, then Galaxy couldn't afford to go on. But now..." Bruiser looked up.

"Damn!" Jason suddenly said. "Are you telling me that Sam and Mike are up there with live ammunition and they don't even know it?"

"Not Fielding and Kelly," Bruiser explained. "Just Fielding. Kelly's guns are loaded with blanks."

"He'll shoot Mike down!"

"Yes, that's what I'm afraid of," Bruiser said.

"You sonofabitch!" Johnny said. He stepped up to Bruiser and sent a roundhouse right crashing into the stunt coordinator's chin. Bruiser went down, but he made no effort to get back up.

"You've got to believe me, it wasn't supposed to be this way," he said.

"Well, can't we do something?" Henry asked. "Can't we call them on the radio?"

"These planes aren't equipped with radios," Jason replied.

"Come on!" Johnny shouted. "I've got to get to a plane! I'm going up there after them!"

———

Mike had flown the Fokker quite a few times since the first dogfight he had had with Sam. Once he mastered the airplane's few idiosyncrasies, he learned to really appreciate its responsiveness. Because of that, he was determined to give Sam a much better fight this time than he had during their last encounter.

The script called for Mike to initiate the attack, just as he did the last time, by dropping down out of the sun and coming up on Sam's rear. Mike signaled to Sam, then to the camera plane, and climbed an additional one thousand feet in preparation for the attack. When he saw that the camera plane was in position, he pulled the stick hard to his right did a wingover, and started down toward Mike, picking up the Nieuport in his gun's ring site.

During his first engagement with Sam, Mike had been surprised at how quickly Sam was able to bring his plane around and latch onto Mike's tail. This time he was determined to keep Sam from doing that. As soon as he flashed by Sam's Nieuport, he hauled back on the stick, pulling the Fokker up into a swooping loop.

Mike's move surprised Sam, who had stuck to his earlier tactic of coming around to follow his attacker down. As a result, Mike was coming out of the top of his loop while Sam was caught going in the opposite direction. With a triumphant laugh into the wind, Mike fell off into a hammerhead stall so that he was, once again, on Sam's tail.

As soon as Sam made his initial maneuver, he realized that he had been tricked, and he knew that Mike would be coming around behind him again. Sam was an outstanding pilot with marvelous reflexes, so he recovered almost instantaneously. Because of his quick reaction, Mike had no more than a second behind Sam before Sam put his airplane into a spin, slowing his descent and letting Mike flash by before he could even line up for a shot.

"You magnificent flying sonofabitch!" Mike screamed into the wind, though he knew Sam couldn't hear him.

Now the two planes separated and started back up for altitude. During their encounter, they had lost the camera plane, so they moved back toward it. Sam slid up alongside Mike and Mike saw him smiling broadly. Sam made a circle out of his thumb and forefinger, then pointed at him, as if challenging him to beat him again. Mike laughed and pointed to his own chest as if saying he was ready for it.

The two planes resumed their original positions, and Mike got ready to launch his second attack.

———————

Because Johnny kept the throttle of the Spad he had commandeered at full takeoff power, the engine was screaming in protest. The cylinder-head temperature was climbing into the danger zone and the RPM was above the never-exceed mark, but Johnny made no effort to slow down. He didn't care if he burned out the engine. All he cared about was that the engine and the airplane held together long enough for him to reach Mike and Sam before they started their aerial combat sequence.

The overworked engine of the Spad began throwing back hot oil. It spattered the windshield and blew back into Johnny's face. As a result, he had to lean to one side to look around the windscreen. And as he had not taken the time to locate a helmet and goggles, he was forced to squint into the hurricane-force wind blast just so he could see where he was going.

Johnny leveled out at about 7,500 feet, then started searching the sky all around him. When he saw nothing, he beat on the instrument panel in frustration. Then, out of the corner of his eye, he caught a flash of light, like sun reflecting off a windshield, and he looked toward it. There, to the north of his position and about three thousand feet below him, he saw three airplanes...a Nieuport, a Fokker, and a DH-4 camera plane.

"Yeah!" Johnny screamed into the wind. "Yeah, I've found you!"

Johnny started toward them, though he wasn't sure

yet exactly what he would do when he caught up. If he could come up alongside Mike and get Mike's attention, he was pretty sure he would be able to make him understand that something was wrong.

Johnny kept the throttle at full power as he closed the gap between them. The cylinder-head temperature climbed higher and the oil leak got worse, but he made no effort to slow down. It was now or never.

Ahead of him, the airplanes separated. The camera plane pulled to one side while the Fokker began climbing. Johnny realized that they were about to start their dogfight.

What Johnny didn't realize was that this was the start of the second dogfight sequence. What Mike didn't realize was that Johnny was anywhere in the sky with him. All Mike could think of was how he was going to handle this attack. He knew he couldn't continue the way he had the first day because Sam had already shown how quickly he could react to that tactic. And he couldn't pull into another swooping loop because he had just done this and Sam would be alert for it. When he peeled off for his second attack, he still didn't know what he was going to do but decided he would just make it up as he went along.

Mike flattened out his dive at the last moment, so that by the time he passed by the Nieuport, he was almost back into level flight, though his direction of flight was exactly the opposite of Sam's. The result was that Mike was heading west at a hundred and forty miles per hour, while Sam was heading east at a hundred and forty miles per hour.

Only Sam wasn't heading east at all. Sam had seen Mike flattening his dive as he came down, and he anticipated Mike's next maneuver. As soon as Mike completed his pass, Sam hauled back hard on the stick and pulled the Nieuport around into an Immelmann turn. He came out of the turn heading in exactly the same direction as Mike, only about one thousand feet higher than the Fokker and on its tail. Also, because Sam was now coming out of the east, he had the morning sun behind him. Therefore, even if Mike had looked around, he wouldn't have been able to find him, because Sam was in the classic attack position...above, behind, and in the sun.

Johnny saw it all. He saw Mike scoot west after the attack, and he saw Sam make the climbing, half-loop turn that put him on Mike's tail. It was too late now to fly up alongside Mike and warn him. The only thing he could do was try to come between them, to interrupt the attack.

Sam could see Mike's head turning back and forth as he searched the sky all around him, looking for his adversary. He knew that Mike wouldn't be able to see him if he kept the proper angle between Mike and the sun, and Sam had done this often enough to know what that proper angle was. He closed in on Mike until he was in position to set up the proper deflection angle.

Of course, this was just for the movies, and as far as the camera plane was concerned, there would be no way to tell whether Sam had achieved the proper deflection angle or not. But Sam would know, and if he was going to do this, he figured he might as well do it right.

He nosed his craft down toward the little red Fokker, then sighted through the ring site of his gun. The three-winged craft in front of him began growing larger, and he reached up to arm his machine guns. He waited. He wanted to be close enough for the tips of the Fokker's wings to fill his site completely.

"Got you!" he shouted into the wind and pulled the trigger. "What the hell?" he gasped.

A third airplane had suddenly and unexpectedly appeared between them just as Sam pulled the trigger on his twin machine guns. He saw a long string of tracer rounds zipping into that airplane's upper wing. As the upper wing was where the fuel tank was located, that meant that incendiary rounds were punching into a hundred and fifty gallons of gasoline. Sam saw the airplane explode right before his eyes.

"Sonofabitch!" he said aloud. "I just shot down the camera plane."

Sam was so alarmed by what he had done that he didn't even stop to think of how he had done it. In the horror of the moment, the fact that his guns had been loaded with live ammunition and not blanks, as he had supposed, had not yet sunk in.

Mike, in the meantime, had figured out at the last minute where Sam had to be, so he was looking back just as the third airplane came between them. He, too, saw the explosion, followed by little bits and pieces of aircraft wreckage. He also saw, coming out of the debris, a larger object. Mike realized, with horror, that this object had to be the body of the pilot.

At first, Mike, like Sam, thought it was the camera plane that had been shot down. Then the camera plane caught up with them and they knew it was someone else.

Shocked, Sam pointed to the ground, then he started back for the aerodrome. Mike and the camera plane followed.

ONE WEEK LATER, ABOARD THE TWENTIETH CENTURY LIMITED, EAST BOUND

"You plannin' on keepin' me locked up all the way back to New York?" Luca Vaglichio asked.

Vaglichio was in handcuffs, sitting on the end of the

seat. Mike, Jason, and Bill had put the table up and were playing cards.

"Yes," Mike said. "We're going to keep you like that all the way back to New York."

"You're crazy, you can't do this," Vaglichio complained. "I know my rights."

Mike looked over at his prisoner. "Mr. Vaglichio, if I were you, I would be quiet now," he said. "I don't think any of us are in much of a mood to listen to you."

"You're sore because of Provenzano and Sangremano."

"Is that a fact?" Mike asked.

"Yeah, that's a fact. I know, you're supposed to be a lawman, but ever'body knows you and Sangremano was friends. Well, I got news for you. It wasn't me that killed him. And you got no proof I killed Joe Provenzano either," Vaglichio said.

"No, I don't suppose we do."

"And anyway, even if you did have proof, it happened in California. They can't try me in New York for a murder that happened in California."

"Oh, this has nothing to do with California," Mike said. "Al Provenzano has made a deal with the governor of New York to testify against you for half a dozen murders in that state. Whether you go to the chair in New York or California, it doesn't matter. It's just as permanent." Mike turned his attention back to the card game.

Vaglichio grinned broadly. "Is that what you're doin'? You're takin' me to New York to stand trial there? Well, let me tell you a few things. First of all, I can't be taken to New York without an order of extradition," he said, pointing to his chest. Then he waved his hand as if he were forestalling a disagreement. "And there ain't been no extradition papers signed. Besides which, you are federal officers. You got no legal right to take me back for murder. Murder ain't against the federal law."

"Did you study law, Vaglichio?" Mike asked sarcastically. "He must've studied law," he said to the others. "He's quite right, you know. Murder is a state offense."

"I always thought he wasn't quite as dumb as he looks," Bill said.

"Yes," Jason said. "I guess if we were taking him back for murder, he might have a case."

"I know. That's why we aren't taking him back for murder."

"You aren't? Then what are you takin' me back for? What are you chargin' me with?"

"We are charging you with being a Communist, fomenting revolution, and advocating the violent overthrow of the United States government," Jason said.

"What?" Vaglichio gasped. "Are you crazy? I'm not a Communist. I don't even know what the hell a Communist is."

"Well, nevertheless we're going to take you back there and see if we can make a case against you," Mike said.

"You'll never make something like that stick," Vaglichio said. "Do you hear me? You'll never make it stick! Why, they'll throw you out of court for something that crazy!"

"Oh, I'm sure you are right, Vaglichio. You know, boys, he's right. I don't expect we're going to be able to make the charge stick."

Vaglichio smiled broadly. "All right," he said. "All right, if you already know that, why are you even bothering to try?"

"Now that I think about it, we probably won't try," Mike said easily. "As a matter of fact I'm pretty sure that what we'll do is look over the evidence we have, then decide that it isn't strong enough to even warrant going to court. We'll probably wind up just dropping the charges against you."

"Of course, the state of New York will be there, ready with their own charges as soon as we drop ours," Bill said.

"What? You bastards!" Vaglichio said, realizing then what was happening. "You tricked me! You're just using that Communist bullshit to get me back to New York."

"And you said he was dumb," Jason said sarcastically.

"No, I didn't. I said he wasn't as dumb as he looks." Bill chuckled. "By the way, I'm hungry. How are we going to work around our dinner?"

"I don't particularly want to take him to the dining car," Jason said.

"We won't have to," Mike said. "You two go eat now and bring something back for our 'guest.' I'll watch him while you're gone. When you come back, you watch him and I'll go."

"Sounds good to me," Bill said, standing and stretching. "Come on, Jason, I could eat a horse."

Mike watched them leave, then he picked up a book and began to read.

"Hey," Vaglichio said. "Kelly. I have to take a piss."

"Why don't you wait until the others come back? You'll want to wash your hands before you eat, anyway."

"I can't wait," Vaglichio said. "I gotta go now."

Mike sighed and put his book down. He stood up and signaled to Vaglichio. "All right," he said. "Let's go."

Mike followed close behind Vaglichio down to the far end of the car. Just as they reached the narrow aisle that ran alongside the "Gentlemen's Room," a rather portly, white-haired man had the same idea. He was large enough to cause some congestion in the narrow aisle.

"Excuse me," he said politely, stepping back to make as much room as he could. "You may go first."

"No!" Mike said, instantly recognizing the potential danger of having the man between him and Vaglichio.

Vaglichio also saw the opportunity, and moving quickly, he stepped around the fat man, then put his arms around the man's neck and pressed the steel cuffs up hard, just under the man's chin.

"What is this?" the man shouted in surprise and fear.

"Vaglichio, let him go!" Mike shouted, pulling his gun.

"Drop your gun!" Vaglichio ordered. "Drop it, or I'll break his neck!"

"Let him loose," Mike ordered. "You've got nowhere to go."

"And I got nothin' to lose!" Vaglichio insisted. "Now, drop your gun." He tightened his grip and his prisoner let out a gargle. "I mean it!" Vaglichio said.

Mike dropped his gun.

"Good for you. Now kick your gun toward me."

Mike did so.

"Give the key to the fat man here. Fat man, when you get the key, unlock these cuffs."

"Please," the fat man gasped. "I mean no one any harm. Let me go!"

"I'm goin' to let you go," Vaglichio promised. "Just as soon as you do what I say. Now, hold your hand out there and get the key."

The man held his hand out toward Mike, looking at him with big, cowlike eyes. Mike stood his ground for a long moment, making no effort to comply. Vaglichio jerked hard on the cuffs.

"Ahh!" the fat man whimpered.

Reluctantly Mike fished the key from his pocket and gave it to the fat man. The fat man, with shaking hands and bumbling fingers, finally managed to get the key in the slot and open the cuffs. The moment the cuffs were open, Vaglichio pushed the fat man hard, toward Mike. Frightened and clumsy, the fat man fell into Mike, knocking him down.

Vaglichio ran toward the rear door of the train car, stooping over to scoop up the gun Mike had kicked toward him. Then he stepped through the door and was gone.

It took Mike another moment to extricate himself. He finally got up and looked down at the shaking, crying pile of flesh who had been Vaglichio's hostage.

"No, don't leave me!" the man gasped. "I need help."

"What's wrong?" Mike asked. "Is it your heart?"

"No, it's...I'm afraid I've soiled my pants," the man whimpered.

"Shit, that's all that's wrong with you?" Mike asked. Unconcerned about the man's potential embarrassment, Mike ran quickly out the door, across the vestibule, and into the next car. He held up his badge so everyone in the car could see him. "I'm a federal agent!" he shouted. "Did a man with a gun come through here just now?"

"No one has come through," a woman in the front seat said, and the others, curious about his sudden entry, concurred.

"Thanks," Mike said, and he returned to the vestibule. If the man hadn't come through the car, then he was going over the car. Mike reached out to the ladder and began to climb.

When he reached the top rung, he saw Vaglichio moving toward the rear of the train. The mobster was crouched over like a gorilla, moving in a sort of loping gait that allowed him not only to keep his balance but also to cover ground rather quickly.

Mike saw at once what Vaglichio had in mind. He was heading toward the rear of the train. If he could reach the rear car, then get to the lowest rung on the ladder, there was a good chance he could jump off without serious injury.

Moving on top of the railroad car of a speeding train is not easy. Mike had to brace himself against a forty-mile-per-hour gale as well as fight against the hot cinders and lung-burning pall of coal smoke that whipped back over the train from the steam locomotive. Here, also, the pendulum effect of the swaying cars was much more exaggerated than it was lower down, closer to the track bed. Nevertheless, Mike didn't hesitate a second before starting after Vaglichio.

Vaglichio sensed that Mike was coming after him and he turned and fired. Mike dropped to the roof of the car to avoid the shot, and when he did, he started slipping over the edge. He grabbed desperately at the top of the car, but there was nothing to give him purchase until he actually slipped over the side. Then, just as he was going over, his hands managed to grab hold of a small rain channel that ran the length of the car. Mike held on tightly, looking down once to see the cross ties whipping by in a blur beneath his feet.

Mike tried to pull himself back up to the top of the car, but as he did so he saw Vaglichio working his way over toward him. The mobster had a broad smile on his face.

"Kelly!" Vaglichio said, pointing the gun at Mike's head. "When you get to hell, give my brother my regards!"

Mike turned his eyes away, not wanting to see the bullet that killed him. When he did so, he saw that the train was passing under a steel signal trestle. Like a croquet wicket, the trestle formed an inverted "U" over the track, its cross beam a little over five feet above the top of the cars. That beam was coming toward Vaglichio at forty miles per hour and it was only two cars away.

"Vaglichio!" Mike called, trying to buy one more second. "Wait!"

"Wait for what, you—"

Vaglichio's sentence was interrupted by a solid thumping sound, following which his head fell to the top of the car, bounced once like a ball, then rolled off. His body stood for a moment longer, squirting a little fountain of blood through the jugular vein and the carotid artery before it, too, tumbled forward, off the train.

Mike held on for a few moments longer, fighting against the urge to be sick. Finally, he managed to use the motion of the train to help get his right leg back on top of the car. Then, slowly, he managed to climb back up. He lay on top of the car for a moment to regain his strength, then he worked his way to the ladder and climbed back down onto the vestibule.

Mike was sitting in his seat, looking through the window at the rapidly darkening desert outside when Bill and Jason returned from dinner.

"Try the lamb," Jason said. "It was delicious."

"We got a sandwich for—" Bill began, then he saw that Vaglichio was gone. "Wait a minute. Where's Vaglichio?" he asked.

"He's delivering a message to his brother," Mike answered.